ARABELLE'S BEAST

ARABELLE'S BEAST

A ROMANCE NOVEL

USA TODAY BESTSELLING AUTHOR
COURTNEY DEAN

LN
P

Arabelle's Beast
Paperback Edition

Love N. Books Press
An Imprint of Wolfpack Publishing
1707 E. Diana Street
Tampa, FL 33610

www.lovenbookspress.com

Cover design by Rachel Chaya Design
Edited by My Brother's Editor

Paperback ISBN 978-1-969876-22-6
Ebook ISBN 978-1-969876-21-9

"We loved with a love that was more than love."

— *ANNABEL LEE*, EDGAR ALLAN POE

ARABELLE'S BEAST

PROLOGUE

My dearest Florian,

I love you with everything that I am. But I'm sorry, my beautiful son. I can't live this life anymore. We've been through too much, and now that you're old enough, I know you can survive this world without me. As a mother, it's been one of the hardest decisions I've had to make, but I feel it's best for you and me because I'm so tired of living, anyway.

I regret a lot of things in my life, one being your bastard father, as you know. But the one thing I will never regret is being your mother. You deserve peace and love, my son. You deserve to experience everything life has to offer you, including love. Don't let your father ruin that experience for you.

Also, get as far away from your father as possible, live your best life, and find someone who will love you as much as I do. I will watch over you from wherever I am as I take the next step in my journey. Don't cry for me. I'm in a better place. I will see you in the next life.

Love Always,
Mor

JANUARY 17, 2005

Standing under the gray cloudless sky, I clasp my frozen hands behind my back, feeling the chill scurry across my body. I do my best to ignore the chattering of my teeth and the numbing sensation in my fingers and toes. The large snowflakes stick to my worn-out suit and cling to my unruly hair, reminding me of the urgent need for a haircut.

I wish this were any other day. Or at least that I was somewhere else other than here. But it isn't any other day. And I'm not somewhere else. I'm standing by my mother's grave, questioning what's left of my life now that she's gone.

I've always hated Swedish winters, but she always loved them. Maybe that's why she ended her life in the dead of winter, so she'd have one last giggle at my misery.

Today, with temperatures dipping well below freezing along with the constant snowfall, I can hear my mother's silly laughter mingling with the cool, crisp winds as she listens to me complain about freezing my nuts off to say a last goodbye to her. That's just the person she is...

Or was.

I run my hand through my snow-covered hair. "Fuck, it's gonna be hard getting used to saying that," I mutter.

She always made me smile when there was nothing to smile about. After today, there'll be nothing to smile about again. This will be the last time I see her.

My heart aches at the realization, and I rub my chest to soothe the pain, although I don't believe that will ever happen. Once her coffin is lowered into the ground and covered with the hard, cold dirt, I'll never set foot back in this cemetery. More than likely, I'll never step foot back in Uppsala. At least, I won't if I can help it.

It's a bittersweet moment because she finally escaped that bastard, which she always wanted, but left me here alone. I'm sure it was tough for her to leave me behind because I know my mother loved me. I shouldn't be mad at her decision because I know the shit she's been through with my father. But I am mad. I shouldn't curse her gods, but I curse them. I'm pissed I'll go through this life without her. She'll never see me become the man she always said I could be.

I howl out my rage, all my frustration and pain, over her deciding to punch her own ticket. However, I refuse to let the tears fall as another shovel of semi-frozen dirt hits the top of the pristine white coffin, the thud as hollow as my heart. The black chunky soil clings to the top, covering the beautiful, immaculate red roses I tossed in earlier, while the rest slides down the sides, leaving a trail of black muck.

With each thump of dirt, the realization sinks in even more, like sharp claws ripping through my chest and tearing out my heart. I used to call it nagging, but now I miss having someone in my corner pushing me forward. I no longer have anyone to love me despite my shortcomings. I used to think it was suffocation, but I would give anything to turn back the hands of time. I would give anything to have her nag or suffocate me as long as she was there with me.

I sigh, causing a white cloud to form in front of my face. It's a longing that will remain, but I need to move forward. I'm no longer a boy but a man, and men don't cry. "Men don't complain," the voice of my bastard father shouts in the back of my mind. But no matter the words on replay in my head, the heaviness in my heart will never leave me. I fight back tears that will soon flow. The only person who loved me couldn't bear this painful life, even for me.

Her only son.

No family or friends are here. Only the cemetery's caretakers burying my mother share in my grief, and I can see the discomfort on their faces as they do. I can't spare them, though I wish I could. Grief and bitterness are all I have. It's all the world will see of me.

I don't know why I expected anything different from my father. When I called, I'd hoped I'd imagined the cheerfulness in his voice when he found out she was dead. But the "good riddance, bitch" he'd sneered before he ended the call told me otherwise. He's happy she's finally dead, freeing him of a burden he could have rid himself of a long time before today.

I was stupid to believe he gave a damn about either of us. He's never hidden his feelings about us or the man he is, and I vow on my dead mother to be nothing like him.

I watch more snowflakes blanket the once-green grass in a sea of white. The snow hasn't stopped falling since I found her lying alone in a pool of her own blood in a bed fit for a queen. The white satin sheets she loved so much, and the cream-colored walls she just painted last year because she needed a change, were stained with crimson and brain matter. The gun she placed against her head had lain next to her right hand, and her suicide note, splattered in blood, laid next to her left.

In the note, she asked me to find peace and apologized for leaving, but she hadn't had it in her to stay any longer. She prayed to her gods, ones I'll never believe in and curse until the day I'm in the dirt, that I find love and get out of life everything I deserve. But finding love and finding peace are not what I'm searching for in this life, whether I deserve it.

Peace, I don't need.

Love, I can live without now that she's gone.

But revenge...now that's a tale as old as time.

I

ARABELLE

NEW YORK

ELEVEN YEARS LATER...

The crowd's thunderous cheers reach the dressing rooms near the back of the theater. After several standing ovations and curtain calls, the energy buzzing around all the dancers is electrifying as we make our way offstage.

The reaction and energy of the crowd are why I love to dance. This atmosphere makes my hard work and all my lonely nights worthwhile.

It's the final show of a month-long performance at the New York City Ballet, and while I'm glad it's over, I won't have time to relax. Tomorrow, I leave for a month-long press tour for the company, which includes photoshoots, interviews, and galas. I'm not looking forward to it. It's the part of my job I like the least. I wish I could dance and not have to do all the extra stuff.

I walk toward my dressing room, accepting congratulations on a job well done from members of the stage crew and by the few dancers who don't hate me. When I reach my dressing room, I push the door open and stop in my tracks.

"Oh. My. God."

I slowly enter, my hands covering my mouth as I look around the room. It's like I've stepped into a beautiful rose garden.

A fairy tale.

"Who did this?" I ask as I take in the room filled with long-stem, blood-red roses in gorgeous crystal vases.

With every performance, I get a private room, which is why the dancers hate me. They see it as preferential treatment. It's not my choice but required by the theater, so I know these bouquets of my favorite flowers are for me. They cover my vanity and the tables throughout the room. There are at least thirty vases of roses.

Who goes through all this trouble? And who spends all this money?

My father, Arthur Williamson, comes to mind. However, I dismiss that thought. My father wouldn't waste his money on something like this if he got no reward for it. He stopped giving me roses a long time ago.

The next person I think of is Dale Austin, my attorney and only friend. He's been more interested in me lately outside of our business relationship. Although flattering, I don't think it'll ever work, so I haven't returned his interest. I don't have that fire or butterflies in the pit of my stomach when he's around, even though I wish I did. He's honest and cares about me, but even this is a little too extravagant for him.

"Absolutely beautiful," I say as I move around the room, smelling the fragrant flowers and brushing my fingers over the delicate petals. I inhale the sweet-smelling aroma. "This had to cost a fortune. And they smell so different."

A knock sounds at the open door. I whirl around, coming face-to-face with Samuel Foster, the company director, and another man in a tuxedo. A very handsome man, but not in the conventional way. He has a rugged, harsh beauty about him. The stranger's long, wheat-colored hair is pulled into a low ponytail, and his piercing gray eyes gaze at me like he's staring into my soul, pulling me closer to him.

However, Samuel's oddly colored green eyes always darken when he sees me, so I keep my distance. He gives me the creeps, and the way he looks at me is worse when I'm in my performance leotards.

Although I'm grateful for the opportunity to perform, he's not one of my favorite people to be around. Samuel doesn't look at you. He leers, and by the look on his face, you can see what he's thinking. I don't like it. It makes my skin crawl, like a thousand spiders are moving underneath the surface. Just thinking about it, my body shivers. I can't stand being around him.

I've heard from the other dancers about what he expects them to do for patrons when attending our mandatory parties. I find it disgusting even if they find nothing wrong with it if it advances their careers. Although I've experienced nothing other than the occasional sexual remark, with Samuel's disregard for my concerns, I wouldn't put anything past him, which is why I try not to be alone with him. Ever. He's sleazy despite what he portrays to people like this guy with him right now.

"I didn't mean to scare you, Arabelle."

Samuel walks further into the room, reaching out to touch my arm, but I step away, which catches the eyes of the stranger. Samuel masks the look of anger that briefly replaces his once stoic face. Samuel doesn't recognize personal space, and when he's close to you, he just wants to touch you with his chubby, clammy hands.

"No worries." I plaster a smile on my face while keeping my distance. "How can I help you, Samuel?"

"Where did all the flowers come from?" Samuel's confusion quickly switches to anger. "I didn't know you had a boyfriend, Arabelle."

"They're beautiful, aren't they?" I ask, ignoring his comment because it's none of his business whether I have a boyfriend, although I don't.

"They are beautiful," the stranger answers. "Someone thinks you're a very special woman, Miss Williamson."

I turn to him and smile. He returns the gesture. "And you are?" I ask.

Samuel clears his throat. "This is Mr. Florian Larsson. He's one of our biggest supporters and a big fan of yours, I'm told. He wanted to speak with you for a moment."

Surprised that anyone would be a fan of mine, my eyes widen. "Really?" I ask. "Well, it's nice to meet you, Mr. Larsson."

I grasp his outstretched hand to shake, but he lifts mine to his lips, kissing my knuckles. I giggle, and Samuel mumbles something under his breath that I'm sure Mr. Larsson heard, too, but neither of us comments on it.

"The pleasure is all mine, Miss Williamson. It is Miss, right?" Mr. Larsson asks, lowering our hands. "I don't want to disrespect you or your husband if you're married."

"No, I'm not married, and you can call me Arabelle, Mr. Larsson."

He maintains his grasp on my hand, his thumb slowly brushing my knuckles as his gaze drops to my lips, then moves back to my eyes. I'm unsure if he realizes what he's doing, but his touch sends a surge of heat across my entire body. I should pull away and turn my head, but I can't. I'm trapped in his gaze.

Samuel clearing his throat again reminds me we aren't alone, pulling me out of my trance. Samuel scowls at me, and I look down as heat crawls up my neck. I've been caught ogling one of our donors by the company director, but I can't help it. There's something about him that interests me. I've never had anyone provoke a visceral response from me like I'm experiencing now.

"Call me Florian."

He smiles, and it's like I've died and gone to heaven. It highlights his rugged beauty even more.

"I just wanted to say that you were absolutely wonderful tonight," he continues. "It was a beautiful performance, and I had a wonderful time."

Something stirs in my stomach. The compliment coming from him seems different.

"Thank you." The flush deepens on my neck and moves across my face. "I'm so glad you enjoyed it."

"I did. Tremendously." He smiles. "I've never seen a terrible performance from you."

"You've seen me dance before tonight?"

"Of course. Work gets in the way sometimes, but I try to see you perform as much as possible."

"What kind of work do you do?" I ask, curious.

Samuel claps his hands. "Okay, Mr. Larsson."

Florian drops my hand as Samuel guides him closer to the door, and I immediately miss the connection.

"There are a few people I'd like you to meet, and I'm sure your fiancée is waiting for you."

Of course, someone like him would have a fiancée.

"And I'm sure Arabelle needs to get ready for the afterparty," Samuel continues, and Mr. Larsson—Florian—doesn't look too happy with him.

"I wanted to say congratulations, Arabelle. Enjoy the flowers. They're almost as beautiful as you."

He gives me one last look before he leaves my dressing room, Samuel following him and rambling about plans for the upcoming season and how he hopes Florian will be donating. When they are gone, I sigh and return my focus to all the flowers.

"What am I going to do with all these flowers?"

Taking one of the roses from its vase, I search for a card. Once I find it, I pluck it from the cardholder, open the small black envelope, and then pull the note from inside. I trace the lovely gold font as I read:

From the shadows, I watch, and in the shadows, I will remain despite the longing of my heart.

Frowning, I place the card back in the envelope. "What does that mean?"

2

FLORIAN

LOS ANGELES

The shadows of the dimly lit room hid me from everyone's view, including hers. I sip from the whiskey tumbler as my eyes clock her every movement. She walks, talks, and laughs just like she dances—with grace.

Two months ago, meeting her in person made me fixate on her even more. I don't know how many performances of hers I've seen in person or magazine covers I've collected where she's on the cover. I've lost count of how many magazine and newspaper articles written about her that I've neatly cut out, which are stored in the safe in my home office.

Fixate may not be a strong enough word to describe my feelings for her. She consumes me. She's everything I want and everything I can't have. However, that doesn't keep me from seeking her out whenever possible.

Just like now.

She stops talking mid-sentence, looks up, and searches the room full of admirers, other dancers, and patrons just like me. No doubt she's searching for me because she senses me when I'm near her. That's one of the reasons I know she belongs to me. It's one reason I know she's the other half of my soul. And it's also one of the reasons nothing can ever happen between us. She's a weakness I don't need. A weakness my father will exploit if he ever finds out she exists. So, I remain in the shadows to keep her safe.

Her eyes stop exactly where I've been standing for the past hour, jealously watching her interact with the people in this room. People who aren't worthy of being in her presence. She can't see me, even though she knows I'm here.

She stares in my direction a few moments longer, trying to decide if it's her imagination or if she's really being watched. As intrigue and fear dance in her eyes, excitement slithers down my spine. I'd love to see that look in her eyes more often. I'd love to see it when I tighten my grip around her slender neck while I'm deep inside her pussy.

Our connection breaks when a hand lands on her forearm, taking her attention away from me. Anger rushes through me. Even though she can't see me, she can feel me, and I don't like her eyes not being on me.

She politely smiles at the older man, who's somewhere in his mid to late fifties. He's in shape, and he looks like he stays tanned ninety-five percent of the year and has the money to make sure he can attract a younger woman that he's too old for, despite the gold band glistening on the ring finger of his left hand.

To anyone who's paying any fucking attention, she's not interested in the conversation, while he's unquestionably interested in her. I can't hear what he's saying from where I'm standing, but I can see the lust hanging heavy in his eyes and the uneasiness in hers.

He touches her arm again, brushing a finger down her bare skin, and I grit my teeth, clenching the tumbler full of whiskey. I force myself not to react. It's not the first time tonight she's had unwanted advances. You'd think the theater would protect the dancers from handsy patrons, but they are the bankrollers, so anything goes.

"I need to have a talk with Samuel if this is how the dancers are treated. If he doesn't keep them in check when it comes to Arabelle, then I will, and I'll keep him in check, too."

She inches away from the older man's touch. Her eyes glance to where I hide in the shadows, like she wants my help. I'd love nothing more than to walk up to her, introduce myself as her partner, and show every one of these motherfuckers eyeing her like they want to fuck her that she's mine. But I can't do that. I'm not worthy, and neither is any one of these motherfuckers. So, I'll stay in the darkness. Watching. Wanting. Obsessing over someone who'll never be mine.

My unattainable beauty.

I reluctantly pull myself from the confines of the darkness and walk outside to keep from attacking the man. As I wait for the valet to bring my car, I debate whether I should stay to make sure that bastard keeps his hands to himself. However, I decide to leave before she does, so I don't miss my opportunity to spend some time with her.

I imagine what life with her would be like if we were together. Can she deal with the beast lurking inside me? Can I let everything go, including the feud with my father, if it would mean that she would be mine? I'm not sure if that's even possible.

The valet pulls my car up in front of me, and it brings me out of my thoughts of things that aren't even possible. He jumps out of the driver's side and places my keys in my hand. I tip him a hundred-dollar bill, then slip behind the steering wheel and drive to her apartment in the city not too far from the theater.

The city's nightlife is waking. The sidewalks are full of people in tuxedos, gowns, and cocktail dresses, ready for a night on the town. Normally, I'd be a part of the crowd with Adahlia on my arm, but tonight, Arabelle takes precedence over anything else I want or need to do.

Once I reach the area near her apartment complex, I pull along the curb close to the building's entrance. There's always a door attendant, and you need to sign in at the front desk if you're not a resident. But I don't leave a record of my visits. There's an alley separating Arabelle's building from the one beside it that's cloaked in the darkness, which I use.

I sneak down the alleyway until I reach the unlocked window of the basement. Even with a doorman and the protocol of all visitors signing in, the security at this place is shit, just like her apartment in New York. Neither place has security cameras outside the building except at the front entrance and the employee entrances at the rear. The owners are more concerned about if their employees are taking smoke breaks on the clock than the actual residents' safety. The cameras have blind spots, which I've memorized, so I can come and go as I please.

When she stays here, this is always the way I get into the building. Sometimes, my man, Hugo, keeps an eye on her, but lately, I've been doing it myself. Tonight, the pleasure is all mine.

There's a narrow window that's always open enough to lift. I slip in, my feet planting with a thud on the cement floor. It's not the cleanest place, but it gets me to where I need to be. So, I ignore the dirt and cobwebs staining my expensive suit and secure the window just in case someone comes down to the basement or the alley and questions why it's open.

Once inside, I quietly ascend the wooden basement stairs leading to the stairwell, then take the stairs to her fourth-floor apartment. When I reach her floor, I peek out from the stairwell door to ensure no one can see me.

There are only four apartments on this floor, including hers. The only one who gives me problems is the nosy neighbor in the apartment across from hers. So, now, I come when it's late at night, and the old bitch is asleep.

Slowly, I approach her apartment door, trying to remain as quiet as possible. I have at least fifteen minutes to get inside and settle in. Arabelle keeps the same schedule. She never spends more than an hour and a half at the after-parties before she excuses herself and comes home.

I unlock her apartment door with the key I made from hers, push the door open, creep inside, and quietly shut the door behind me before twisting the lock.

When I first decided to visit her myself, I'd pick the lock. I've been doing it since I was a kid in Sweden. I started off as a petty thief to help my mother since my father was a piece of shit. I learned many things, like picking locks, kids shouldn't have to learn so we could survive. The things I had to do and witnessed shaped a lot of my views on family and people, neither of which I have much tolerance for, especially my family.

A smile graces my face as I step inside and look around her apartment. It's been a few weeks since I've been able to stop by in person because I've been working nonstop and dealing with my youngest brother. Although I've seen her through the cameras I secretly installed a few months back, it's never enough.

I've spent so much time in her apartment that it feels like home. It smells like her—rain mixed with mandarins. It's a calming scent, one that settles the beast inside me.

Glancing at my watch, I now have at least ten minutes before she's home, so I can't linger even though I'd love to.

My dress shoes echo on the bamboo floors that run throughout her entire apartment as I walk the familiar path down the hallway to her guest bedroom. It's right across the hall from her bedroom. When I reach it, I step inside to wait until she arrives.

I've lost count of how often I've done this same routine. Creepy? Sure, it is, but I don't mind being creepy as long as I can spend time with her.

Like clockwork, the echo of the lock turning sounds throughout the apartment. She tosses the keys in the basket, which sits on a table beside the door, like always, and then the lock on the front door clicks into place.

She sighs as she makes her way down the hallway and then into her bedroom. She sleeps with the bedroom door cracked, making it easy to sneak into her room once she drifts off. Like I said, she sticks to the same routine, which in reality isn't good for her but is very good for me. She's a creature of habit, so it has made it easy to see her whenever I can without getting caught.

Some would say I'm insane, especially to enter her apartment and watch her while she sleeps. But it's the only time I can get close enough to her, and it brings me peace. If that makes me crazy, then I have no problem being that crazy motherfucker as long as I get to spend some time in her presence. I need it like I need air to breathe.

The shower switches on, and her beautiful voice touches my ears as she hums a song I recognize from tonight's performance. I've imagined so many times slipping behind her while she's in the shower, running my calloused hands down her wet, naked flesh as I thrust in and out of her tight cunt from behind. Then finally, I fall to my knees and worship that juicy cunt full of my cum with my tongue.

I groan as the images fill my head. I grab my hardening cock through my dress slacks, wishing the friction was coming from her cunt or mouth instead of my hand.

"Fuck." Shaking my head, I try to remove the very enticing images that have me wanting to act instead of remaining in the shadows as I should.

The sound of the shower shutting off brings me out of my head. I watch, transfixed on the sight of a naked Arabelle as she exits the bathroom with a trail of steam tailing her. One of the upsides to seeing her at night—she always sleeps naked.

The moonlight shining through the window hits her sexy body perfectly as I catch glimpses of her as she moves around the room preparing to go to bed. Her toned frame causes my dick to twitch.

She's fucking magnificent.

When she finally disappears from view, instead of her light snores filtering into my ears, it's her moans. Moans that cause my ears to perk up. Moans that travel straight to my cock, which has gone from twitching to being hard as fucking steel.

I step carefully across the hallway, making sure not to be heard, although I'm sure the sexy sounds she's making will drown out my footsteps. I peek through the crack she's left in the door, which is wide enough for me to see her lying on her bed. Her ebony legs are spread wide open.

The light from the moon filtering through the open venetian blinds of her floor-to-ceiling window glistens off her gorgeous pussy. Anyone who wants to see what she's doing has a great view.

There's no doubt what she's doing and where she's doing it is on purpose. Maybe my sweet little Belle is a temptress who loves for someone to watch her.

I wish I could test my theory.

Maybe I'll buy the building across from her so I can see her up close and personal without relying on the cameras.

Her nimble fingers of one hand are moving through her bare cunt, giving me an excellent view of her moist petals, a gradual shift from brown to pink, while the other tweaks her pert brown nipples. I suppress the moan climbing up my throat as I watch, entranced as my tame beauty looks like a sex goddess calling me.

Her mouth is slightly open, and her plump lips are wet from where she's licked them before trapping the bottom one between her teeth. Her eyes are closed tightly, her hair slightly disheveled, and the most serene look graces her stunning face. My dick is so fucking hard watching as she masturbates that it's challenging to stay rooted in place. I have to remind myself she has no fucking clue who I am and why I'm in her apartment. So, if I want to keep any kind of connection with her, she can't know I exist. Or that I've been watching her.

I slowly unzip my dress slacks, pull my hard cock from its confines, and grip my cock so tightly I have to force myself not to groan. I've never jacked off while this close to her, but I might have to make an exception if this is how it's going to be. I can see myself getting addicted to this.

I stroke my dick while watching my obsession fuck herself, her nimble fingers moving in and out of her wet folds. And it's one of the most erotic things I've seen or experienced in my life.

I've been with many women over my lifetime. Fucked in many places. I've even had my share of orgies, but none of that compares to watching Arabelle's gorgeous cunt on display while she gets herself off.

Fucking magnificent.

"Yes," she moans as she rides her fingers while I imagine it's my cock. She tweaks those perfect dark nipples that I wish were in my mouth instead.

"Fuck, yes," I mumble, stifling my groan as I jack off to the rhythm of her movements and to the hypnotic melody of her lovely moans and whimpers.

Planting one arm above my head against the frame of the door, I tighten my grip on my length and speed up my stroke while gathering precum from the head of my cock with each pass, hissing at the sensitivity.

Damn, she's so fucking close, and so am I. The way her entrance is gripping her fingers, her juices leaking down the crack of her ass, I wish I could make it last longer because I don't know when I'll have this chance again. So, I'm not coming until she does. I want to close my eyes and relish in the delicious feeling getting ready to take over my body, but I don't want to miss the look of rapture on her beautiful face either.

The sound of her moans and the smell of her drenched cunt fill the space. Fuck, I wish I could step inside the room, but if this is as close as I can get to watching the euphoria cross her face when she comes, it'll have to do.

At least for now.

Her body tenses, then trembles. She releases the most sensual whimper I've ever heard as she finally pushes herself over the edge, which forces my own orgasm to barrel through my body. My legs tremble as I release my load. Thank fuck she's so caught up in her own bliss that she doesn't hear my deep guttural groan when I come in my fucking hand.

I expect her to go clean her cum from between her thighs, but she doesn't, which gives me more dirty images of licking her cunt clean as I watch like the creep that I am while she gets comfortable and closes her eyes with the sweetest smile on her face.

I wonder how often she masturbates. She has no man, and all the times I've been through her home, I've never come across a vibrator. Her not having a vibrator is definitely something I need to change.

Maybe I'll leave that along with the roses she loves so much next time.

I close my eyes as I imagine her pussy becoming wet as she uses a vibrator against her clit and her entrance. Now, that would be a show to die for.

After a few minutes, she's lightly snoring. I push her door open and move into her room. I close my eyes, inhaling the fragrance of her space.

"Fucking heaven," I mutter.

When she finally does crash, nothing wakes her, so I don't expect her to catch me while I'm here. Quietly, I walk to the bathroom and grab some of the cleansing wipes from the bathroom counter. I clean the cum from my hand and wipe off my cock, then discard the wipe in the small trash can in the corner. I push my shit back inside my pants, then zip them back up.

I haven't come that hard in a long time. I should leave and get some rest, but then, if I do that, I won't get to spend time with her, so instead of doing what I need to do, I walk back into her bedroom and focus on the most beautiful woman I've ever seen–the only woman who makes this cold dead heart inside my chest beat.

Bathed in the moon's gentle light, her small form appears ethereal. I've missed her. I've missed her presence. I wish I could kick off my shoes, slip into bed beside her, and wrap her in my arms, but I know I can't. And wishing is for fools. This is as close as I will ever get to having her.

I slowly walk toward her bed as she sleeps curled up with one of her massive pillows. I wonder if she has so many pillows because she dislikes sleeping alone. She's so beautiful, and my heart aches that I can't be with her the way that I want to.

When I reach her bedside, I lightly brush my finger down her cheek, relishing in the smooth, silky texture of her skin against mine. She sighs, and her eyes flutter as she leans into my touch.

"Damn, how I wish things could be different, my Beauty," I say low enough I don't wake her.

Resigned to my fate of never being able to touch her in the way I desire or be with her in any way other than this, I walk to the chair in front of her window. The same chair I use every time I get to spend time with her.

Peace engulfs me as I sit and watch her sleep, and I release a contented sigh. At this very moment, there's no other place I rather be.

3
FLORIAN

After I left Arabelle sleeping comfortably in her apartment, I decided that once I returned to New York, I would have a much-needed conversation with Samuel Foster. I've been at the theater waiting for him to arrive so we can get a few things straight. Now, I'm sitting in his office, which is the last room at the end of a long dark corridor nestled at the back of the theater, not too far from the dancers' dressing rooms.

The seclusion will come in handy just in case the theater isn't empty like I think it is. Alrick disagreed with me doing this right now once I contacted him to get eyes on Samuel until I returned. He argues that this wouldn't be the best use of our time since Olan is gaining some momentum in his war against me. But I can't see any other way around it. He's putting not only every dancer who works at the theater in danger by letting handsy patrons accost them, but also Arabelle. And that's something I cannot and will not let happen.

His cheap cologne mixed with the scent of even cheaper cigars lingers in the air, filling the small, cramped office. Sitting behind his small oak desk, the eerie glow of a desk lamp casting the only light in the dark room, I casually sip the scotch he has stashed in his desk drawer. It might not be top-shelf scotch, but it's better than nothing.

The family photographs he proudly displays on his desk capture my attention. He's standing beside what I assume is his wife and two young daughters, the girls standing in front of them with huge smiles on their faces.

I'm not a family man. I don't see myself having children in the future, but I am curious about the type of man who preys on women despite having a family. What kind of man would put women in such a vulnerable position, especially when he knows that his own wife and daughters could become prey for men with the same intentions?

Samuel needs to be taught a lesson he will never forget. I prefer that he doesn't live because once a threat, always a threat, so we'll just have to see how things progress before I decide which way this goes.

When I first met Arabelle, I couldn't help but notice the fiery jealousy and anger burning in his eyes and resonating in his voice, especially when he caught sight of the vases full of flowers I gave her. Of course, neither had known the flowers were from me, but it showed his utter disdain for anyone who shows her any attention. I also couldn't help but notice the deliberate distance she kept, as if trying to create a barrier between them while he persistently tried to invade her personal space. It pissed me off then, but I had to maintain my composure. At that time, I had been just a wealthy donor and a fan of hers. Now, it's time he pays for his actions.

The doorknob rattles, and his hushed whispers echo through the wood panel door of his office. He's not alone, but that won't change the course of what I need to do.

When the door opens, Samuel steps in, tightly gripping the hand of a woman who looks like this is the last place she wants to be. She looks like she's being forced to come in here with him.

She reminds me a lot of Arabelle, with beautiful ebony skin, a dancer's body, and dark hair in a neat bun at the nape of her neck. At this point, I don't think it's a coincidence that he's meeting up with someone who looks like her. With the appearance of this Arabelle lookalike, it means he's fixated on Arabelle, which means I cannot let him live.

Neither have noticed me yet because I'm shrouded in darkness. He closes the door behind them, the sound of the lock clicking into place echoing through the room.

"I'm not sure about this," the woman says.

Irritation crosses Samuel's face. Either her refusal isn't something he's used to, or he's pissed she's not going along with whatever he has planned.

"I think I need to leave," she continues.

She tries to pull her hand out of his grasp, but he grips it tighter.

"Arabelle, this is what you have to do if you want to dance at my theater. I want to see how well that mouth works, and if you're unwilling, there's the door. I can fill the spot with someone else tonight."

"That's not my name."

When he finally lets her hand go, he walks to a long brown leather couch in front of a bookshelf, unbuttons his pants, pulls them down along with his briefs, and then sits on the down, palming his erection.

"It doesn't matter what your name is, darling." He moves his hand up and down his dick. "What matters is that you are here to get on your knees to show me that you really want this opportunity."

The woman looks completely mortified, and I have no doubt she's not the first one he's done this to. Did he try this same thing with Arabelle?

The anger surging through me at the thought makes me see red. I hate a fucking predator, especially one that's preying on my beauty. It's time to put an end to this.

"Sweetheart, whoever you are, I need you to leave," I say from the shadows. "Now!"

She wastes no time rushing to the door, quickly unlocks it, and slams it behind her.

"What the fuck!" Samuel shouts, jumping up from the couch with his hardened length still on full display. "Who are you? You can't be in here!"

"Put your shit back in your pants, asshole," I sneer.

His eyes widen in disbelief as he realizes he has been caught with his hard dick out in the open.

"I don't know who you are, but you're not supposed to be in

here," he says as he tries his best to stuff his shit back inside his pants, then zips them up. "I'm calling the cops."

"Are you sure you want to do that? I can just tell them everything I just saw. Sounds like you were trying to force that young woman to perform sex acts to be considered for a job. I'm sure she's not the only one you've coerced, and I'm sure she and others will confirm it once the cops start asking questions."

"I have no fucking idea what you think you heard, but if you don't—"

"Have a seat," I say, cutting off his lie.

He stops what he's doing and then looks at the door like he's thinking about making a run for it. It's probably the best thing for him because his death will be quick, but what fun will that be for me?

"You'll be dead before you make it, Mr. Foster. Have a seat."

I lean forward so I'm no longer hidden in the shadows. I need him to see who he's dealing with.

"Mr. Larsson?"

"Sit, Foster. Now!"

Flinching, he races to the chair placed in front of his desk. "What are you doing here, sir?"

I can hear the confusion and fear in his voice. He knows that I donate a healthy amount of money to this theater, and I have enough pull in this city to cause a hell of a lot of problems for him if I ever speak about what I just witnessed. However, he doesn't have to worry about everyone discovering what he's been up to.

"I'm here to have a little chat with you, Foster, so we can get some things straight when it comes to Arabelle. Imagine my surprise to see this little interaction between you and the young lady."

"Oh, that was nothing. That was definitely not what it looked like. We just had a few things to discuss."

"With your dick hanging out?" I ask, my brow arched. "The same things you tried to discuss with Arabelle?"

I can't be certain if he's attempted the same thing with Arabelle, but if he did it once, chances are he has done it before and would repeat it.

His eyes widen before he quickly conceals his shock. "I've done nothing wrong and have no idea what you're talking about, Mr. Larsson." He jumps to his feet. "I don't think this line of questioning is appropriate. I think it's time for me to leave."

I rise from behind his desk, circle it, and approach him. Standing just inches in front of him, I see pure fear in his eyes. He's so scared that his body visibly shakes with terror, and I absolutely love it.

"You're not going anywhere."

"Please, I've done nothing wrong. No matter what the bitch has told you."

Without warning, I punch him in the throat. His eyes brim with tears as he hunches over, his shoulders shaking. He struggles to scream, clawing at his throat, but all that comes out is a faint, muffled noise.

"Watch your fucking mouth!"

He raises a hand. "Please...I..."

I yank his head back using his hair, forcing him to look at me. "When I first came here, I wanted to talk to you about how the patrons were treating the dancers. Then I saw firsthand how you treat them. I saw firsthand your fixation on Arabelle. Now, my decision has changed."

"Please. I can just quit and leave. You'll never see me again."

I force him to his knees, never releasing my grip on his hair.

"Please, I'll do anything you want me to," he begs. "Just don't hurt me."

I stand behind him and remove my knife from its holster with my other hand. I lean over near his ear. "No amount of begging will save you," I whisper. "She's mine. No one else can have her."

As the sharp blade glides across his neck, a metallic smell fills the air. It's a familiar smell, one that I've come to love, but I don't have time to relish it. The theater will be open in a few hours.

Pushing his body to the floor, I watch as he desperately clutches at the wound to no avail. It will only take a few seconds for him to bleed out. With a deep sigh, I watch as his body goes limp, and then I reach for my phone to dial Alrick.

"It's done," I say as soon as he answers the phone. "I need the body removed and this place cleaned up."

His deep sigh reverberates through the phone line. "On the way."

I ignore Alrick's aggravated sigh, end the call, and stuff my phone in my pocket. I will never regret what I have to do to keep her safe. If it comes down to it, I will not hesitate to kill anyone who's a threat to her.

4

ARABELLE

CHICAGO

After ordering room service, I fall backward onto the bed of the master bedroom of the hotel suite I've been staying in for the past week. I've been doing promotional photoshoots and interviews for the dance company, which the new company director scheduled for me to get my name and face out there. It's almost set in stone that I'll be named principal dancer. Hopefully, this will be the final push I need.

I had been discussing it with Samuel before he suddenly left everything behind to take on a new position in a European theater company, as confirmed by the theater company. No one, including the dancers or even the new director, knew anything about this new position or which company. I arrived one morning at the theater, was informed about his departure before meeting with the new director and was then thrust into rehearsals. Although I find it strange when he had so many new ideas for the upcoming season, I can't say that I will miss him. He was creepy as hell. Hopefully, the new director isn't the same kind of man.

This is my last day in Chicago. Tomorrow, I'll be flying back to New York, and I can't say I'm looking forward to it because my phone has been ringing nonstop for the past few days. When he calls, he wants something, and I don't have the time or the patience to deal with my father.

I jump at the sound of a knock at the door. Since I've been here, the attendant has been flirting with me when he brings my food. I don't believe he knows who I am, and I'm glad because I don't want to scare him away. I'm not that comfortable around guys, but he makes it easy, and I like it.

I fluff my curls, straighten my oversized shirt to make sure I'm presentable, and then walk to the door. I'm not one for wearing makeup unless I'm performing, so if he's the type that likes glitz and glam, I'm not that girl.

I check the peephole, but I don't see anyone there or the room service cart.

"Hello," I call out instead of opening the door. However, I'm met with silence. "Hello," I call out again.

After a few moments with no response, I unlock the door, pull back the security latch, slowly open the door, then peek out. When I don't see anyone, I open the door wider and look back and forth down the hallway, but it's empty. However, when I close the door, I notice the red rose and black envelope on the floor.

I look down the hallway again before I pick up the rose and envelope. Just one day, I would like to see who's leaving these for me. I've been getting a lot of roses lately, ever since my dressing room was decorated with them in the most beautiful crystal vases.

Excitement races through me as I close the door when I should be freaked out. The only people who know I'm here work for the theater. But I'm not freaked out. I love all the roses, and the notes are always so nice and eloquent.

I sit on the couch and smell the flower, then smile. I can't pinpoint the fragrance, but they always smell so good, nothing like any flower I've smelled before. I've tried to track down the person who's been sending them to thank them because they always bring me joy, but I've come up empty so far.

I place the rose on the couch beside me, then pick up the envelope and pull out the black card with lovely gold writing.

This rose, although beautiful, will never compare to the light of your soul that battles the darkness of my heart. You will always be my unattainable beauty.

I sigh. "I wish whoever this is would make themselves known."

I'm not scared, though I can admit it's a little creepy. They always know where I am. I should be scared, but I've received so many flowers and notes now that I actually look forward to getting them. Dale says I've got to be experiencing some type of Stockholm syndrome. Maybe he's right.

Despite my petite frame, men are intimidated by me once they find out I have a career and can support myself. Also, being recognizable to people, especially in the media, has made men shy away from trying to date me. I understand because who wants to be on the cover of tabloids if you didn't sign up for it? The few who've tried didn't stay around too long, and I never heard from them again.

Another knock sounds at the door.

Room service!

The sound of his voice sends a surge of excitement coursing through me. Every time I request room service, Pierre Gaultier, a cute server with a delightful French accent, brings my meals. He's soft-spoken, very cordial, and has a killer smile.

I spring up from the couch in my excitement at seeing him again and completely forget about the rose and the note.

I look through the peephole before opening the door. I stand back, and Pierre enters, pushing the food cart, then closes the door behind him. The delicious aroma fills the space, and I can't wait to dig in. For the past few months, I've been eating light meals to keep my weight in check, but tonight I'm going all out. I'll need to put in extra effort to ensure I burn off the calories.

"Bonjour, Arabelle," he says, and my stomach flutters. "How are you today?"

I can't stop the smile from crossing my face. His dark hair, slightly disheveled, adds to his sexiness. And that voice, I can't get enough of it. Hearing his French accent takes me back to my time in France.

"Hello, Pierre," I say, almost unable to get the words out. "I'm doing well. How are you doing today?"

"It's been hectic, but my shift is almost over, so that's good. Where would you like me to set up your meal?"

"Over by the couch is fine."

I motion to the small living area of the suite. He nods, and I follow him as he pushes the small dinner cart toward the couch.

"So, what are your plans for the rest of the day?"

He removes the lids from the plates on my tray.

"Nothing." I sit down on the couch. "Eat, then watch a movie. Maybe read a book, I guess."

I don't do much when I travel for work. Staying in, reading books, and watching movies is what I do in my spare time when I have it. My life is monotonous, filled with work and a constant stream of smutty books and old black-and-white films.

"What are your plans?" I ask as I open the bottle of water he hands me.

He takes a step back from the dinner cart, looks at me, then smiles. "I was hoping you would go with me to get a drink."

"You want to get a drink with me?"

I'm not much of a drinker, but I do like the occasional glass of wine.

He laughs. "Yes, if you would like or if you don't have a boyfriend?" His gaze shifts to the rose, then back to me. "I don't want to cause any problems."

No boyfriend, but I do have an admirer.

I shake my head. "No, I don't have a boyfriend, and I would love to get a drink with you."

He releases a breath, and a look crosses his face that I can't make out before he masks it.

"I get off in a couple of hours," he says. "Would that be a good time?"

I look at my watch, and it's still pretty early, so I won't be out too late. A couple of glasses of wine won't hurt.

"Sure," I say. "Give me your phone."

He reaches into his back pocket, grabs his phone, puts in his password, and then hands it to me. I add my name and number to the contacts, then return the phone.

"Text me when you're available."

He smiles. "I'll see you in a few hours."

"It's a date," I say, and his smile widens.

He walks to the door, then leaves, and I settle down to eat.

"I can't believe I have a date."

I cover my face with my hands and scream. Even though it's just drinks, it's the first date I've had in a long time.

5
FLORIAN

It turns out Arabelle is in Chicago, and it's just a coincidence that I'm here, too. As soon as Hugo gave me her whereabouts, I sent a rose and note to her hotel suite to show her my thoughts are always with her.

The day was off to a fantastic start, and I eagerly looked forward to seeing her. I wasn't about to let this chance slip through my fingers since she's so close. I've been longing to see her in person for weeks now, but business has prevented it. However, today, I cut my business meeting short when I received an urgent phone call from Hugo, who revealed that my beauty is on a date.

As I crack my knuckles, a wave of anger washes over me, intensifying my urge to kill this motherfucker. When she's with other men, I spiral out of control. It's frustrating how Arabelle has an unsettling ability to make me feel like a wild animal, even though I prefer stability. She drives the beast inside me crazy, and she's the only one who can calm me.

"Where's she now?"

The sounds of laughter, music, and the distinct clinking of pool balls reverberate through the air. She's only been in Chicago for a few days, and now I'm on my way to where she's hanging out at a bar with some fucking guy. My irritation is only rising the more I think about what led up to her actually going out with this guy.

She doesn't date.

"They're sitting at the bar at The Black Star Bar and Grill, and she's having a glass of wine." Hugo sighs. "Don't you think this is a little too much, Beast? You've had me following this woman for months. You've also been following her when I'm not around."

"Are you questioning my orders, Hugo?" I ask, annoyed he's even saying anything about what the fuck I'm doing. One thing I don't tolerate is anyone questioning me about my business. "I don't see how what I've had you do affects your pay, so what's the problem?"

"I just don't understand what I'm doing here, Florian. What's the point of following this woman twenty-four-seven? She has no life. All she does is dance, travel for her job, and go home. This is actually the first date she's been on the entire time you've had me keeping an eye on her. Don't you think my time would be better spent on your father?"

His time would probably be better spent on keeping an eye on Olan, but I need him here.

"The point is I pay you to do what I ask regardless of whether you think it's a waste of time. What I've asked is for you to watch her. If you have an issue doing that, you can always be replaced. The choice is yours, Hugo."

I don't expect anyone to understand my obsession with her. I don't understand the shit myself. But what I expect is for my men, who I pay very well, to do what I want. No questions asked. If they don't want to, there's always someone out there who will gladly take their place. While this job is perfect for Hugo, all he needs to do is say the word, and he'll be on the next plane back to New York. I'll hate to do it because he's one of my best men, and I can trust him to do everything in his power to make sure Arabelle is safe, but I can easily replace him with someone who won't question me.

"I'm good." He lets out a deep, exasperated sigh. "It's just fucking weird, that's all."

"Who the fuck is this guy?" I ask, suppressing the annoyance I feel toward Hugo. Yes, it may have been weird, but I don't give two shits what he or anybody thinks about what I'm doing. He's here to do a job.

"He works at the hotel she's staying at," Hugo says, breaking through my thoughts. "His name is Pierre Gaultier. He's the son of a French diplomat."

He's getting ready to be the dead son of a French diplomat.

"Before you get any thoughts in your head, Florian, he's the son of a very *high-ranking diplomat*," Hugo warns, like it will make a difference in my decision. It won't. "One who can bring hell down on you if you harm his son. It's not worth it."

Only I have the authority to decide if it's worth the effort. If Arabelle is on a date with him, then it's worth it.

"Why the hell is a diplomat's son working at a hotel?"

"He attacked some girl and got kicked out of school. His parents refused to fund his lifestyle because of ruining the family name," Hugo says. "But I will repeat, it's not worth it."

Even more reason for him to be far away from Arabelle.

"My driver is pulling up outside," I say, ignoring his comment. "When they leave, keep your eyes on her."

"And what are you going to do?" he asks, sighing because he knows whatever he's concerned about, I don't give a fuck about.

"I'm following him."

"I'm going to sit at the bar next to them so I can keep a close eye on them."

"Good," I say, ending the call.

I don't need to hear anyone tell me what I'm doing is wrong. I know it's not right. I just don't give a fuck. She belongs to me. If I want to follow her around or have my men follow her, that's what I'm going to do. If this guy even tries to touch her, I'll kill him.

My driver stops across from The Black Star Bar and Grill, the bar where Arabelle and this motherfucker are having their date. Tonight is the first time in a long time she's changed her routine, and I don't like it one fucking bit.

"I can't believe she's on a fucking date," I mumble, waiting for an update from Hugo. "Her laughs and smiles are mine. Not this motherfucker's."

As soon as my phone rings, I grab it. Before I can speak, all that fills the air is the sound of Hugo's loud breathing, music, and laughter.

"I think the motherfucker drugged her, Beast. Move the fuck out of the way!"

Anger surges through my body like a tidal wave. "I'm going to gut that motherfucker."

"I'm following them toward the back of the bar," Hugo continues. "She's stumbling, and her words are slurred from what I can hear. They haven't been here long enough for her to have drank that much, Beast. He had to have drugged her."

I can hear the genuine concern for her safety in his voice, which sends another surge of anger and panic through me.

"I'll meet you around back." I end the call, and without hesitation, I exit my vehicle and sprint toward the back of the bar, where a narrow, dimly lit alleyway separates the bar from the neighboring business.

The air is saturated with the scent of damp wood and the sour smell of garbage. Stacks of crates lean against the brick wall of the bar, contrasting with the rusty green dumpster nearby. I dodge greasy-looking puddles of God knows what, maybe dried vomit or piss, and shards of broken glass.

The metal exit door to the bar swings open, creating a loud bang as it slams against the building. Pierre Gaultier steps out, his arms wrapped tightly around Arabelle. She can barely walk, her footsteps are slow and heavy, and she can't keep her eyes open.

I'm going to kill him.

He hasn't seen me yet, and I look over his shoulder when Hugo steps out of the bar. He quietly closes the door behind him.

As Pierre Gaultier pulls Arabelle along, she trips over her own feet, and one of her heels comes off, her bare foot hitting one of the many puddles of muck.

"Come on, bitch!" He slams her tiny frame against the grimy brick wall of the bar and pushes her skirt up above her waist.

Mumbling and resisting, she tries to push him away, but whatever he gave her has left her disoriented and powerless to fight off someone who has at least seventy-five pounds on her.

While he tries to undo the button on his jeans, her head falls onto his shoulder.

"Whoa, is she all right?" I ask as I approach them. "She's not looking too good."

I'm trying to stay as calm as possible when all I can see is red. He looks up and stops fumbling with his jeans. He grabs her and begins pulling her toward the end of the alley while attempting to maneuver around me.

"Yes, she's fine," he says. "You know how drunk bitches can get."

I stop him in his tracks by placing my palm on his chest. At the same time, I remove my knife from the sheath attached to the waistband at the back of my dress slacks. I like carrying knives better than guns. They're silent and efficient.

"I'm just trying to take my girlfriend home," he says in an irritated tone. "Get the fuck out of my way!"

He hasn't noticed Hugo moving up behind him.

"Your girl?" I chuckle, arching my brow. "She's mine, Pierre. Not yours."

Ignoring any possible response, I thrust the knife into his abdomen, warm blood instantly staining my hands. As I observe his eyes widening with shock and then filling with fear, a twisted pleasure courses through my black soul. He releases his grip on Arabelle, and Hugo catches her before she hits the ground.

I glance at Hugo. "Take her to the hospital," I order. "Call me."

Seeing the dazed look in her eyes and hearing her struggle to speak tightens my heart in my chest. Despite the consuming need to go with her, I need to deal with this asshole first.

Hugo nods and disappears from the alley, carrying a confused Arabelle.

My attention is drawn back to the man, his hands tightly gripping my shoulders while blood slowly trickles from his mouth. Fury, rage, and determination surge through my veins, igniting every fiber of my being—fury because he thought he could get away with raping her, rage because he tricked her to get her in this position in the first fucking place, and determination to protect her from anyone who wants to harm her, including myself.

"You think you can touch her and get away with it?"

The knife sinks deeper into his stomach, and his face twists in agony. "Please," he begs, his voice trembling. "Do...don't kill..."

"Please...please, don't kill me," I mock, my voice rising. "No amount of begging will save you, motherfucker. How many women have you done this to?"

I don't really need to know the answer.

Arabelle definitely isn't the first woman he's done this to. There's no telling how many single women he's lured to this bar from that hotel. However, she will be the last.

"Anyone else involved in this?" I ask.

I'm not sure how he was able to spike her drink, but if anyone else is involved, they will end up just like him.

"I...I didn't do anything," he says, stammering over his words. "You have no idea who I am, but if you let me go, you won't get into any trouble."

"Of course you did something, Pierre," I say, ignoring his comment about who he is because I don't give a fuck. "You drugged her. You were in the middle of taking something she wasn't going to give to you willingly. And one thing I do not tolerate is anyone fucking with her. You picked the wrong woman. I'll see you in hell, motherfucker."

With a swift motion, I remove the knife from his gut and drive it back in, over and over. The noise of the surrounding city drowns out his screams, grunts, and pleas for mercy. Pleas for me to stop. However, no one will hear him, just like no one would have heard her desperate cries for help if Hugo and I hadn't shown up. He deserves this and so much more.

I stab him until he's no longer a threat to her. Until he's no longer a threat to anyone. With a final gasp, his eyes roll, then close before he collapses, his body crumpling to the filth-ridden alleyway. I wish I could piss on his body, but I have to make sure not to leave any evidence behind.

I pull my white handkerchief from the inside of my coat and try my best to get most of his blood off my hands and the knife I used. Once I've gotten rid of his body, I'll ensure that there's no trace of evidence left behind.

I pull out my phone and dial my driver. Once he answers, I instruct him to bring the car into the alley. I wanted to make him suffer more for what he did to her, but his quick death will have to do for now.

As my driver pulls into the alley, I make a plan on how to dispose of his body. I have to be careful since he is the son of a high-ranking diplomat, as Hugo warned.

This isn't how I thought my day would go, but at least she's safe, and he's no longer a threat to her.

6

ARABELLE

The strong, distinct odor of antiseptic, rubbing alcohol, and bleach immediately filters into my nostrils. Slowly, I peel my eyes open and squint as the overhead fluorescent light blinds me, while the incessant beeping sounds and constant humming grate on my nerves. I've never in my entire life had a headache this bad.

"Shit," I groan, grasping my head. "Shut it off."

"Thank God. Arabelle."

I face the familiar voice, although I don't understand his concern. My brows dip in confusion. "Dale..."

"You're all right." He tightly grips my hand like if he lets go of it, I will disappear. "You scared the shit out of me, sweetheart."

Along with his appearance, the relief in his voice is confusing for me. What the hell happened?

"Dale, what are you doing here?"

The last thing I remember, I was at the bar with Pierre having a few drinks. Then, I started feeling queasy and dizzy after having a couple glasses of wine. Then my memory fades to black. I remember absolutely nothing.

"Where am I?" I ask. "Where's Pierre?"

"You're in the hospital in Chicago, honey."

My eyes widen as I look around the room. The room is filled with the smell of antiseptic, bright lights overhead, and the sterile feeling of medical equipment surrounding the bed where I lay and the chair where Dale sits.

"That explains the smell and all the noise. What am I doing here?"

"Someone dropped you off at the emergency room because they believed someone drugged you. Thank God whoever it was found you."

"Drugged?"

Even more confusion swirls inside me.

"Yes. They believed you were roofied. Sweetheart, what the hell happened? Who's Pierre?"

I groan when I try to sit up in the bed. The room spins as unbearable pain pounds against my skull. "Ow!" I grasp my head.

Immediately, Dale jumps from the chair and adjusts the pillows behind my head to make me more comfortable and to help me sit up straighter.

"Thank you."

"Don't worry about it, but you need to slow down. Let me help you. They said you may experience some pain and severe headaches. It's the effects of the drugs."

"What kind of drugs?"

"I don't know. I'm not family, so they wouldn't give me any information other than you were stable."

"I went on a date." I rub my temples, trying to help relieve the excruciating pain pounding in my head. "We were at the bar not too far from the hotel. I can't remember the name. But, after that, I don't remember anything."

"And this was with someone named Pierre?"

I nod. "Yes."

"Do you remember his last name?"

"I don't. Dale, I don't even know if I asked for his last name. Is he the one who brought me to the hospital?"

He sighs. "They don't know, but whoever it was knows who I am. They gave the hospital my contact information so they could get in touch with me. They also hid their face from the hospital's security cameras."

That causes even more confusion. There's no way Pierre would know anything about Dale. So, if it wasn't him, then who was it?

"Pierre works at the hotel I was staying at. So, there's no way he would know who you are. I've only been there a week and never mentioned you. How would he know any of that?"

A look of bewilderment blankets his face, his brow furrowing in confusion.

"If Pierre wasn't the one who brought me to the hospital, it must mean he's the one who drugged me, right? I have no recollection of what happened, so I can't say for sure it was him, but who else could it be? He's the only person I've been anywhere with since I've been here."

Before we can continue our conversation, there's a knock on the door, and a doctor walks in.

"Ms. Williamson, I'm Dr. Morgan," she says as soon as she enters the room. She walks toward the machines and jots down notes on a clipboard before turning her attention to me. "I'm the attending physician on call. How are you feeling?"

"Hello, Doctor. I've got a massive headache, but other than that, I guess I'm doing okay."

"The headaches are to be expected. That's the effects of the drugs in your body, but we are flushing your system. I'm going to ask you some questions about what happened."

I release a heavy breath. "There isn't much I can tell you, doctor. All I remember is having a couple glasses of wine with my date. Anything after that is blank."

"Well, you had Rohypnol, what's better known as the date rape drug, in your system. Also, with the defensive wounds on your hands and arms, I would like to perform a rape kit to rule out sexual assault. The police will also like whatever evidence we can collect for your case."

I stare at the scratches and cuts on my hands and arms that I hadn't even noticed, and my eyes fill with tears as reality hits me square in the stomach.

Someone tried to rape me.

Dale grabs my hand, giving it a gentle but firm squeeze. "It's going to be all right, sweetheart."

No matter the conviction in Dale's voice, I don't know where my life goes from here. How can I trust anyone after something like this? I can't believe that I'm in this position. All I wanted to do was go out with a cute guy, have a little fun before my reality took back over. Now, I'm in the hospital and can't remember what's happened in the last twenty-four hours. All I want to do is wake up from this nightmare.

It took me a couple of hours to get Dale to leave once we got back to New York. Even though I understand why he wants to hang around to make sure I'm safe, I just want to be alone. I need time to process what's happened to me.

The cops said they will be in touch with me once the results are back from the examination. However, the examiner confirmed that I wasn't raped, so they are treating the case as an attempted sexual assault. I felt an overwhelming sense of relief that I struggled to put into words when I found out I hadn't been violated. All I could do was let the tears freely fall.

They meticulously inspected every inch of my body, poking, prodding, swabbing, and taking photographs where they suspected evidence might be found. They even scraped under my nails just in case I had been able to scratch my attacker. It was the most invasive exam I've ever experienced. The most humiliating thing I've ever been through.

I'm so grateful to be home. Finally, after hours of questioning and going over the same details and finally getting nowhere other than I was last with Pierre, they allowed me to return to New York. Hopefully, through their investigation, they will find out who drugged me and find the person who brought me to the emergency room. I'd at least like to thank that person for saving me.

Wrapped in a cozy blanket on my couch, I stare blankly at the flickering images on the television screen. I haven't been able to focus on anything other than trying to recall details of what happened to me, but my mind is completely blank. I can still feel the effects of the drug the person gave me lingering in my system, which is probably still clouding my memory.

Did Pierre do this to me? The cops haven't been able to find him.

The sound of my cell phone ringing causes me to groan in annoyance. I grab it from the coffee table and let out a sigh when I see the caller ID. Talking to my father is the last thing I want to do right now, especially considering the circumstances. So, I silence it. If he's calling, he wants something, and I'm not in the right frame mentally to deal with any of his bullshit. After everything that has happened, all I want to do is sleep and forget the last few days.

"I need to sleep."

Before I can close my eyes and finally relax, a sharp knock on the door makes me sigh in frustration. I just want to be left alone.

I rise from the couch, my limbs heavy and stiff, and shuffle toward the front door. It has to be Dale.

As I look through the peephole, I expect to see Dale's handsome face, but no one's there.

As I slowly open the door, my frown deepens when I spot the single rose and black envelope with gold script. Instead of the usual giddiness apprehension fills me.

I pick up the rose from in front of my door, feeling its delicate petals in my hand, then the envelope, and close the door. Leaning against the door, I close my eyes and breathe in the unique sweet, floral scent of the rose.

I remove the card from inside the envelope and brush my fingers across the words printed in elegant gold script as I read.

Nothing compares to the beauty you possess and the

grace you present to the world. But, most of all, the strength you carry is beyond anything imaginable. You are a survivor. Always remember that.

"I'm a survivor," I mumble to myself. "Does this person know what happened to me? Did they do this to me?"

7
ARABELLE

LOS ANGELES, CALIFORNIA

THREE MONTHS LATER

"Again, Arabelle!"

The sound of Madame Rostova's intricately carved walking stick resounds on the concrete floor, perfectly in sync with the music. Her thick Russian accent fills the air as I catch a fleeting glimpse of her in the mirror. For the past twenty minutes, she's been fixated on this section of the performance, her unhappiness apparent in her expression and relentless criticism.

Madame Rostova is an old-school hard ass. She's a prima ballerina from the fifties who danced with one of the most elite Russian companies. I was introduced to her about two years ago through a mutual contact on the ballet circuit, and she's been my dance instructor ever since. Almost every day of the week during the offseason, I train at her Los Angeles dance studio.

"Focus on the quality of your movement, Arabelle." The pounding of her cane echoes again. "Pay attention to details! It's all in the details! If you aspire to be great, if you aspire to be principal dancer, you need to earn it!"

As I repeat the same motions over and over again, the pressure to meet both her expectations, and my own, becomes overwhelming, causing an intense urge to scream and to rip at my hair.

Earn it! Goddamn it! All I've been doing since I was a kid is earning it! I want to scream, but it would all be in vain. She's not here to listen to me complain or argue. Ever since I started working with her, my dance has seen remarkable improvement. So, without objection, I push myself, feeling the strain in my muscles.

Harder.

Faster.

Higher.

Perfection is what Madame Rostova wants, and although I know I'm far from perfect, excellence is what I aim for with every jump, with every spin, and with every movement of my body. While perfection can't be obtained, in my opinion, it is possible to get close to it. That's the story I've been telling myself as far back as I can remember.

We've been going at it for close to two hours. I'm okay with practicing because there are always areas I can improve on. I'm not one of those dancers who believes my ability to captivate an audience comes naturally even though I've been told most of my life what I do can only be done by a natural. A prodigy. But I believe that it only comes through hard work, and it's something I've been working toward since my childhood.

However, no matter how much I love what I do or how much the ability comes naturally, I need a break. I need a long vacation because, during the offseason, I still have little time to relax. My mind and body are running on empty, and it's been that way for a long time, even though I've refused to acknowledge it. I never believed I'd ever get burned out with dance, but I think I'm getting close.

"Keep your core engaged, Arabelle," Madame Rostova shouts, her frail but stern voice rising above the music. "Yes! Yes! That's it. Keep going. *Sauté*."

Her instructions infiltrate my thoughts. Following her direction, I leap off both feet and gracefully touch down on both feet again before transitioning into a *jeté*, where I leap from one foot and land on the other.

"Perfect! Beautiful! Beautiful!"

She claps her hands, and then the music comes to an abrupt halt. I come to a standstill as well.

"That is it for today."

Placing my hands on my hips, I take deliberate, deep breaths, allowing the air to enter my nostrils and exit in long, controlled exhales to calm my racing heart. I shake out the tension from my legs, feeling a sense of relief washing over me. They burn along with my lungs, and my body's drenched in sweat, but I had a pretty good practice. I'm definitely getting better.

"You're almost there, Arabelle," Madame Rostova says, her stoic face never changing. "You need a little more work. A little more discipline, and you'll be there."

I want to roll my eyes at her statement. Almost there? What the hell do I need to do to get there?

There's no point in arguing, so I just nod my head in agreement. "Thank you, Madame Rostova. I will keep working on it."

"Bright and early tomorrow, Arabelle."

She doesn't wait for a response as she hobbles out the door of the dance studio toward her office. She knows I'll be here on time.

Like always.

Since I became a part of the dance company a few years ago, it's been nonstop for me. Training, rehearsals, photoshoots, and shows. Then I do it all over again. It's not like I hate it. I actually love it, but it gets tiring and lonely.

Lonely more than anything else.

I walk around the room as I try to decompress. I've been going without a break for the last few months, and my calendar is full for the rest of the year except for the couple of days I have lined up to go home. It's the grueling life I chose. It's the grueling life I love.

I take another deep breath and then take a drink of water from my water bottle before I pack up. I slide on my sweatpants, sneakers, and pull my long-sleeve shirt over my head.

In a few hours, I have to do another photoshoot for one of the top African American publications in the country because everyone believes I'll be named my company's first Black principal dancer. I've been trying not to get my hopes up, but it's hard not to. It's a big step in my career.

Despite the excitement for the photoshoot, I want to rest before I have to head to the studio. Then, I'll have practice for the next few weeks with no events scheduled before I go home to New York for a few days.

I wasn't looking forward to going home because I know when I get there, I'll wish I was somewhere else. My family can be the most draining part of my life. The only reason I am going back is because memories of my mom help me recharge, and being there helps put everything in perspective, which is what I need at the moment.

With my bag slung over my shoulder, I step out of the dance studio and onto the bustling streets of Los Angeles. Even though I'm not a fan of crowds, there's something about this place that I absolutely love. It's my home for only a portion of the year, as it serves as my training ground during the offseason.

The rest of the year, when I'm not traveling for work, I live in my New York apartment during the dance season, much to the disappointment of my father. His insistence that I live under his roof isn't driven by genuine concern for my well-being as a single woman in the city. Rather, it stems from his desire to have power over me. Have control over my financial situation. Which is why I have my own place and have no financial ties to him.

When my career started to gain momentum, I left my home at fifteen, motivated partly by a desire for distance from my sisters and father. It was the best move I've ever made. Even though I still have to deal with them, it would be so much worse if we lived together.

The weather is a balmy seventy degrees, which is one of the reasons I chose Los Angeles over New York during the offseason. I want to be able to relax in the sunshine instead of the cold weather.

I wish I had the time to relish the beautiful day and enjoy the warm sun kissing my skin and the gentle breeze tousling my hair. But duty calls.

Walking from Madame Rostova's studio to my apartment building takes just around twenty minutes. Earl, my doorman, greets me with a warm smile as he opens the door, and I wave at him in return. Then I make my way to the bank of elevators.

"There are never enough hours in the day," I mumble as I press the elevator button and wait for the doors to open.

Usually, I opt to take the stairs to give my legs an extra workout, but today, I just don't have the energy. I wouldn't make it up the first flight before I would start to cramp up.

Madame Rostova has been demanding more of me during this offseason. She insists it's the only way I'll make principal dancer when the season starts in September. She's an expert with over forty years of experience, so I'll do whatever I have to do to achieve a dream I've been chasing since I was a little girl.

The doors to the elevator slide open, and I step in, feeling the cool, smooth surface of the walls against my fingertips as I take a deep breath. I wish I could stay inside for the day, watch TV, or read a book and just relax. But wishing is for fools.

When I reach my floor and the elevator doors open, I toss my bag over my shoulder again and step out. However, as soon as I reach my door, Mrs. O'Donnell's door creaks open. It's like she has an Arabelle radar that alerts her, so she knows exactly when I'm coming or going.

With a deep breath in and a long exhale, I gather my composure and plaster a smile on my face as I approach my elderly neighbor. She's a widower in her late eighties, and her large tabby cat named Gertrude is just as ornery as she is.

I know she doesn't mean any harm, but she's incredibly nosy and insists that my boyfriend is secretly coming in and out of my apartment. She keeps warning me I need to make him stop before she reports it to the apartment manager, concerned that I'm violating the lease agreement. News flash—I have no boyfriend and haven't had a boyfriend since high school, and that only lasted a few weeks.

"Mrs. O'Donnell, it's so nice to see you again. How are you doing today?"

Even though it isn't nice to see her, I make sure I remain respectful.

"That boyfriend of yours was here again today while you were out, Arabelle." She grasps Gertrude tighter as Gertrude tries to wiggle out of her arms. "You know if he's not on the lease, he's not supposed to have a key."

I sigh, rubbing my forehead. "Mrs. O'Donnell, I don't know how many times I have to say this, but I don't have a boyfriend. I promise you no one has a key to my apartment."

She huffs. "I know what I saw, Arabelle. There's a man coming in and out of your apartment. He's been doing it for a while now. And after all the times I've told you about it, you've still done nothing about it."

"That's not possible, Mrs. O'Donnell, because I don't have a boyfriend. Now, if you'll excuse me, I need to go."

I don't have time to deal with this nonsense. I don't have a boyfriend, and no one is coming in and out of my apartment.

I would know.

"If you're not going to abide by the rules, Arabelle, I'll just let the office manager handle it."

"You do whatever you need to do, Mrs. O'Donnell." I dismiss her threat because I have nothing to hide. "Try to have a nice day."

As I unlock my door and push it open, she huffs once more, muttering something under her breath, before her door slams shut.

Once inside, I lock the door and drop my keys into the bowl on the table. For a long time, Mrs. O'Donnell has claimed that I have had some man sneaking in and out of my apartment, and I have no idea who she's talking about. I have no boyfriend. Hell, I don't have any friends besides Dale, and he doesn't have a key.

"She's crazy, or maybe she has some type of dementia," I mumble as I make my way to my bedroom. "Or she's just lonely and needs someone to talk to. I know how that feels."

I enter my bedroom, drop my duffel bag at the foot of my bed, and then make my way to the bathroom. In less than fifteen minutes,

I'm in and out of the shower, feeling refreshed and ready to take a quick nap so I can finish the rest of my day.

I wrap myself in a towel, walk out of my bathroom, and stop dead in my tracks as soon as I see it perfectly placed on my pillow. A single long-stem red rose along with an envelope.

"What in the hell?"

How did I not see it? Or did he put it in here when I was in the shower?

I slowly walk to the bed, grab the black envelope, and remove the card with shaky hands. I furrow my brows. I've been able to deal with the flowers and cards being left at the theater, outside my hotel room, and even at my apartment door in New York. The attention is flattering. But this is something different. He's been inside my apartment.

From the shadows, I've watched, but in the shadows, I can no longer remain because of the desires of my heart.

I drop the envelope and rush back down the hallway toward my door, not caring that I'm wrapped in nothing but a towel. I fling the door open, rush across the hallway to Mrs. O'Donnell's apartment, and knock on her door. When she doesn't answer, I knock a few more times, a little louder, just in case she can't hear.

The door slowly opens. "Arabelle?" She looks me up and down with her eyes as wide as saucers, but then they narrow. "Why are you in nothing but a towel, child?"

She looks down both sides of the hallway, I assume, to see if anyone else has seen me standing basically naked in front of her apartment door.

"Mrs. O'Donnell, can you please tell me what the man looks like you think you've seen come in and out of my apartment?" I ask, ignoring her question about my towel.

She huffs. "He's your boyfriend, Arabelle. Shouldn't you know what he looks like? Unless you have more than one?"

She gives me a look full of judgment and disdain.

How many times do I have to tell her I don't have a boyfriend? And I definitely don't have more than one.

"Please, Mrs. O'Donnell, this is important," I plead, attempting to hide my annoyance. I have to remind myself of her age and that I need her help. There's no point in pissing her off just so she'll slam the door in my face. "What does the man look like that you think you saw?"

"I don't know." She shrugs. "Tall. Dresses very well. Other than that, I can't tell you anything because I can't see that well anymore. And he always has his head turned anyway from the door. So, I can never see his face."

He's intentionally hiding his face from her. He must know how nosy she is.

"And you're sure he's going inside my apartment?"

She sighs, rolling her eyes, her annoyance very clear on her aged face. "Arabelle, I watch that man every time he comes here. He unlocks the door with his key and walks right inside."

I don't correct her about him having a key. Nobody has a key but me.

"And today was the last day that you saw him?"

"Yes, Arabelle. He left a few minutes before you came home today. Is that all?" she asks with a sigh. "It's almost time for my shows to come on, and I don't want to miss them."

Thank God he left before I got here.

"Yes, that's all. Thank you again, Mrs. O'Donnell."

She says nothing else and closes the door in my face. I walk back across the hall to my apartment and immediately call the front desk. All visitors are required to sign in with the front desk attendants. It's why I picked this place. There are security protocols, along with a doorman, which right now are shit.

"Front desk, this is Nathan speaking."

"Yes, Nathan. This is Arabelle Williamson in apartment 432. Have I had any guests sign in today?"

"Give me one second, Ms. Williamson, to check."

I can't believe someone has been inside my apartment.

"Our records show no one has signed in. Is there a problem?"

"Yes." I run my hands through my hair in frustration. "I believe someone's been in my apartment."

Silence filters through the line for a few minutes.

"Have you given a key to anyone, Ms. Williamson?" he asks. "You know it's against complex policy for someone not on the lease to have keys to any of the apartments. That can be a reason for us to end your lease."

"I'm well aware of the policy, Nathan. That's why I haven't given anyone any keys."

"According to our records, we've also received a complaint from Mrs. O'Donnell, your neighbor, that you've had an unauthorized visitor who has a set of keys."

"Well, Mrs. O'Donnell is old, and she has no idea what she's talking about. No one has keys to my apartment but me. Has maintenance been scheduled to do any work?"

"No, ma'am. Not that I can see."

"Okay." I pinch the bridge of my nose. "I know it sounds crazy, but is there any way I can get my locks changed today?"

"I can put in the order today for maintenance to change the locks. But it will take twenty-four to forty-eight hours for the work to be done, and you will be billed for the lock changes."

"The cost isn't an issue."

"Okay, then I will put in the order. The new keys will be up here at the desk for you to pick up when available."

"That's perfect." I breathe a sigh of relief. "Thank you, Nathan."

I finish the call and make my way to my bedroom to put on clothes. What do I need to do from here? If I call the cops, they'll think I'm crazy. Someone has entered my apartment, and according to Mrs. O'Donnell, it has happened on multiple occasions.

"There's no way I can stay here until the locks are changed. I need to find somewhere else to stay."

"Breaking News..."

As I search for my clothes in the dresser, my gaze shifts to the television on the bedroom wall. There's a reporter standing in front of the Peninsula Chicago, the hotel where I met Pierre.

Filled with anger and confusion, I sit on my bed, releasing a deep sigh.

The police believe that I'm the last person Pierre was seen with. They grilled me for hours about him and our date. I can't recall anything after I had my second glass of wine, so I don't know what happened to him. Since he didn't answer any of my calls, I suspect he's the one who drugged me. I only found out he was missing when two Chicago police detectives appeared at my door in New York. I let them know I thought he drugged me, which led to more questions.

> *Authorities have located the body of Pierre Gaultier, a foreign exchange student who was last seen with Arabelle Williamson, a professional ballet dancer and the daughter of Williamson Holdings' CEO, Arthur Williamson. Three months ago, Pierre Gaultier, son of French Ambassador Jean Gaultier, disappeared without a trace. Authorities questioned a witness who claimed to have seen Ms. Williamson, who they recognized from a magazine cover, and Mr. Gaultier leave The Black Star Bar and Grill together, where he was last seen. The police have not named Ms. Williamson as a person of interest in his disappearance, but detectives say no one has been eliminated as a potential suspect in his disappearance and death. At this time, the police have not disclosed the cause of death. The family is offering a reward in the amount of $250,000 for any information leading to the capture of any individual involved in this case. Don't miss our exclusive interview with his father at six o'clock to hear his thoughts on his son and how the police investigation is progressing.*

I turn off the TV and throw the remote onto the bed.

"We went on one date. Jesus Christ!" I run my hand down my face in frustration.

I ignore the sound of my cell phone ringing and groan. I know who it is before I even look at the caller ID. My dad will want to know why I didn't tell him about this, but not because whatever happened to me that night matters. Because now, his name is in the news and linked to someone's death.

I don't want to talk to anyone, especially him. Pierre is dead, and I have absolutely nothing to do with it because he drugged me.

8

FLORIAN

THREE WEEKS LATER...

She's all I want.

She's not just someone to spend my days and nights with, sweaty and wrapped in tangled sheets to help slay the demons wreaking havoc in my mind. I just want her. If I can have the one person I need, I know everything in my life will be worth living.

However, I've tried to forget her. After leaving that flower and note inside her apartment, I realized I may have gone too far. She's too innocent, too pure to taint with my wickedness, but no one else will do. To strip her of everything she is and make her into what she deserves to be will be my greatest reward. If I have the chance to be with her, it will be unreal. But it's not to be.

With a tightening grip on my whiskey, a stream of images showcasing her beauty fills my mind as the sun rises. While she doesn't know I exist, she's become my obsession. She's the one thing I can't live without but have been forced to. To keep from destroying her, I've hidden in the shadows for months, wishing she wasn't my unattainable beauty. As a reminder of my devotion to her, I send her roses because they're her favorite, and still, nothing has changed since I first laid eyes on her.

She's still my unattainable beauty because I will always be Beast. Her light will always shine, while my hands will always be stained with blood.

Standing at the floor-to-ceiling windows in my office on the sixtieth floor of *Larsson Industries,* I gaze at an impressive view of the beautiful New York skyline. The sky is filled with shades of pink, purple, and orange rising above the city's skyscrapers. The morning dew covering the windows sparkles like diamonds as the sun filters through the large panes of glass as the city below comes to life. It seems like a different world looking down on everything below. In this perfect world, I'm not the man I am, and I have the woman I've always wanted. But nothing's ever truly perfect, is it?

I sigh and take a sip of whiskey, wishing some things in my life were different. But I should know by now that wishing is only for fools. And I'm no fool. My life is what it is, and there's nothing I can do to change things.

A little after seven in the morning may be too early to have a drink, but the need to remove her from my thoughts is more intense today, and I'm not sure why or if it even matters. Nothing good comes from obsessing over the impossible, and for this next meeting, my anger needs to be in check, so I don't give in to my rage and kill him.

Five years ago, at twenty-six, I *acquired* Larsson Industries and many other businesses, expanding my reach into the business world and the criminal underworld outside my hometown of Uppsala, Sweden. My network in both worlds is now extensive and is only getting larger.

After emigrating to America and becoming a US citizen, I worked tirelessly to achieve what my father never could, taking Larsson Industries places he only dreamed of. His bastard took over his company and his criminal organization, expanding both beyond anything he could ever do. And he absolutely hates me for it. His *legitimate* sons hate me for it. On many occasions, they have all wished for my death, but it's hard to kill the *Beast.* I should know. Many have tried.

And I still live.

I'm ruthless, merciless, and some say cruel, but no one can deny that I'm fair. Stories of the *Beast* being unable to die circulate throughout the criminal underworld—an exaggeration, of course, because I bleed like any other man. However, the stories, I don't deny. They strike fear in my enemies. Fear that fuels me. Fear that I relish in. Fear that allows me to remain at the top even though many have tried to topple me.

Heavy is the head who wears the crown, so they say. Now I'm the one sitting on the throne while my father withers away. I manage the weight of my crown well, and my reach is far, much farther than my father's.

Olan Larsson should look at me as his enemy since that's what he has forced me to be. He never gives me credit for what I accomplish, or what I'll gladly take from him because, in his eyes, I'm nothing more than a weakling. The bastard son of a whore, not worthy to have the Larsson name or wear the Larsson crown. But I'm always the predator and never the prey. He will do well to remember that with the little time he has left on this Earth.

I glance down at my watch, downing the last of my whiskey when there's a knock at the door.

Right on time.

The large mahogany door swings open. However, I keep my back to him. Every time he's in my presence, it takes everything in me not to kill him with my bare hands, forcing his last breaths from his body.

"Son."

My body stiffens. I hate it when he calls me his son. I am not and will never be Olan's son. He made sure of it a long time ago.

I've learned every facet of my father while I plotted against him. When he uses the term of endearment, it means he wants something from me.

"Florian," he calls out when I don't respond.

I break free from my thoughts, make my way to the desk, and sit down, placing the tumbler on top of a coaster. With a glare, he stares at the empty glass, narrowing his eyes. His judgmental glower, I ignore. It doesn't matter to me if the motherfucker doesn't approve of my choice of drink.

Olan's beliefs are strange when it comes to certain indulgences, such as alcohol, drugs, and sex. He believes they are vices, weaknesses for his children even if he partakes in them, which he does often, and so do my brothers.

The prostitute whom he's fucking and sniffing coke from her cunt tells me all his secrets—for a price, of course. While it's disgusting to hear all the vile things he's into, I'll listen to it as long as I learn how to destroy him.

Such a fucking hypocrite.

This meeting needs to end as soon as possible. Today, I've been on edge more than usual, barely hanging on to the little sanity I have left. Many think I lost it a long time ago. Sometimes, I can't disagree with that assessment.

He's standing, flanked by Asva and Alrick Persson, twin brothers who have been with me since I took over the Larsson Syndicate, to Olan's disgust. He doesn't like anyone not associated with the families of Uppsala to be a part of the Syndicate. However, I've learned that the people from Uppsala, my people, can't be trusted, especially if they're going to be close to me. Most remain loyal to Olan, which is why I recruit from outside Uppsala's borders.

I grab the bottle of high-end whiskey from the drawer, pour two fingers into the glass, and then slip the bottle back into the drawer. Olan's scowl only deepens when I take a sip, enjoying the burn of the smooth amber liquid sliding down my throat.

"You're drinking this early in the morning?" He doesn't hide his disgust for my choice of an early morning beverage. "You should know better than to do that."

I ignore his judgmental attitude. I haven't cared what Olan thinks about my decisions for a long time.

"I have a busy day, Olan." I sigh. "Why did you need to meet with me this morning?"

I ignore his question and ask one of my own, although I know the answer. His old friend Arthur Williamson has been in touch with him to see if he can stop the inevitable—the takeover of Williamson Holdings, a shipping company I've been after for a very long time.

It isn't going to happen, no matter what Olan says.

"You know why I'm here, Florian. Don't play stupid. As my son, it's beneath you," he growls. "Why are you trying to destroy everything I've built? I've formed many relationships over the course of my lifetime. These men trust me, and you would steal from them?"

I don't steal. In fact, I can't stand a thief and have killed many throughout the years for stealing from me. But what I am is a savvy and shrewd businessman who provides struggling individuals with capital with the promise of repayment of the loan in full plus interest. If payment isn't made in full by the time determined within the contract, I confiscate their companies or whatever I deem worthy as payment. Sometimes, I've used less-than-honorable means to get what is owed to me. I've broken a few bones, maimed a few men, and taken a few lives, but I always get what's owed to me, no matter the means of compensation, whether it's by blood or money. It's not thieving. It's called good business.

"Everything you've built?" I scowl, steepling my hands and leaning back in my chair. I take offense at his statement.

When I assumed control, Larsson Industries was in a state of complete chaos. Complaints of sexual harassment, mainly about him, grievances about wages, and employees were jumping ship as fast as they could. Larsson Industries was hanging on by a thread. Now, things have changed. My employees are happy, and work production has multiplied tenfold under my leadership. So, he hasn't done shit.

"You haven't built shit, Olan. What you see around you," I motion around the room with outstretched arms, "I've built with my blood, sweat, and tears. If it wasn't for me, there wouldn't be a Larsson Industries. Remember, you came to me just like Arthur and the rest of your friends because you needed my help. Not the other way around."

He doesn't like me to mention the deal we made. He doesn't like to admit he needed his bastard's help. My little brother owed ungodly amounts of money due to his drug habit, but Olan wanted to save face. He didn't want the other families catching wind of a Larsson being addicted to drugs, although I'm sure everyone already knew. So, he asked if I would pay my brother's debts because even though I held the Larsson name, no one at the time knew I was his son. And if they did, they didn't speak of it because he threatens anyone who questions who I am.

He believed he was using me, but I saw it as my opening to take him down, and I took it. He put Larsson Industries on the line, and now I own it while Olan's precious image remains intact.

I don't mind helping my youngest brother. In fact, I would have done it for free. Out of all my family, Didrick's the only one I will ever help, but Olan presented me with an opportunity I couldn't refuse. I saw it as my chance to destroy my father. I saw it as a chance for all of us to be free of him.

"You ungrateful little shit!" He takes a step forward, but Asva and Alrick grab him by the arms. "This is my company!" He struggles against their hold. "We are supposed to be a fucking family, and you stole it from me!"

Family?

"Let him go." I wave my hand dismissively, and Alrick glares at me. "There's nothing he can do to me," I assure both Asva and Alrick. When they release him, I tilt my head, smiling at my old man as he smooths non-existent wrinkles from his expensive Armani suit. "I haven't stolen shit from you, Olan. If you would've paid your debt like everyone else who comes to me with their fucking hand out, you'd be in a different position."

"You tricked me!" He points his finger at me. "And you know it."

I smile, and he narrows his eyes at me. "Tricked would not be the term I would use, Olan. No one tricked you. You knew exactly the terms of my deal before you agreed to it."

He isn't as smart as he thinks, and as a businessman, you should always read the fine print. Olan didn't. He automatically assumed I'll do anything for him, that I crave any kind of attention he's willing to give me. Maybe when I was a kid, but I haven't wanted his attention for years. I only want what is owed to me as his firstborn son.

The Larsson empire. I want it all, including his life.

When I was old enough to learn that he was nothing more than a money-grubbing bastard who couldn't care less that I have his blood running through my veins, everything changed for me. That knowledge stripped me of any hope he'd be the father I need and deserve.

He made it clear I wasn't his son, and that's when I knew I had to do things my way. Getting close to Olan and pretending to beg for whatever scraps of attention he'd give me, was the easiest part of my plan to oust him from his company and claim my place on the Larsson throne from the age of sixteen.

Every day, I groveled for whatever scraps he was willing to give me, inching my way closer to my goal. After I did the dirty work for him with the Larsson Syndicate, gaining the trust of some of his soldiers, I took it, along with Larsson Industries. Everything he cares for is now mine.

I wouldn't change anything I've done to get to where I am today, and Olan got everything he deserves. He left my mother with nothing because, to him, she was only good enough to be his whore. Even though he had no interest in her or me, Olan mistreated her and prevented her from moving on to a better life.

After she took her life when I turned eighteen, he refused to acknowledge who she was to him. I stood alone as they lowered her white casket into the ground, the only one who mourned her death and shed tears that mixed with the cold Swedish snow as I said goodbye. I'll never be able to forget that day, a day which fuels my anger today. The day the loving, caring boy turned into Beast.

Just as he took the most precious thing in my life away from me, I took the most precious thing to him. Although she pulled the trigger, he's fully responsible for her death. If it's the last thing I do, I'll be the cause of his.

"Olan, you and your friends aren't exempt from the rules." I try to rub away the building tension in my forehead. This conversation is wearing my patience thin, and when it comes to him, I already have very little tolerance. "Everything I do is legitimate and legally binding. Arthur knew the terms when he took my money, and so did you. If you were so concerned about Arthur's predicament, why didn't you put up the money to help him? Why don't you put up the money now so he can keep his business, and life can go on as it should?" I ask, although I know the answer.

Olan doesn't help anyone who isn't a Larsson. Well, except for me, the Larsson bastard. The one who is a perfect likeness of him.

Arthur and Olan have been friends for decades, but that doesn't matter to him. Arthur isn't his blood. So, Arthur came to me for help like so many others.

When Olan doesn't reply, I shake my head. Every shred of empathy for him was wiped away a long time ago. His threats and pleas for people who don't deserve them are useless. He didn't listen to hers. Why should I help anyone because he asks? He refused to help the one person I needed in my life, so now, I will repay the favor.

My mother, Freja Ek, begged for our freedom. She pleaded for him to let us go so she could find someone who would love her and me in return. But he refused and threatened to kill us both if she ever found another man to be her husband and my father. To him, we were his property even when he didn't claim us. Even if he didn't want either of us.

He stripped her of everything she ever knew. He forbade her from seeing her family or having friends. She couldn't come and go without his permission or without a guard who was supposed to report her every move to him. So, she became isolated from everything and everyone she loved. With my birth, the restrictions became worse. She was his prisoner until she took her own life.

The only way to escape him.

Now, I refuse to do anything he asks of me. He doesn't deserve my help nor my mercy, and nothing will change the outcome for Arthur Williamson. I gave him my hard-earned money in exchange for him signing the contract. Unless he pays me with interest in the next few minutes, I will own Williamson Holdings.

"Your day is coming." Olan points his gnarled, trembling finger at me, spit flying from his mouth. "And I pray I'm alive to see it."

"But you won't be, Olan," I respond calmly. "If I have anything to say about it, when my time comes, you won't be alive to see any of it."

"Is that a threat, boy?" He narrows his ice-blue eyes at me, the same color eyes I stare at each morning in the mirror with disdain. "You would dare threaten your own father?"

"See, this is where you and I differ." I take a sip of whiskey, enjoying the burn as it slides down my throat, the heat calming the rage boiling in my gut. "I never threaten anyone. I only make promises."

His face pales.

"Now do you understand, Olan?"

The beast he's created always lurks just beneath the surface, and now, he sees him clearly. Now, he sees that the threat is real.

"You wouldn't dare." The tremble in his voice and fear in his eyes say he knows otherwise. He knows the truth. I mean every word. His time in this life is coming to an end sooner rather than later. "I'm your fucking father!"

"Of course, I would, *Far*."

Father.

"You son of a whore!" he shouts. "You can go straight to hell, Florian."

"You first, daddy dearest." I wink, and his features darken. Olan has no idea the destruction I can cause, but he will soon enough. "Asva will see you out. Oh, and Olan, before you go..." He glares at me. I've never seen so much hatred in his eyes. "Make sure you stay away this time." I shuffle the papers on my desk to keep my hands occupied. Now isn't the time to kill him, I remind myself. "We have nothing more to discuss."

"You bastard!" he seethes. "I tried to get your bitch of a mother to get rid of you. I wish I'd done it myself. Put you in the same goddamn hole with her and be done with the both of you. You're no son of mine."

My jaw tics.

I can't kill him now. Stay calm.

I regain my composure. I won't let him see that he's gotten under my skin. "You're right, Olan. I'm definitely no son of yours. That's the most coherent thing you've said in a long time." I wave my hand. "Asva, escort him out, now. There's nothing more for us to discuss."

"This isn't over, Florian!" Asva grabs Olan by the arm, pulling him toward the door. "This isn't over!"

Despite the yelling, I try my best to ignore him. It's not finished yet because I'm not ready for it to be over. Justice for my mother hasn't been served yet.

Once the door slams shut, my focus shifts to Alrick. His eyes, a frosty shade of blue, grow narrower. His features always show concern following a visit from my father. I understand why. Despite his diminishing power and fragile look, Olan Larsson is an extremely dangerous man. Alrick thinks I'm reckless and that I don't take necessary precautions, but I never underestimate him.

"Everything will be fine, Alrick." I sift through the stacks of papers on my desk, looking for a copy of Arthur's contract among the many others. "You worry entirely too much."

"And you don't worry enough, *Odjur!*"

Beast.

When I look up at him, he sighs. I lean back in my chair, giving him my full attention. Alrick is the most vocal of the twins. Although I'm sure Asva has concerns, he keeps them to himself. While they are my employees, I look at them both as brothers, but Asva understands that, as a leader, I make all the decisions. Alrick doesn't care that I'm the leader; he speaks his mind. And that keeps me grounded.

"You know he has men who are still loyal to him," he continues. "I don't understand why you're waiting to take him out. It'll take too long to weed out the ones who aren't loyal to you before Olan strikes. You need to strike him first."

He doesn't even flinch when I slam my palm down on the top of my desk. "Because he hasn't suffered enough! He will suffer until he is left with absolutely nothing. Until he grovels and begs for *my* mercy!"

He sighs. "But it's not smart to keep him alive, Florian. You are letting your need for revenge cloud your judgment. He'll gather the others together to go against you soon if it's not already happening."

While he might be right, I won't alter my plan. I need to do this my way.

"I appreciate the concern, Alrick. I really do, but you're overstepping." I take a calming breath and remind myself that Alrick is only looking out for me. "I will handle Olan as I see fit. Let it go."

My plans for Olan are not open for discussion. It has been brewing for as long as I can remember, and nothing will sway my determination on the execution and timing.

Alrick wants to say more, but whatever it is will be in vain, and he knows it. The decision on what to do with my father was decided a long time ago. He'll die on my terms.

"I'm only trying to look out for you, Florian, as your friend. As your brother."

"I know, and it's the only reason I allow you to speak your mind. It's the only reason I haven't slit your throat."

He huffs, rolling his eyes, even though he knows I'm telling the truth. Alrick doesn't understand the depth of my hate for my father. No one understands what he has put me through. The suffering he caused my mother when she was alive. The torment. The violence. He deserves no mercy and will get none from me.

I glance at my watch. It's ten minutes after the time Arthur's loan was due, and it looks like he's making no effort to handle his debt.

"Enough about my father. Go pick up Arthur Williamson and bring him to me."

9
FLORIAN

"I only need a few more months, Florian. Please." The begging starts as soon as Alrick shuts the door behind him. It's annoying as hell, but I expect it. It always happens. "And I'll have your money."

"With interest?"

I arch my brow, then he looks away, and I sigh.

Of course, he won't have it. He's drowning in debt, and when I take over Williamson Holdings, I'll gain all his other debts, too. It's nothing I can't manage, but the promises Arthur's making, he can't deliver, and he knows it. His business hasn't been producing for years, and the man loves to gamble. A lot. Which is why he's in the position he's in. Now, everything has caught up with him, and he's on the verge of losing everything, including his shipping company and all its holdings.

It was only a matter of time before he came to me. All Olan's friends have come to me at one time or another. Either they were saved by my hand or destroyed by it.

Today, it looks like Arthur Williamson will be destroyed by it.

Although this is the usual tactic when it's time for payment, I can't deny that it coming from him is different. Arthur isn't himself. Dark circles highlight his dull eyes, emphasizing the ashen skin of his sunken face.

Maybe he's sick?

Not your concern, Florian.

I like Arthur. Although I don't know him all that well, from what

I've seen, he seems fair. I'll never understand the connection between him and Olan or how they became friends. His reputation as an upstanding businessman precedes him. But if I take pity on him, I'll have to take pity on everyone. And I'm definitely not willing to do that.

"Arthur, the terms of our agreement haven't changed." I rub my temples, the pounding in my head increasing. "Unless you have payment plus interest today, there's nothing I can do."

Of course, he doesn't have payment. Rarely do any of them. However, Arthur looks like a broken man. Like he's lost everything. But his loss isn't my concern. His loss is my gain. He understood the deal when he came begging for my money. They all do. He agreed to the terms when he signed his name on the dotted line after I gave him out after out, which I do with everyone because I know it eventually ends like this. Now, he has to live with the consequences of his decision to enter into a contract with me. He has regrets, but there's nothing I can or will do about it.

"I understand the terms of our agreement, Florian, but I'm out of options here. I need the money for Arabelle, so I can't repay you right now."

Arabelle.

I feel a stir at the sound of her name, and I shift to get more comfortable. Her name stirs something primal in me.

Arabelle Williamson, better known as my obsession. She's the most beautiful woman I've ever seen. The first time I saw her, she was performing in *Don Quixote*. It was then that I became consumed by my desire for her.

The beast in me wants to strip her bare and have her screaming my name until she can't scream any longer, her body slick with my cum and limp under me. But Florian, the sane side of me, stays away to keep from ruining her, destroying her with my demons.

My need for her won't distract me. Arthur just lied. He doesn't need the money for Arabelle. She has her own money and keeps him and his other children afloat as her career soars. What he needs the money for doesn't matter to me, but I know it isn't for her.

I hate fucking liars.

"She'll be named principal dancer soon, Florian," he continues, "and with that title comes more opportunity."

More money for him to take from her.

The excitement gleaming in his eyes at the prospect of the money Arabelle will garner being named principal dancer causes my stomach to lurch. Now, it makes sense why Arthur and Olan are such good friends. He'll exploit her like Olan exploits all his children, damn the consequences.

When I narrow my eyes, his smile disappears.

"So, you would use your daughter, your goddamn flesh and blood to repay *your* debts?" My temper and disgust rise. He'll make her work twice as hard, so he no longer owes me money or anyone else. "They're your debts to pay, not hers."

"I'm not using her."

His chin lifts as he crosses his arms over his chest. He knows I'm right, but the old bastard refuses to admit it to me even though he admitted it to himself a long time ago. He's a fucking snake in the grass.

"She's a good girl, Florian. She'll do what is necessary to help her family. To help me."

Like always.

I sit back in my chair, interlacing my fingers and eyeing the man who's now lost what little respect I held for him.

"Arabelle doesn't need to work harder than she already is, Arthur."

Although Arthur doesn't need to know, Hugo, one of my soldiers who is also former Mossad, follows Arabelle and sends me a report every weekend detailing her movements. She practices, performs, and attends the required after-parties for the dancers and photoshoots, fulfilling her obligation to the theater. That's all. Her life revolves around dance. Taking care of Arthur's debts would add even more pressure. Besides her attorney, Dale Austin, whom I despise, she has no interaction with anyone.

I see how he looks at her, how much he wants her, which I think she's oblivious to. If she's not oblivious to the way he feels about her, she doesn't see him the same way and ignores it.

Asva and Alrick both discouraged me from killing him a while ago because, in their words, no matter my feelings for him, Dale Austin protects Arabelle from people looking to prey on her, including her family. It's the only reason he's still breathing.

"You know nothing about my daughter," Arthur growls. "So, you have no place to say anything about what she needs to do."

He has no fucking clue what I know about his daughter, but I'll keep that thought to myself. He doesn't need to know she is my obsession. No one needs to know that I've killed for her.

"She'll do what is necessary for her family," he continues. "And Arabelle isn't your concern."

Arabelle will always be my concern.

I shake my head, repulsed by the idea of her working harder. I won't allow him to exploit her for his own benefit anymore. Now, I can have what I've always wanted—her.

The beast inside me stirs with interest.

"I'll tell you what, Arthur. Since I'm in a good mood today, maybe we can come to another agreement." Hope blooms in his eyes. How long it will last remains to be seen. "I'll forgive your debt and pay off all your creditors on one condition." He smiles, and I hold up my index finger before he can thank me. Before his hopeful attitude plummets. "If you give me Arabelle's hand in marriage."

"What!" His caramel skin deepens in shade. His polished dress shoes echo off the bamboo flooring as he paces in front of my desk like he has a fire under his ass. "She's not ready to be married, Florian, especially to a man like you."

I raise my brow. "Please tell me, Arthur. What do you mean a man like me?"

He comes to a sudden halt, and his eyes grow as large as saucers, revealing his disbelief at accidentally letting his true thoughts about me slip. I'm just fucking with him. I know what he means, but I like to see him sweat.

Everyone knows who I am. I don't hide it. I'm ruthless, merciless, and cruel when I need to be, which is most, if not all, of the time. I don't claim to be anything other than who I am. I've earned the name *Beast* and fully embrace it. But Arthur has only scratched the surface of the person I can be, and he has no other option but to give me Arabelle or his company. Whether I have her, I still end up winning.

"You can't be serious, Florian." He runs his hand over his thinning salt-and-pepper hair while he paces again. "What if I give you my eldest daughter's hand instead?" He's nodding like that's the best idea he's had in a long time. "She's not innocent and is more suitable for your world. She would love a man like you."

From the information I've gathered on Angela Williamson, Arabelle's older sister, she's a woman who loves any man with money. Regardless of his age, morals, or how he made his fortune, as long as he can keep her living in luxury, she doesn't care.

I must admit Arthur is right. She is more suitable for someone like me. She's perfect for the criminal underworld. A morally bankrupt beauty can be useful, but she's also untrustworthy. She'll never have any loyalty as long as money is involved. Either way, it doesn't matter. She's not who I want.

Arabelle isn't ready for a man like me. However, I've grown tired of staying away. We're made for each other, and this way, she'll have no other choice but to accept me as hers.

I want my beauty.

"No."

He merely stares, tongue-tied. He was so sure I'd accept his offer.

"Well...well, what about Raven then?" he asks with a little more hope in his eyes than he should have. "She'll also make a wonderful wife."

"Ah yes, the alcoholic."

I lean back in my chair, steepling my hands.

"She's sober now."

He's lying through his teeth. The bitch can't stay sober if her life depends on it, and he knows it.

While Raven Williamson is also beautiful, she can't stay sober long enough to make anything of her life. Just like the eldest sister, she'll cause more problems than I'm willing to deal with.

Arabelle is the one I want. Nobody else.

"It's Arabelle or no deal, Arthur. In exchange for her hand in marriage, I'll tear up our initial contract." I dangle the small stack of papers in the air in front of him, giving him even more of an incentive to give me what I want. "Your debt to me will be paid in full, Williamson Holdings will remain in your possession, and any other debt you have incurred with other creditors will also be paid. But there is one stipulation."

"Stipulation?" His brows draw together.

"Yes."

"Okay, what's your stipulation?"

"Arabelle will not be deceived. You will be upfront with her and tell her about our deal. If I find out you have not, your company will revert to me, and you'll also owe me all the money I used to pay off your debts."

He runs his hand down his face. "Florian, I can't tell my daughter I'm giving her to you so I can keep my company. She'll never forgive me."

"Then there's no deal, Arthur. Give me my money now, or your company is mine."

"Florian..."

"I will not start our marriage off based on a lie," I say, interrupting whatever excuse he wants to give me for lying to her. "She'll agree to our arrangement knowing the truth, or there's no deal, and Williamson Holdings is mine as of today. This is not negotiable."

The room is filled with tension as silence surrounds us. I allow him some time to process my offer. I'll forgive his debt if he gives me Arabelle. Finally having her will be worth more than the millions I'll pay his creditors and the loss in revenue from obtaining Williamson Holdings.

"Florian...I," he stammers.

For a moment, I believe he may do the right thing for his daughter and keep her far away from me. I'll ruin my beauty, and Arthur knows it. Deep down, he knows Arabelle being with me will destroy her.

"On one condition."

I let out a disappointed sigh as he proves me wrong. He's exactly like my father—only out for themselves, no matter the damage they do to others around them, especially their own children.

"I don't think you're in a place to make any demands of me, Arthur." I lift a brow. "Do you?"

He lifts his chin. "Maybe not, but it's for my Arabelle's protection."

Do I believe the concerned father act? Fuck no. Not for one minute. When it comes to Arthur Williamson, I'll keep my eyes open because I'm sure, somewhere down the line, there'll be some type of ploy.

I motion for him to continue.

"If you aren't faithful to my daughter or don't give her the life she deserves, then she's allowed to get out of the marriage without a fight from you, and my company will remain mine and my debts will remain clear."

"Agreed."

He stares, complete surprise on his face as I agree to his demands. Did I have to? No, I didn't have to agree to any of his shit demands. But I'll never mistreat or be unfaithful to Arabelle. She's the only woman I want and will ever need. So, it's easy to agree to his terms, especially if it gets me closer to having her in my life. I'll do absolutely nothing to mess up this opportunity, including being the asshole I know I can be.

"Well, if I can get Arabelle to agree, then you have yourself a deal."

"Like you said, Arthur, she'll do anything for her family, right?"

He nods, but I don't miss the uncertainty in his eyes. He's asked a lot of his daughter throughout the years, but this just might be the first time she puts her foot down and says no to him. I won't blame her if she does. She needs to stand up for herself, especially against her family. She's taken enough of their abuse. If I lose out on my chance to be with her because she finally does something for herself, I can't be mad. I'll definitely be disappointed, but it will be what's best for her.

"Will she be in town soon?" I ask, although I already know the answer. According to Hugo, she's already boarded her plane. That puts her touching down in about an hour. "I'd like to get this done as soon as possible."

"Today, as a matter of fact."

"Perfect. I'll have the papers drawn up immediately and delivered within the hour. I expect them to be returned to me within forty-eight hours, Arthur, and not a minute past that time."

Standing up from behind the desk, I extend my hand. Knowing he has doomed his daughter to the Devil, he reluctantly takes hold of it.

"It was nice doing business with you, Arthur."

He grunts and leaves as quickly as he can. I grab the office phone and call my secretary. "Lilian, have Roger come to my office. I need a contract drawn up as soon as possible."

After I hang up, I place my hands on my desk. I lower my head and exhale, attempting to soothe the mix of anticipation and nervousness within me. I finally get to have the one thing I can't get out of my mind. The one thing I long for. The one thing I don't deserve in this life or the next.

"I finally get to have my beauty."

That's if Arthur can convince her to sign the damn contract.

10
ARABELLE

Exhaustion. I can't escape it.

My life revolves around rehearsals, performances, after-parties, and photoshoots. It's not a complaint because I love to dance, and I work hard to do the one thing I love to do. My mom used to say that there's always a downside to the things you love to do. With age comes understanding, and now, I get it.

At three, I put on my first pair of ballet shoes. Dance comes naturally to me, which has led some to call me a prodigy. The stage is where I find peace and feel at home. Even now that I'm older, the excitement of performing remains.

Dance is everything to me. It's in my bones. It's the very air that I breathe. But I can admit it gets lonely.

I'm lonely.

I have nothing outside my life at the theater. The women around me are untrustworthy because they are always looking for any weakness so they can take my place. So, I have to be conscious of that fact anytime anyone tries to befriend me. I learned my lesson a long time ago when it comes to my colleagues. They are not my enemies, but they are not my friends either. This career is cutthroat, and I have to always remember that, especially with the more fame I gain.

So because my life centers around the theater, I have no friends to hang out with, and I have never had a real boyfriend. Not even my family comes around unless they want something.

I lost my mother at a young age, and it's hard for me to recall much about her. The memory that always stays with me is her guidance to *plié*, her knees bending perfectly, and her arms extended gracefully. Despite her small size, her voice remains firm yet proud, offering words of encouragement as I follow her guidance, saying, "Great job, my lovely Belle." Her words of praise always echo in my mind whenever I achieve something.

Although my mother has passed, my father is still alive and well. However, he only contacts me when he wants something or believes I need to work harder for his benefit.

In the past year, he's been bothering me more because of the rumors circulating about me becoming the principal dancer. I've become a way for him to get money more than anything else. It's sad, but I believe if it weren't for dance, I wouldn't have any contact with him or my sisters.

My sister, Raven, who is the middle child, needs rehab and medical care due to her alcohol addiction. My oldest sister, Angela, is a vindictive bitch always trying to get ahead in her life on my name and on her back. My father is addicted to gambling and always expects me to bail him out financially. I've come to terms with the fact that I'm my family's meal ticket. Without my money, they would probably not give a damn about me or what happens to me.

"Do either of you know what this is about?" Raven asks.

She gulps down the last of her beer sitting in front of her before taking the cap off another one.

I respond with an eye roll and with a glare directed at her. She hasn't been out of rehab for very long. To ensure she received the best care, I covered all of the expenses for her stay in an exclusive rehab facility out west, even though my father didn't contribute one dime after he made me believe he would help. At this point, she's had no less than three beers while we've been sitting here. God knows how many she's had before now, and she'll have at least six more before calling it quits with the beer and moving on to the wine cabinet.

Although I'd like to question her about it, she gets defensive, and I lack the energy to argue with her about something she doesn't want to change.

I used to feel sorry for her and Angela. I believe our mother's death set them on their destructive paths, Raven's being the path of alcoholism. Angela surrounds herself with countless men who care nothing for her, hoping they'll make her life easier. But now I just believe neither gives a shit about anything, and both are determined to continue down their destructive paths, regardless. So, I don't feel sorry for them anymore. We've all handled our mother's death differently, including my father. Now, all of them are just using her death as an excuse.

I've been back in New York not even an hour, and my father has already called a family meeting, so whatever he's got to say can't be good. The flight from California was long, and all I want to do is sleep for a few days before I go back to work. I want to have no worries. Just relaxation.

"It's something to do with Belle, like always," Angela scoffs. "Raven, you know Belle's all daddy cares about, anyway."

Raven grunts, nodding in agreement. I ignore my older sister's snide remark. She hates me, and it's only gotten worse the older we've gotten. As the youngest, I've never been close with either of my sisters. Both would rather use me than have a real relationship with me. I've come to terms with their jealousy and hate for me.

"I don't know why he's called a meeting," I say, scrolling through my phone, returning emails from my agent confirming my schedule for the next month. I've got two one-week performances, rehearsals, and a few photoshoots. Three days of rest isn't enough time, but I'll have to make do. "I just got here."

"Good," my father says as he walks in and sits at the head of the dining room table, interrupting our conversation. "I'm glad you're all here."

He places a manila folder on the table in front of him.

"What's going on, Daddy?" Raven asks, sipping from the bottle of beer. "You said it was urgent."

My father's eyes narrow on her while she continues drinking like nothing's wrong. Like I didn't just spend my hard-earned money to get her help. And for a brief second, it looks like my father will say something to her, but the disapproving shake of his head is the only acknowledgment he gives to Raven while she continues to drink.

The money I spent on rehab was a waste. I'm going to have to cut them off sometime soon.

"Well, I need each of you to know that our family company and name are on the line with this deal."

I sit back in my chair and eye my father with a critical gaze. While he's speaking to all of us, he only looks at my sisters, and my hackles rise.

"What's going on with the company?" I ask, hoping to get the truth, knowing it's unlikely.

"It's nothing for you to be concerned about, Belle," he says, looking at me for the first time since he walked into the room, which did not ease my concern. "None of you need to worry. Not anymore. I've handled it."

The effortlessness with which he lies is quite alarming. If he insists there's no reason for me to worry, that usually means I should start worrying.

Has he always been like this?

When I was young, like most little girls, my dad was my hero, especially after my mother passed away. Without fail, he'd bring us gifts from his business trips whenever he was away. Of course, my sisters would always ask for something expensive—jewelry, designer clothes. Anything they could flash at their friends, they had to have it. All I wanted was my favorite flower: a single red rose from wherever he had visited. Now, there are no longer any roses. Not from him, anyway. I'm the one who's always giving. He has become unrecognizable to me.

A leech.

His eyes are heavy with trepidation and fear, as if weighed down by an invisible burden. In fact, as I pay closer attention to him, I realize his entire appearance is unusual. His designer suit doesn't conceal his noticeable weight loss, the paleness of his skin, or the lackluster expression in his eyes.

"Are you sick?"

Both my sisters' lack of reaction to my question is typical and unsurprising. They're less concerned with what's happening if the conversation doesn't revolve around them. Despite knowing my father only values me for what I can provide, I can't help but worry about him more than I probably should because he's still my father.

"No, I'm not."

I nod, relief sinking in instantly. I'm not sure if it's the truth, but something has caused his sickly appearance. Maybe it's this deal concerning the company.

"Are you going to keep us in suspense?" my oldest sister asks, picking at her manicured nails.

Her nonchalant attitude has always irked me. She doesn't have a care in the world because everything with this family always sits on my shoulders. She doesn't have anything to worry about as long as I fund her existence.

"We know it has something to do with Belle," she continues. "It always does. Let's get it over with because I have a date."

"Of course, you do," I mumble. "The unlucky bastard."

"It would do you some good to get fucked too, ice princess," she sneers.

I roll my eyes. "Having sex is the least of my worries, Angela, especially when I have to work. You know, make a living? But, of course, you wouldn't know anything about that since I'm the one funding your lifestyle."

"You bitch!" she screams, jumping up from her seat.

"Could you both stop this damn bickering? Sit down, Angela." My father runs his hand down his face. "This is too important."

"Sorry, Daddy," I apologize.

Of course, Angela won't apologize even if her life depended on it. Even as adults, some things will never change. I should stop expecting them to.

"I've been offered a business proposition," my father says, a rare smile gracing his face. "A very lucrative business proposition."

"What kind?" Raven asks before I have the chance to. "And what does it have to do with me?"

"It has nothing to do with you, Raven, or Angela," my father responds. "But it concerns the Williamson legacy, so that's why everyone is here. Angela is right. It does have to do with Belle."

"Of course, I'm right," she sneers. "Doesn't everything always have to do with your precious Belle?"

My father's palm slams against the oak dining room table, echoing throughout the room, and we all flinch. The beer bottles my sister emptied earlier clink against one another.

"Because Belle is the only one of you that has made something out of their goddamn life! If it wasn't for her, both of you would be dead or penniless. We all would be."

Both my sisters roll their eyes. Although it's shocking to hear my father finally acknowledge what I've done for all of them, they don't care what I've sacrificed so they can have a decent life. Not just a decent life, but a better life than they would have had if I wasn't keeping them afloat. They never will. I stopped waiting for them to care about me and what I've done for them a long time ago.

"Daddy, calm down," I say, trying to diffuse the tense situation.

Although my father is telling the truth, I don't need more hate from my sisters. I don't need any more to deal with. He's always the reason we've been in these positions. His gambling doesn't help and not pushing my sisters to do more causes everything to fall on my shoulders. Although my sisters are bitches, he could have put an end to how they treat me a long time ago. He just refuses to do so.

"Tell us about this deal, and if I can help, I will."

"Yes." He releases a breath, relief covering his features. "I told him as much."

"You told who?" I ask as unease builds inside me even more.

"Florian Larsson. He's asked for your hand in marriage, and I've agreed."

I scoff, shaking my head. This is not happening. What the hell?

"This isn't the 1800s, Daddy. Why in the hell is he asking to marry me if I've never met him, and why the hell are you agreeing to it?"

"*The* Florian Larsson?" Angela interrupts. It's the first time she's actually smiled since I sat down at the table. "Billionaire Florian Larsson? One of *Forbes's* most eligible bachelors? That Florian Larsson? Are you fucking serious?"

My father ignores my sister and lasers his focus on me. "I owe Florian money, sweetheart."

I run my hand through my hair. Of course, he does. He owes everyone money.

"A lot of money."

"How much?" I pick up my phone and start scrolling through the contact list to call my accountant. "I'm sure I can pay it if I move some things around. Oh, and I have an upcoming shoot..."

My father shakes his head. "You don't have this kind of money, Belle. And neither do I." He sighs and moves his hand over his salt-and-pepper hair. "I'm sorry, but this is the only way. He's agreed to let me keep the company and pay off any other debts I owe if you say yes to his proposal."

Proposal! This isn't a damn proposal! It's blackmail!

I stand up and pace back and forth, my restless energy filling the room. This can't be happening. How in the hell have I been pulled into my father's business deal, and who the hell is Florian Larsson?

I stop pacing. "Angela said she'll do it." I toss my hand in her direction while she enthusiastically nods her head. "Why not her?"

"Yes, Daddy, I'll do it," she responds eagerly. "I have no problem walking down the aisle, especially if I'm going to marry Florian Larsson. He's so hot. We'll make the perfect couple. I'm sure he's great in bed, too."

"Don't forget rich," Raven chimes in, pointing the neck of her beer bottle at Angela.

"Yes. Very rich," Angela says.

If this were a cartoon, her eyes would be flashing dollar signs with how excited she is that it's possible she's landed a handsome billionaire.

It's not surprising to see that hungry look in her eyes and her eagerness to marry a stranger, considering she's always searching for a wealthy man to support her while living off my money. She's a leech just like my father, and if she can take my place, this deal would be perfect for her and a blessing for me. I can finally stop supporting her lazy ass, and it'll be one less person or thing I'll have to worry about.

The thought of getting married fills me with anxiety and uncertainty. I'm so awkward around men, it's pathetic. The only time I've come close to having a man in my life is the mysterious man who sends me flowers and a note, which I've found myself pathetically looking forward to receiving. Even after he violated my privacy by entering my apartment without my permission, I still look forward to his gifts.

I've been seeing a therapist to reconcile my feelings of dealing with the trauma of being roofied, while also the invasion of privacy by the mysterious man. According to my therapist, I may have some type of ambivalent attachment to him where I have mixed feelings even though he causes me comfort and distress. So, other than him, I'm completely clueless when it comes to the male species. That'll make for a very embarrassing wedding night.

Yes, Angela will be a much better choice. Hell, even Raven would be a better choice than me!

My father shakes his head and leans back in the chair like the entire conversation exhausts him. "I offered Angela and Raven because they're both better suited for a man like Florian, but he insists it has to be you and no one else."

A man like Florian? What the hell does that even mean?

"Why me?"

My heart plummets to my feet. I can't breathe.

As I receive the news, my chest tightens, and it's like someone sucker-punches me in the gut. With my hand against my chest, I sit when my knees buckle under me.

My father lets out an exasperated sigh. "I don't know, Belle."

"Does it even matter? Belle, it's Florian Larsson for fuck's sake. Do you know how many women would kill to be in your place? Do you know they call him *Beast*?" she asks me, like she's ready to divulge some deep dark secret.

"Beast," I say, my heart rate picking up faster.

Why in the hell do they call him Beast?

"I heard they call him Beast because he has his enemies killed," Angela says, shrugging like having people killed isn't a big deal.

Panic surges through my entire body. "I can't do this, Daddy. There has to be another way. I can't marry someone they call Beast who has his enemies killed!"

"There's no other way, Belle," he says frustrated like I have the nerve to go against what he wants. Go against what Florian Larsson wants. This is my life we're talking about. "You marry Florian, or we'll lose everything."

"You'll lose everything, not me."

He glares at me, but he knows it's the truth. No matter how much I've helped my family, I'm wealthy outside of what my father has. His debts are not mine.

"Stop thinking about your damn self for once!" Angela scoffs, and Raven nods while she sips on another beer. "It could be a hell of a lot worse than Florian Larsson. Suck it up and do what the hell you need to do for this family."

She stands and stalks away from the table.

"Angela's right, Belle," Raven says. "Stop thinking about yourself for a change. This affects all of us. Not just you."

She stands and staggers out the same door as Angela. I slump in my chair. Besides dancing, my family consumes my life. I never think about myself. It's always about them.

My father reaches over and places his hand on top of mine, giving it a light squeeze. It takes everything in me not to snatch away. He's put me in an impossible position again.

"I'm so sorry, Belle."

"Are you?" I snap. "How could you do this to me! You fucking sold me to some man they call Beast!"

He narrows his eyes, sliding the manila envelope over to me along with a pen. "I wish it didn't have to come to this, but I'll do everything in my power to get you out of this mess. I promise."

Promises, promises, promises. He always makes promises he can't keep. He's an addict. His gambling addiction is so severe that it's become a serious problem. Until he acknowledges it and takes action, nothing will ever change. I'd be naïve to think there's a possibility he can rescue me from this predicament. As long as he's taken care of and doesn't lose his precious company, he'll always be content, no matter my situation. I'm doomed to marry a man I don't know to save my family. A man known as Beast.

I remove the papers from the envelope and scan the contract. If I sign the contract, my father's company will remain in his hands, and all his debts will be paid. There's also a stipulation that I must be treated well, and Florian must remain faithful to me for the contract to remain legally binding. Although it's straightforward, I still want my lawyer to review it for added assurance.

"I'll sign it if Dale okays it."

My father shakes his head. "Everything's on the up and up, Belle." He sighs. "Just sign the damn papers so we can get this over with. I don't want to keep Florian waiting."

"I'm not signing this,"—I wave the documents in the air—"until Dale looks it over. Florian Larsson can wait, and so can you."

He glares at me but says nothing. I learned a long time ago not to sign anything without having a legal professional read over it, especially if it's connected to my father. He's dishonest, and I have no doubt that it's a very real possibility there's something in here I might overlook that Dale would pick up.

Against my father's wishes, I hired Dale as soon as my career took off. I remember arguing with him for hours about it, and that told me that I was doing the right thing. Of course, he wanted his attorneys in control of my legal affairs, which would have given him access to my money while I was underage. If I'd done that, I would be broke today, no matter how hard I worked.

From the beginning, I made it clear I wanted to keep my career completely disconnected from anyone associated with him, and that remains true today. My father isn't a trustworthy person, which didn't take me long to figure out. And I have no idea about Florian's character, but I can only speculate with a name like Beast and his affiliation with my father he must not be very admirable either. I'd be stupid to sign this contract without letting Dale read over it.

I pull up my contacts and scroll until I come across Dale's number. It rings a few times before his calm voice comes through the receiver.

"Hey, sweetheart. Is everything all right?"

This won't go over well with him, but he's the only person I can trust.

Dale just turned thirty-seven. With sandy blond hair and a towering height, he possesses a physique that would put most twenty-year-old men to shame. But beyond his appearance, he's the sweetest person I know.

When my career took off at seventeen, my dance teacher highly recommended him to oversee my legal affairs. At nineteen, he began extending dinner invitations to me that I politely declined every time. He's mentioned his feelings for me on many occasions, but I can never move beyond a friendship with him. Not because of him, he's a wonderful man, but he's got more to offer and better things to do than waste his time on a workaholic like me.

"Hey, Dale. And to answer that question, I'm not sure." I chuckle, but it's hard to keep the uneasiness out of my voice. I have no idea what my father has gotten me into, but it makes me wary. It may be something I can't get out of. "Are you available like right now? I need you to look over a contract."

"Whatever you need, Belle. Come on in. I'll let Alice know to send you on up when you arrive."

"Thank you, Dale. I appreciate it."

"No problem. See you soon."

"It's all pretty straightforward, Belle." Dale leans back in his chair and steeples his fingers. His face is tinted red in anger. "Marry Florian Larsson, and your father is covered. But why in the hell would you even think about signing this?"

"So, this is legal?"

"There isn't a *legal* obligation to the marriage stated in the contract, Belle. It's written as a long-term business partnership instead of marriage, which is a loophole Mr. Larsson is using. It's not enforceable if it's written any other way. So, yes. It's legal."

I can hear the anger in his voice, and I know why he's mad. Hell, I am, too. But I know what needs to be done so my family isn't left with nothing. I need to step in.

As usual.

He grabs the contract, stands, and moves to the front of his desk. He leans against it, folding his arms across his muscular chest and crossing his legs at the ankles.

"Because I have no choice, Dale." I sigh. "I've already told you this."

"But that's not true, Belle. You have a choice. It's past time you stopped bailing your father out. You've been doing it for years now."

"I know, but what do you expect me to do? Let him lose everything?"

"That's exactly what I expect you to do. You'll want for nothing until the day you die, Belle. You've done wonderfully for yourself. You've invested wisely and saved your money like a responsible adult, unlike your family. Your father's debts are just that, his debts. Not yours. It shouldn't be left up to you to save him *again*. To save any of them."

Even though I know Dale is right, I can't turn my back on my family. While they treat me like trash, they're the only family I have left. What does it say about me if I don't save them from ruin? I'll be just like them. Selfish. I refuse to be a selfish person, even to those who are that way to me.

"You know I can't do that, Dale. No matter what he's done, he's still my father. I have to do this."

Defeated, his shoulders sag. As he stands to his full height, the anguish in his eyes sends a pang through my chest. The thought of causing him pain fills me with guilt and sadness. He's been a good friend, and I care a lot about him, but I don't love him.

If I'd lived a different life, I believe I'd easily fall for Dale, but he has too much to offer someone who's more worthy than me. Someone who will give him everything he needs and deserves. At this point in my life, that person isn't me. Maybe it'll be in the future, but not now. Right now, I can't give him anything but lonely days and nights since mine are consumed by my career.

I stand, make my way toward him, and then gently place my hands on his face. "Whoever you fall in love with is going to be one lucky woman."

"I've already found that woman," he says with sadness in his eyes. "Unfortunately, she's getting ready to marry another man."

"Dale, no matter how much I would love to be that woman, and no matter how much you want me to be her, I'm not. But she's out there. Trust me."

I stand on my tiptoes and try to kiss his cheek, but he has other things in mind. With his strong arms wrapped around my waist, he pulls me in, pressing our bodies together. Another look of sadness passes over his handsome features. I don't want to be the cause of his pain, and I wish I could make it all go away, but there's nothing I can do. I have to marry Florian to save my family.

His kiss is slow and thoughtful. Although nice, I don't feel any kind of excitement or spark. No butterflies. No increased sense of longing for more or heartache that we can't take our friendship to the next level. Immediately, I know I've made the right decision. Dale is not the man for me. As he lifts his lips away from mine, his gaze locked with mine, I can see the spark of realization replacing the lingering pain in his eyes. He felt nothing either.

"Don't be a stranger." He steps away from me and hands me the contract. "Call me if you need me. I'll always be there for you."

"I know you will." I wrap my arms around his waist and lay my head against his broad, muscular chest. Although things will be different from now on, Dale will always have a special place in my heart. "Thanks, Dale. For everything."

I don't know why it seems so final, but after I put my name on this contract, I have a feeling that things in my life will never be the same. I pull back and give him a final wave before exiting his office.

II

FLORIAN

With a groan, I toss the crumpled sheets off my body, instantly feeling the weight of exhaustion in my limbs as I rub the tiredness from my eyes. With each passing day, sleep seems to slip further away, and I cherish the couple of hours I've been able to get.

As I gaze at Adahlia, her blonde locks cascading onto my black satin sheets, any remnants of contentment from the few hours of sleep I had evaporate, leaving behind a sour mood.

I'll never understand why I put myself through the agony of sleeping with other women, knowing deep down that no one can truly fulfill me. Nobody can replace *her*. There's only one person who possesses my black heart, and her presence consumes my soul.

"Fuck!" I groan when I stand and sway.

The unending pounding in my head serves as a constant reminder of the fleeting nature of sleep and the ceaseless stress that plagues my existence. The migraines can be debilitating at times, but I manage them, determined to keep my weakness a secret. Adahlia's presence only amplifies the fucking pressure, making the pounding in my head unbearable. But I have no one to blame but myself because when she calls and begs for me to fuck her, I can never say no.

I love it when she begs.

I lazily make my way toward my balcony, not bothering to put on any clothes. I gaze through the tinted panes of glass, wondering what she's up to today. According to Hugo, Arabelle visited her lawyer, but I haven't received the contract yet. Her time off is nearly up before she goes back to work. It's not nearly enough time to rest for the amount of work she does, but who am I to judge? Like I said, I may get a couple of hours of sleep myself. I know how it is to work yourself too hard to where your life becomes consumed by your work and nothing else.

I can't wait to change that.

I wish I could catch a glimpse of her. It's been weeks since I've been able to see her beautiful face. Of course, I get daily updates on where she's been and who she's with, but nothing ever changes where she's concerned. Outside of her job, she has no life. While I pity her sometimes because she's alone, and that can't be easy for anyone, I'm grateful all the same.

I'm a bastard.

The last time Arabelle's schedule changed, she ended up being attacked in a grimy alley behind a bar. It was through no fault of her own, of course, but he paid for it with his life. I did what needed to be done. However, they discovered Pierre Gaultier's lifeless body only because I was driven by emotion. I had done a piss-poor job disposing of the body, but I'll make sure Arabelle and myself will be protected. I have a lot of people in my pocket, and they are always looking to get their pockets lined.

No man will ever share her space and breathe the same air she breathes. Not while I'm alive, especially someone she didn't give consent to. No one deserves to have even the smallest piece of her. Not even me.

I make my way back toward my bed, each step filled with a growing sense of dread for when Adahlia wakes up. I open my nightstand and pull out the pack of cigarettes inside. I promised my mother when she was alive that I would quit, but like everything else I promised her, I haven't been able to do it.

At the click of the lighter, Adahlia's beautiful blue eyes peer up at me through long lashes. A small smile graces her face. In her mind, she's convinced herself she's in love with me, but in reality, she's not. She's in love with my cock and the idea of us.

Throughout the years we've been intimate, we've had this conversation countless times: she believes it's love, while I always emphasize it's purely physical. It will never go beyond us having sex. I will never open my heart up to her.

She props up on her elbow, and the silk sheets fall, showcasing her palm-sized breasts and pink nipples. "Come back to bed, Florian," Adahlia says, her husky voice going straight to my cock. "It's still early."

It's time to walk away. It's been time to end this.

"We can't do this anymore, Addie." I sit at the end of the bed, pull on the cigarette, and blow the smoke into the air. "It's gone on long enough."

Adahlia Karlsson, the daughter of Andreas Karlsson, was born into one of the most influential Uppsala families. There are six families who possess an equal share of power, all with their own territories. Some alliances are stronger than others, and most of the alliances are made through marriage. At one point, I saw an opportunity to solidify my power by marrying Adahlia after taking over the Larsson Syndicate. However, everything changed that fateful night I attended the ballet and saw Arabelle. That night, I met the other half of my soul, although I don't think she even remembers me.

Adahlia scoots up next to me, her hand finding its way to my semi-hard cock. With just a few strokes, she elicits a low groan from me, and I can't help but revel in the exquisite pressure and friction of her smooth hand.

Naturally, she goes back to relying on sex. It's what has always worked in the past because I'm a man who loves a beautiful woman. However, it won't work this time. The Larsson and Karlsson Syndicates have already formed an alliance. Therefore, there's no longer a necessity for a marriage with her. She's not the person I want anyway and definitely not the woman I'll call my wife.

"I think you just need to let me take care of you, Florian." She slides off the bed, and her beautiful, lithe body settles between my knees. "You've been so stressed lately."

She's completely clueless about the amount of stress I've been under. Shit never stops when you're at the top, and I don't complain because it's where I want to be.

Although I know I need to stop her, Adahlia's so fucking talented with her mouth, it's hard to say no. My silence she takes as her cue to go ahead.

With her painted nails, she traces a tantalizing path down my chest and over my abdomen, igniting a surge of desire. I embrace it all —the heat, the slickness, the pressure. One more time won't hurt, I convince myself.

After I stub out the cigarette in the ashtray on the nightstand, my fingers tangling in her golden locks, pulling them hard as she moans in ecstasy. However, in my mind, it's not Adahlia pleasuring me but Arabelle—the one who captivates me. Instead of blonde hair and thin lips, it's Arabelle's dark curls and plump lips bringing me pleasure, filling me with an intoxicating desire.

As she moves up and down my firm length, a surge of adrenaline floods my senses, amplifying every sensation as she plunges me deeper into her warm, wet mouth.

"Damn, that feels good, Beauty," I praise as she hums, rejoicing in the attention I'm giving her. The sensation sends a surge of electricity moving through me.

Using her tongue, she traces a path along the length of my shaft before engulfing me once again. I tighten my grip on her golden strands, lifting my hips and guiding her head down to meet my thrusts.

"Fucking take all of me like a good girl," I order, speeding up my movements. "You know how long I wanted those fucking lips around my cock? Hmm? I'm going to fuck that pretty mouth of yours until I come down your throat, and you choke on my cum."

The sight was absolutely breathtaking. Tears welled in her eyes, spilling over and staining her cheeks. Her skin is adorned with scattered splotches of vibrant red. The way her tongue dances across the head of my shaft is pure bliss, edging me closer to the point of no return.

With a groan, I apply even more pressure and force her head down further, craving the sight of those tears. Needing to feel her throat close around the head of my cock. She gags when the reddened mushroom tip hits the back of her throat over and over, but she doesn't try to push me away. She takes everything I'm giving her like the good girl I know she is.

I'm in heaven as my orgasm barrels through me.

I throw my head back and close my eyes. "Fuck! Belle," I shout as my orgasm barrels through me like a freight train. "That's it, Beauty, swallow all of it. Don't lose one single drop."

I maintain my grip on her until I completely empty myself into her mouth. I open my eyes, and my dick slips from her mouth when I let go of her hair, then she jerks to her feet.

"Who the fuck is Belle, Florian?" Adahlia shouts with her hands on her hips.

I can't help but admire her body. With her slender hips, flat stomach, perky breasts, and flawless skin, her beauty is undeniable. However, the sight of her ruins my perfect fantasy. She's all wrong.

"What the fuck are you talking about, Adahlia?"

I reach for the cigarette in the ashtray and light it again, relishing the flavor as it envelops my mouth and coats my tongue. After shooting your load, there's nothing quite like the satisfying taste of tobacco.

"You called me Belle, you fucking asshole."

In a hurry, she snatches her clothes from the floor and dresses. This isn't the first time I've imagined Belle while fucking her or someone else, but I don't think I've ever said her name out loud. That's a new one. Or if I have, no one has ever called me on it. Do I care that I called out her name? Not really. The person whose name echoes from my mouth is the one who occupies my thoughts and heart. The woman I'm with at the time doesn't matter to me. They never matter to me. They are only there to serve one purpose.

"Is that why you don't want to be with me anymore?" she asks as she slips on her heels. "You've found someone else?"

Adahlia doesn't deserve an answer because, although we fuck each other often, we aren't exclusive. I've never told her this goes beyond what we do in the bedroom. Belle is my secret. The object of my relentless fixation. And it will remain that way until I'm ready to introduce her to the world as my better half, which may be never if she doesn't sign the contract.

"It was always going to be this way, Adahlia," I say, ignoring her questions. "That's something I've never hidden from you. I've never said we were exclusive. That's why you're not the only woman I fuck, and I know I'm not the only man you fuck."

I shrug, indifferent to who she sleeps with, but she winces, unable to escape the sting of the truth. I'm a powerful man in this city. Whenever I attend functions, Adahlia is usually perched on my arm. Because of that, people think we're in a relationship. So, it's not uncommon for men who are looking to impress the Beast to inform me when she's with other men. Not that it matters to me.

"Fuck you, Florian!" she screeches instead of acknowledging the truth.

Maybe she's embarrassed that I know what she does with other men, but she shouldn't be because I couldn't care less. She's a piece of ass to me and most likely to them too. A very nice piece of ass, but not special, which I've told her many times. It may make me a bastard, but I would never lie to her, no matter the situation.

"You think you can just get rid of me? Just wait until my father hears about this."

She storms out of my bedroom, then out of my penthouse, the door slamming behind her.

I'm not worried. I've already spoken to her father, and I let him know there is no chance of me marrying his daughter. He understood, and we forged an alliance because he can't stand my father. He'd rather deal with me and give the middle finger to my father, even if I'm not married to Adahlia.

"One thing off my plate."

12
ARABELLE

Ignoring any sense of etiquette, I storm into my father's study, the door crashing open, and throw the envelope onto his desk. This used to be one of the places I had very fond memories of from my childhood, when my father was still a loving and supportive parent. Now, he's turned into a parasite who exploits me. I'll always look at him and this place differently. He's tainted every memory I have of him.

His eyes meet mine, filled with disappointment as if my abrupt entrance into his sacred space has upset him, but he keeps his silence. He picks up the envelope, opens it, pulls the contract from the envelope, and flips through it until he reaches the last page.

"I signed it."

I cross my arms over my chest. He lets out a tired sigh and places the papers on the desk before lifting his gaze to meet mine.

"I didn't want this for you, Arabelle. Believe me."

"Believe you? You can't be serious? Why the hell do you think I'd believe anything you have to say!"

"Do you think I want you to marry a man like Florian Larsson?" he asks. "He's heartless. He's a ruthless man who shows no mercy."

He shakes his head like he's so distraught at my situation. Yet, he had no problem handing me a contract and asking me to sign my life away because he knows I can't say no, regardless of how much he uses me.

"And yet, I have to marry someone who will treat me like I'm less than nothing because you're an addict who can't take care of his sick daughter! Raven's an alcoholic who has liver disease! Or did you not give a damn because you know I wouldn't let anything happen to her if I can help it?"

Do I believe he's sorry for putting me in this position? No, I don't. Do I think he cares he's ruined my life? As long as he can keep his money and company, he couldn't care less about me. That contract shows me all I need to know about what my father thinks about me.

"Arabelle." He sighs, pinching the bridge of his nose. "I never wanted this to happen, especially to you."

"Of course you did, Daddy. You're the one who put me in this position, knowing you couldn't pay a goddamn thing!"

"Watch your tone with me, young lady!"

"My tone!" I toss my hands in the air. "My tone! That's what you're worried about right now? You're worried about how I'm talking to you when I've just signed my damn life over to a man who I don't know because of you!" I yell, pointing at him. "And you want me to watch my tone? You're so fucking unbelievable."

He jumps to his feet. "Now you wait one goddamn minute, Arabelle Michelle Williamson. If it wasn't for me,"—he points to himself—"you wouldn't be where you are! I've done everything for you!"

"When, Dad? Tell me when you've done anything for me when it didn't benefit you or my sisters?"

"Who do you think paid for all those goddamn lessons, Belle?" He places both palms on his desk and leans forward, glaring at me. "It sure as hell wasn't your mother! It was me, whether you want to acknowledge it or not!"

Of course, he would bring up that he paid for all my dance lessons, travel expenses, and whatever else I needed when I first started dancing. But isn't that what he was supposed to do as my father?

Although he paid for everything, he seldom showed up to watch me dance. He never took me to rehearsals or recitals. Even after my mother died, the nanny took me to all those things.

When I was younger, it bothered me that he didn't show up for anything that I did. Now, I don't care if he ever sees me dance again. He just reaps the benefits of my hard work. He and both my sisters sit on their asses and do absolutely nothing.

I huff. "And I've paid you back tenfold for any money you dished out for me when I was a child! I've been paying you back since I got my first paycheck, but no more. This is it. Don't ask me for another goddamn dime. Your daughters, who don't want to work, who I've been footing the bill for since I was fucking fifteen years old, are cut off too. I'm no longer your or their personal piggy bank! I'm done with you and them. You no longer have a daughter, and they no longer have a sister. From here on out, every one of you will make your own damn way, just like I have."

"Arabelle, we're your family! You know we need your help!"

"Family?" I chuckle. "None of you know the damn meaning of the word. My family died when my mother did."

I storm out of his study with him calling my name, but I ignore him. When I say I'm done, I'm done. There will be no more handouts given, no more saving him from shit he got himself into. No more funding my sisters' extravagant lifestyles or wasting money on exclusive rehab. This will be the last time I save my family.

Sleep doesn't come. I've been tossing and turning since I got to my penthouse. I love New York, but being here stresses me out. Little did I know this short trip to relax for a couple of days would spiral into a complete shitshow. It's a reminder that when it comes to my family, things are never simple.

Florian should have the papers by now. If not now, he'll get them first thing in the morning. Will he be happy with this arrangement? Because I'm definitely not.

Unable to sleep, I open my laptop and start searching for information about my future husband. The thought that I'm going to marry someone I don't know sends a burst of terror racing through me.

"What the hell am I going to do?" I mumble as a picture appears on the website. I instantly recognize him by his rugged beauty. "That's the man Samuel introduced me to. One of the theater's donors."

I scroll through the many articles that have popped up about him.

Even though he's been photographed a lot with a mesmerizing blonde bombshell, Florian Larsson is still considered one of the world's most eligible bachelors, according to the popular tabloid *Exposé*.

"Someone who looks nothing like me."

One article's headline suggests that a wedding is on the horizon for them. Despite what the papers say, his body language doesn't convey that he's in love with her. Our arranged marriage is further evidence of this.

"Either she's a great actress, or she's in love with him," I mutter as I continue to scroll through picture after picture of the beautiful couple. "She's going to be a problem."

In some of the photos, her eyes are fixed on him with such intensity, like he's the only thing that matters in the world. In other pictures, they pose for the camera, giving off the impression of being the next sought-after couple. However, I can say that the way he looks at her falls short of the way she looks at him. He maintains a cold and distant demeanor. In every photograph, his gaze never meets hers and is always fixed on the camera.

"But she has to mean more to him than just someone to take to fancy functions, Belle," I say to myself as I search through even more photos and articles of the couple that go back years.

Since this isn't a real marriage, will he have a mistress even though it says in the contract he must remain faithful? Will it be her?

I push those thoughts out of my mind, but it leaves behind a lingering feeling of sadness. While I don't know him, and this marriage won't be real, I still don't want to imagine I've given the rest of my life to someone who'll disrespect me in that way because that's not something I would do despite this being a farce. But his relationship with her is something I'll deal with when the time comes. It's definitely a conversation we'll need to have. Right now, there's something more important I need to know.

"I need to find out why the hell they call him Beast."

After doing a little more digging, I stumble upon another article from *Exposé*, this time written by investigative reporter Amy Moreno.

It's unclear whether this is a ploy for attention or fact, but the reporter alleges that he's the head of one of the six established Swedish Syndicates who have made waves in the criminal underworld in the US in the last few years, especially with Florian at the reins.

"Oh my god." I rub my temples, the pain increasing in my head as reality sinks in. "My dad sold me to the mob."

Known for his cutthroat tactics in business, Florian has become a prominent figure in both legitimate business circles and the shadowy realms of criminal activity since succeeding his father, Olan Larsson, according to Amy Moreno.

He lost his mother at a young age and basically worked his way into the position he holds now. Despite his reputation for cruelty, people still view him as an enigma because he effortlessly moves between both worlds.

"Who is this man, and how in the hell does my father know him?"

Although he seemed nice when I met him after my performance, what my family had to say about him let me know that I totally misjudged the person he is.

I shut down the laptop, its screen going dark, and place it on the bedside table, adding to the clutter of books. There has to be a way to prepare for this, but how do you prepare for someone you don't know? Someone known as Beast.

"I'm so screwed."

13

FLORIAN

Closing the front door to my penthouse, I grip the large brown envelope in my hand like it's my lifeline, and if I let it go, it might vanish into thin air. Or maybe I might wake up, and it all will be a dream.

Hugo just delivered Arabelle's contract, and I'm in total disbelief. I'd believed that she would finally stand up for herself and tell her father to go to hell, but I guess she isn't at that point yet. While this works in my favor today, I know eventually, she'll be able to cut ties with her family because all they are doing is holding her back from living the life she deserves.

"She signed it." I shake my head in disbelief. "She fucking signed it."

I can't believe it repeats through my mind. It's almost too good to be true. Sitting in my penthouse on the thirtieth floor in Soho, exhilaration courses through my veins as I gaze at the contract. I stare at the bottom of the page where her name is signed on the dotted line in elegant script, like if I blink my eyes or turn my head for a second, it will disappear.

Today feels otherworldly. Today feels like a dream. It's something I've wanted, but I never believed that I could actually obtain. And now, I'm still struggling to grasp the fact that she's finally mine. Maybe not by choice because I did force her hand, but the day I've been longing for has arrived.

With a sigh of relief at seeing her name, I toss the papers onto the glass coffee table in the sitting area and head toward the sliding door that leads to my terrace. I slide open the glass door, step out, and walk to the black railing. I grip it while taking in the breathtaking view of the New York skyline.

The sky is filled with billowing gray clouds casting a shadow over the landscape, while the crisp, cool air nips at my face. Inhaling deeply, I fill my lungs with cold air and marvel at how different life seems with just the sight of her name elegantly written on the dotted line.

She'll be mine in a matter of days.

Eleven years ago, I buried my mother. This day serves as a bittersweet reminder of both the past I've left behind and the future that awaits me. The future that awaits me with her.

My Beauty.

My mother's hopes for my life may come true after all. There's no doubt in my mind that Arabelle will fall head over heels in love with *Florian.* That side of me will lavish her with love and shower her with gifts to show her how much she means to me. She'll never want for anything, including love. She already has my heart, and I'll give her whatever her heart desires. But can she accept the beast that lurks inside? The beast will always be a part of me.

I don't want this to be just an arranged marriage where we are both living separate lives. I hope that's not what she wants either because I want a marriage filled with genuine love and commitment. I want a wife I can worship and who'll also worship me as her husband and the love of her life. The person she can lean on for anything and everything.

Will she accept our relationship without any conditions? Will she open her heart to me so we can have what we both desire?

The rapid knocks on my door tank my mood immediately. I just want to enjoy this one win before being brought back to reality. Stepping inside, I walk to my front door, then look through the peephole and confusion blankets my face. Opening it, I'm faced with two men in cheap blue suits.

"Florian Larsson?" one of the men asks, flashing a badge.

Fuck!

"How may I help you?"

"Mr. Larsson, I'm Detective Regan, and this is Detective Logan. We're from Chicago PD, and we have some questions about the disappearance of Pierre Gaultier."

"I don't know how I can help you with that. I don't know any Pierre Gaultier."

"If you let us in, we can discuss this matter further," Detective Regan says.

"Well, I'm sorry, gentlemen, I'm on my way out for an important meeting, but I can give you my attorney's card, and he will set up a meeting for a later date."

"An attorney? If you have no involvement, what do you need an attorney for?" Detective Regan asks.

"Gentlemen, I'm a very wealthy man. I don't go anywhere or discuss anything without the advice of my attorney."

"Were you recently in Chicago?" Detective Logan asks as I retrieve my wallet from my back pocket.

"Depends on what's recent. I travel a lot," I say as I pull my attorney's business card from inside my wallet. Detective Regan grabs it, looks at it before focusing back on me.

The insistent ringing of my cell phone is a welcome intervention. I reach into the other back pocket of my dress slacks and groan at Alrick's name on the caller ID, which means my evening is about to change.

"Sorry, gentlemen, I have to take this."

"We'll be in touch," Detective Regan says, and I nod before shutting the door in their faces.

"Alrick?"

"We have a problem."

I pinch the bridge of my nose, feeling the pressure and tension building. Of course, we have a problem. I can't even fucking celebrate my upcoming nuptials. No matter what, life seems determined to crush my happiness at every turn.

"What kind of problem?"

"Didrick." He sighs. "He was in the alley behind the warehouse in Hell's Kitchen."

I can't help but feel sorry for my brother. He's always had a tougher road than my other brothers, which has led him down a path of addiction that he can't seem to overcome.

"I'll see you in twenty."

A few of our warehouses are behind Sully's Dry Cleaners. Along with the three warehouses, I also own four multistory apartment buildings in front of the warehouse we've named *The Pit*. It's where we handle most of our business.

In Hell's Kitchen, the residents turn a blind eye to the shit surrounding them as long as their beloved buildings are well-maintained. So do the Irish, who I have cultivated a close relationship with, which allows the Larsson Syndicate to operate in their territory as long as I give them what they want.

"What's he doing here?" I ask Alrick as soon as I enter the building.

He shrugs. "Don't know. I didn't ask because he's out of it. He looks like shit, Florian."

"Of course, he does. That's what fucking drugs will do to you."

As we walk toward the coolers at the back of the warehouse, the sound of my footsteps reverberates through the space, bouncing off the smooth tile floors.

When I bought the place from the O'Connors, I almost took the coolers out. Alrick had the idea they might make a good soundproof room just in case we needed to get information out of our enemies.

I agreed.

The air in the warehouse is filled with the sound of clanging crates as the boys work diligently, stacking the newly arrived ghost guns from my supplier, a powerful one-percenter motorcycle club based in Las Vegas. It's not uncommon for me to be present at any of my operations, so no one wonders why I'm here.

They continue to do their jobs as I make my way to see what condition my little brother is in. That being said, I can't help but worry about someone else spotting him here.

"Did anyone see him other than you?"

It's not about my brother's drug addiction. It's about someone using it against me. In this kind of work, I can't have that kind of weakness. Anyone can keep him supplied if they think I'd spend any kind of money to help him.

"I don't think so," Alrick replies. "I found him sleeping against the dumpster. I don't even think he tried to make it inside. He's not looking so good."

I paid thousands of dollars to get him clean after I paid off his debt. My father doesn't care if he's an addict as long as it doesn't affect his reputation.

My half brothers and I don't have the best relationship. The truth is, they can't stand me. But what can I say? I have a soft spot for the kid because I know he's fucked up in the head because of our father. He's still young, and his behavior can be corrected. The others don't have an excuse for their behavior.

I thought Didrick would be tied to a chair like the others, but he's not when we enter the cooler. My eyes are filled with curiosity as I glance at Alrick. He knows I'm not close with any of my brothers, even though I've tried to help Didrick in the past.

"He's still your brother." He shrugs. "I didn't think you'd want him treated like everyone else. And, like I said, he's not doing too good. Tying him to a chair served no purpose."

I remain silent. Alrick is right. I don't want to treat Didrick like my enemy, but if it was one of my other brothers, those motherfuckers would be tied to a chair and getting the shit beat out of them for lurking around my business. Didrick is different. He always has been. I guess it's because he reminds me of myself at that age.

His current state causes my heart to constrict inside my chest. Even at seventeen, he has his entire life ahead of him if he can break free from this addiction. His drug of choice is heroin. From my understanding, it started with a pill addiction and morphed into this after a nearly fatal motorcycle accident.

I lower myself next to his feeble body, observing the fresh needle scars on his arms, and a swirl of guilt consumes me. Damn, he's lost so much weight since the last time I saw him.

How long has it been?

Lying in the fetal position, Didrick has his arms crossed over his chest and his knees pulled up to his stomach. His body is so thin that it looks like his skin is stretched tightly over his bones.

I watch for the slow rise and fall of his chest, then breathe a sigh of relief when I see it.

Good. He hasn't overdosed.

I brush his usually pale, matted hair away from his sunken eyes, now darkened by dirt, giving it a grayish hue. His clothes are covered in dirt, blood, and what looks like vomit, maybe food. As I slide my thumb across the dirt smudged on his pale skin, anger surges within me. He's been on the streets for a long time, and I didn't know.

How am I any better than our father if I don't take care of him?

"Didrick." I nudge him. "Didrick. Wake up."

As he squirms, his eyes slowly open. When he catches sight of me, a frown appears on his face. Tremors rack his frail body as he tries to sit up, forcing me to help.

"Florian, what are you doing here?" he says with a little panic in his voice and fear in his eyes as he looks around the freezer. "You can't be here."

"But I came to see you, little brother."

I force a smile. I hate treating him like a fucking baby, but he's high out of his mind. He doesn't know up from down right now, so he has no fucking clue he's in my warehouse. It's not the best time to give him my hardened attitude.

"Do you know where you are right now?" I ask, even though I know he doesn't.

"I'm at home." He looks at me with confusion. "But why are you here? You know Dad's going to lose his fucking shit if he finds you here." His breathing picks up as panic sets in even more. "You got to get out of here, Florian! He can't find you here. He'll kill you."

He's more worried about what our father will do to me if he finds me here than being high out of his mind.

"Didrick, calm down." I place my hand on his arm, careful to avoid his track marks. "Don't worry about me. I can handle our father. Everything's going to be fine. I want you to come with me."

"You think that's such a good idea?" Alrick asks. "You need to meet with Arabelle soon."

I glare at him over my shoulder. He holds up his hands.

"I didn't forget, Alrick. But I need to take care of this first. He's high out of his goddamn mind, and he's been living on the fucking streets."

I shift my attention back to my brother and gently lift him onto his feet, which are barely covered by shoes with gaping holes in them. His pants and shirt also have holes in various places.

The foul odor wafting from him is almost too much to handle, but I force myself to ignore it. He's my damn family.

"Come on, Didrick," I say as I escort him toward the door. "Let me get you out of here." I turn my attention to Alrick. "Have Daniel pull the car around back."

"*Ja, Odjur*." Yes, Beast.

As Alrick leaves, my little brother grabs onto my hand, seeking comfort and reassurance. I feel like a piece of shit for not making sure he was all right. Even though we don't have the best relationship, it's up to me to prevent him from becoming something I know he loathes. He dislikes being an addict. He dislikes being a burden to me, which I understand. However, burden or not, he's my blood.

"Where are we going?" Didrick asks, his frail body shaking in my arms. "I have nowhere to go."

I continue to ignore the sour odor coming from his body and his breath, bearing the majority of his body weight as we make our way toward the back of the warehouse. He's dropped so much weight. He's always been a lanky kid, but now, he's as light as a feather. I'd be shocked if he weighed over eighty pounds.

"He said I'm a disappointment, and I'm no longer his son. He doesn't want me at the house anymore, Florian."

It's hard to ignore the pain in his voice. Despite how I feel about our father, Didrick and my other brothers actually care for him, even though he doesn't give a shit about them.

"Then you can come home with me."

It's not the best idea, especially now that I have Arabelle. But he's my brother. I can't turn my back on him.

As I help Didrick get clean, I can't shake the heavy burden of guilt. How did I let this happen to him? He's nothing but bones covered in filth.

Didrick, being underage, still has a lot of growing up to do. It's not his fault our father is a piece of shit, and his mother is the typical wife of a mobster. She keeps her mouth closed so she doesn't face his wrath, no matter if her children face the consequences of her silence.

Yes, I helped Didrick once, getting him into the best rehab in the US, but I failed to stay in his life. I failed to make sure he stayed clean. If I had stayed around, or at the very least given him a job to keep him occupied and away from our father, he wouldn't have found himself in the same position as before. Right now, he would be clean and living a new life, not living on the streets in filth.

I know how our father is. If he sees anyone excelling above him, he sucks the life from them. That's what he did to me when I was younger. That's what he did to my mother, and now, he's done it to Didrick.

"Florian, you don't have to help me," he slurs as I pour shampoo onto his matted, shoulder-length hair. "I'm not a goddamn baby. I can wash myself."

He's still coming down from whatever he's on. He barely removed his soiled clothes before getting into the shower. There's no way he can clean himself properly, sitting on the shower bench as I watch the dirt from his hair and body swirl down the drain.

Do I want to give my brother a shower? Fuck no. But the condition he's in, there's no way he can do it himself, so I ignore his outburst.

"I know you're not a baby, Didrick, but I want to help, okay? Let me help you."

He sighs but nods. I returned to trying to clean the dirt from his soiled hair.

"What are you on?" I ask as I try my best to get the muck out of his hair. "Heroin or something else?"

He's going to need a haircut.

His head droops. "I couldn't handle it. I tried, Florian. I swear I did. But when Father kicked me out, I had nowhere to go. I got a hit of heroin, hoping I wouldn't wake up. And just like that, I was hooked again."

"Why didn't you reach out to me?"

Anger rushed through my veins. I'd made it clear to him that I would help him anyway that I could, and that I didn't fault him for our father being an asshole. However, I needed to compose myself and help, not push him away.

"I would have helped, Didrick. You know I would."

"I know Father came to you to help me the first time, and he's never let me forget it. I didn't think you would help this time," he says, sadness in his voice. "I know you don't like me, Florian. I don't even blame you, not after Father pitted us against one another."

"You're my brother, Didrick. No matter what *Far* does, nothing changes that. I will always help you if you need me. All you ever have to do is pick up the phone, and I'll drop everything."

A series of sobs escape him, causing his body to shake with each one. For the next few minutes, I listened to the youngest Larsson release the anguish and hurt that not only my father caused him, but me as well. I'm determined to make this right. Unlike my other brothers, Didrick hasn't been totally corrupted by our father, and I refuse to let it happen. I can still help him escape the destruction that is our father. He still has time to make something of himself as long as he's far away from Olan.

"I'm going to get you some help, Didrick," I say once his sobs slow. "I'm your big brother. I'm going to fix this."

He nods, but he says nothing else. I'm sure his body is suffering from agonizing pain. He's ashamed of the person he's become and needs time to process what's happened. So, I continue to clean him in silence as he comes down off his high.

Tomorrow, I'll make sure he's on the first plane out of the country. In order for him to get clean and stay clean, he needs new scenery. New people. Most of all, he needs to be as far away from our father as humanly possible.

14
ARABELLE

The moment I step into the opulent foyer of Laila's of New York, I'm immediately struck by the luxurious marble floors beneath my feet and the intricately lofty ceilings, with a multi-tiered chandelier hanging from above. A massive abstract water feature dominates the center of the area, its cascading streams creating a soothing ambiance to the space. I have never seen something so sophisticated.

As I approach the hostess's podium, I can't help but notice the young, dark-haired woman in a black-and-white uniform. The name Laila's of New York, written in large, shimmering gold letters, looms behind her.

Many times, I've wanted to come here, but it's nearly impossible to get a reservation. The last time I checked, the wait list was seven months long. It made me wonder how much power Florian actually has to pull this off in less than a week.

"How may I help you, ma'am?" the hostess asks, her beautiful smile on display.

"I'm meeting someone," I reply as butterflies flutter in my stomach.

She opens the reservation book. "Name?"

"Ms. Williamson. I'm here to meet Florian Larsson."

"Oh yes!" She closes the book. "Ms. Williamson, Mr. Larsson said you would be joining him tonight. Giancarlo will take your wrap and clutch." She points to the young man standing a few feet away. "You can pick them up at the end of your night."

"Thank you."

I remove the black cashmere wrap and hand it to the young man along with my black, diamond-encrusted clutch. He tags both items with my name and then disappears into a room off to the left of the hostess station.

"Let me take you to your table." She grabs a menu from behind the podium. "You're in the private dining room. Right this way."

"Thank you."

Stepping into the dining room, I'm greeted by the soft glow of candlelight dancing off the crystal chandeliers above. With a deep breath, I square my shoulders and lift my chin, refusing to let the anxiety churning in my stomach overpower my confidence. I'm about to meet my future husband. The man known as Beast.

Whispers of his alleged connections to Swedish organized crime have been floating around, but so far, none of it has been substantiated. The papers suggest a connection, but they also mention that his name originates from his involvement in the corporate world. I don't know what to believe. I've lost any hope that my father wouldn't get me involved with someone who would put me in danger because he doesn't care. As long as he gets what he wants, I now know he doesn't give a shit about me.

I push down the negative thoughts intruding on my night. I have to make the most out of it. He's going to be my husband. I've signed my life away, so there's no going back now.

Despite my nerves, I can't help but take a sharp breath in awe of the vast, beautiful, and elegant space. The dim lighting creates a romantic mood. The black tablecloths draped over the round dining tables contrast elegantly with the tall crystal vases brimming with exquisite white roses.

It's absolutely breathtaking.

We maneuver through a crowded dining room, the clatter of dishes and chatter of voices filling the air. The mouthwatering smells are impossible to ignore. Although I'm training, it's not often I get to dine in one of the world's most exclusive restaurants. Tonight, I definitely plan to indulge.

As we approach the private dining room, I touch the hostess's arm, signaling her to stop before she opens the door. I need a little extra time to compose myself.

"Could you give me a minute before we go in?"

"Sure thing." She smiles, holding our menus against her chest. "Let me guess, blind date?"

"Something like that." I return her smile. "How did you know?"

"You're a nervous ball of energy," she says, chuckling. "I can feel it from here. Just take deep breaths. Remember that you're a beautiful woman, and he's the lucky one, and everything will be fine. At least, that's what my mama always told me in these situations."

I laugh and can already feel the nerves start to dissipate. "Your mom sounds like a wise woman."

"She was." A forlorn look crosses her face before she clears her throat, and then her smile returns, though it no longer reaches her eyes. "Ready?"

"Yes. And thank you."

She winks and pushes the door open, and it's like I've stepped into a fairytale. I gasp, and so does the hostess.

What the hell? It's just like my dressing room.

Everywhere I look, vibrant red roses adorn the room. As I enter, my eyes are drawn to the sight of rose petals scattered across the pristine, white marble floor. The room is beautifully decorated with lit candles and large bouquets of long-stem red roses in clear crystal vases, creating a romantic ambiance. In the back of the room, there's a glass table adorned with a blanket of red roses, their familiar sweet fragrance filling the air. Glass vases with flickering candles decorate the top of the table, casting a warm, yellow glow, illuminating the entire room.

My breath catches in my throat, leaving me momentarily speechless. Behind the table stands the man who will be my husband. The man who made my heart race with excitement when I first laid eyes on him.

As I take the first step toward the rest of my life, my heart rate quickens, reminiscent of the first time we met. I'm feeling a mix of confusion and uncertainty at the moment, to be honest. I'm a twenty-two-year-old woman who has never had a serious relationship, and now I'm expected to marry someone named Beast, who possesses the looks of any woman's wet dream.

I've hit the jackpot when it comes to my future husband. With his tall stature and captivating presence, he possesses that irresistible aura women are drawn to. He still exudes that rugged beauty vibe, but what unsettles me is the mystery behind all of this.

Standing at least six foot three, possibly four, with tousled, dirty-blond hair, his cobalt-colored eyes captivate me, drawing me closer like I'm in a trance. Among all the women he could have chosen, he picked me. There has to be a reason.

As my eyes linger on him, a sudden rush of heat engulfs my cheeks. However, I push aside my embarrassment and continue to examine him. If I'm going to marry the man, I have every right to look at him as he devours me with his intense stare. He doesn't seem to mind, anyway, as a small smile tugs at the corners of his mouth.

He steps from behind the table, his dark-blue slacks clinging to his muscular legs. His baby-blue button-down shirt, undone at the collar, reveals a glimpse of his tattoos, adding a hint of sinful allure to his appearance.

The butterflies that were fluttering earlier have taken full-blown flight now. The feeling has shifted from nervousness to an overwhelming desire.

His gaze explores every inch of me, his eyes moving up and down my frame. I aimed for a sophisticated yet understated look tonight. My choice was a black cocktail dress that exposed my shoulders and reached my calves, hugging my slender figure and modest bust with precision. I'm glad I chose the four-inch black strappy stilettos. They add an extra touch of elegance to my outfit, and I need all the height I can get.

"It's nice to see you again, Arabelle." He kisses me on the cheek and then pulls out one of the chairs. "Please have a seat."

I give a small nod and take a seat. "Thank you."

He pulls out the other chair and settles down next to me, creating a sense of closeness as my arm and thigh brush his. There's no space between us, and I'm actually okay with it.

The man has a jawline that looks like it's been chiseled from marble.

His loud laughter resonates throughout the room. I would never believe a man could get any more beautiful just by a carefree laugh if I hadn't seen it for myself.

"Did I say that out loud?"

My face flushes with embarrassment.

"You did." He reaches for the bottle of wine that's on the table. "Would you like a glass of wine?"

I'm not much of a drinker, especially since I was drugged, but I think I might need some liquid courage to figure out why this man wants to marry me. He has the power and money to have any woman, but he's chosen to be with me.

"Sure. But just so you know, I'm not much of a wine drinker. Or really any alcohol."

Anger flickers in his eyes, and before I can question him about his change in mood, he shuts it down, and a charming smile graces his face.

"Are you scared you might fall head over heels in love with me?"

With humor in his voice, I know he's trying to lighten the mood and distract me from his mood change. This is an odd position for me to be in, so I'm happy he's trying to make it less stressful.

I chuckle. "Something like that."

He pours a glass of wine for each of us. "One can't hurt." I can't resist melting when his intense eyes lock onto mine. It feels like he can see right through me. "Let's make a toast."

"And what are we toasting?"

"New beginnings." He raises his drink.

With a raised glass, I toast to "new beginnings" and take a sip of wine.

"But I have to ask..." I sit my glass on the table. "This question has been on my mind since my father brought this arrangement to my attention."

"You can ask me anything, Arabelle." He places his wine glass on the table. "Nothing is off limits if it's appropriate for this setting. You deserve answers to all of your questions."

"Why?"

He smiles, and it seems genuine. Not forced. "Could you please be more specific?"

"Why do you want this marriage? I don't know you, and you don't know me. I'm sure you're a great guy, but don't you think all this is kind of weird?"

He shrugs. "Maybe."

It's definitely weird.

"I need you to be honest with me. This has got to be as strange for you as it is for me."

"I'll always be honest with you, Arabelle, even when you don't want me to be."

"Well, that's good to know," I say. "But you're not answering my question. I want to know why you want to marry a stranger. You're wealthy and very handsome. You can get any woman you want."

"You think I'm handsome and can get any woman I want?" he asks with a smirk.

I can't stop myself from laughing. "Of course, you're handsome, and you know you can."

He directs his gaze toward me but doesn't respond to my statement.

"I just can't figure it out, and it's something I need to understand."

After another smile from him, I have to pause, take a deep breath, and refocus my thoughts. The man makes my heart race and my pussy weep.

It's been entirely too long since I've slept with anyone. I'm not sure my fingers are doing the trick anymore.

I'm thankful when the waitress comes in and takes our order. It allows me to breathe and regain my composure.

I understand exactly why my father took this deal. He's greedy. He saw a way to have his debts cleared and maintain control over his company. What I don't understand is why this man would want to marry a stranger.

"The reason I made the offer to your father is because I've wanted you since the first night I met you." I gasp, and he chuckles. "You want the truth, right?"

"I do," I say without hesitation.

"You can't be surprised that a man would want such a talented and beautiful woman as yourself."

Honestly, I am surprised. I've never been hung up on beauty despite others telling me how beautiful I am. I'm just an ordinary girl who loves to dance and who receives compliments about my dance skills and beauty. Yet it has a different feel when he says it.

"Thank you for the compliments, but I want to know why you want to marry me, Florian. It has to go beyond beauty and talent for me. Marriage is a big step, especially getting married to someone you don't know. Both my sisters are beautiful, too, and you explicitly told my father no when he offered them to you."

I'm not gonna comment on their talents since it won't paint either one of them in a good light.

He groans and licks his lips. "Say it again."

My eyebrows furrow in puzzlement. "Say what again?"

A smile spreads across his handsome face. "My name."

"Florian," I say without hesitation and with a little confusion. "You want me to say your name?"

Leaning back in his chair, he runs his thumb along his bottom lip. "You don't know how long I've waited to hear my name come from your lips since that first time I met you. It's not quite the way I've imagined it, but it will definitely do for right now."

A wave of heat slowly rises up my neck. My entire body warms from embarrassment.

I'm relieved when the waitress brings in our food. She puts it down in front of us and then leaves the room. We both focus on our food, and all thoughts of me saying his name disappear. Even though I haven't received an answer to my question, the silence between us remains tension-free.

With each bite of the grilled salmon, the tender flesh melts in my mouth, releasing a burst of savory flavors.

I groan.

"Is it good?" he asks, a mischievous smirk playing on his lips.

"Umm...very."

When our eyes meet, the intensity in his gaze sends another surge of heat coursing through my entire being. I lick my lips, and I notice his gaze briefly shifts to my mouth before meeting my eyes again.

"I've been wanting to come here since the place opened, but it's hard to get a reservation. And what about yours?" I point my fork at his steak.

"Laila's never disappoints." He cuts a piece of steak and points his fork at me. "You want to try it?"

"You want me to try your steak?"

Trying someone else's food is a little intimate, in my opinion.

He nods, and a small smile tugs at the corners of his lips. Despite not knowing each other, I lean in and take a bite from his fork, savoring the taste of the tender meat as its juices and flavor coat my tongue.

As I swallow the steak and take a sip of wine, he looks at me with satisfaction.

"Good?"

"Yes. Oh my god. It's so delicious."

He takes a sip of the rich, velvety wine and carefully places the glass back on the table.

"I purposely stayed away from you after meeting you that first time. On occasion, I've been weak and visited you."

My mouth drops open in surprise. "What do you mean 'visited' me?"

Memories flood back to me, specifically of the stranger who Ms. O'Donnell was adamant about seeing coming in and out of my apartment, leaving me with a sense of curiosity and concern.

"If you knew how obsessed I am with you, Arabelle," he says, ignoring my question, "it would scare the shit out of you."

The red roses.

"The rose in my bedroom? All the roses in my hotel rooms? They were all from you?"

Anger is moving through me, and so should fear, but it doesn't. This man knows every place I have been. It's very possible he may have been in my apartment. More than once. But if he had any intention of hurting me, he would have done so a long time ago. So, what's the purpose of all of this? It's definitely not to harm me.

"I can see your mind working overtime, Arabelle," he says. "I want you. I always have."

"You're stalking me."

"I am."

As I slide my chair away from the table, the sound of its legs scraping against the floor fills the air. When I try to stand, he firmly grasps my arm, preventing me from getting up. His grip isn't tight, but it's firm enough to keep me in my seat.

Even though I know I should be scared, fear never comes, but I am pissed. I'm angry he believes that it's fine for him to invade my privacy.

"Please stay."

"The roses and the notes have been beautiful and have brightened my days more than once," I confess, not to excuse his behavior but to tell him the truth. "However, you were in my apartment without my permission, Florian. And, according to my neighbor, it's been multiple times! I thought she was going crazy."

"I know, Arabelle. I understand what I did wasn't right and an invasion of your privacy. I would never claim that it was the right thing to do, but what else was I supposed to do?"

A flicker of something almost like fear passes through his eyes before he hides it away.

"Maybe approach me like a normal human being instead of sneaking around doing stuff like a crazy person!"

"I want you, Arabelle." He sighs like he's got the weight of the world on his shoulders, and it's hard to discuss this with me. "But I'm a dangerous man. I have many enemies, which has kept me single for a long time. However, when I saw the opportunity to have you in my life for real, not just from the shadows, I took it. I'm not the prince in the fairy tale. I am the Beast. I take what I want. And what I want is you. So, please stay."

"Why should I stay?" I ask, not sure I want to hear his answer, but the need to know or hear him say it is overwhelming.

"Because I'm never going to let you go, Arabelle."

"What?"

"You're mine now, and I plan to cherish every moment with you."

I relax in my chair even though I know I should run as far away from this man as I can possibly get.

"And why does my father owe you money?" I ask, my voice filled with suspicion.

"As you know, he has a gambling problem, which you've been saddled with taking care of for a long time."

"You've looked into me?"

I should have expected it, but it's still difficult to listen to him discuss my family problems.

"I have. Just as you've looked into me," he says, giving me a pointed look. "I gave your father a loan, and he put his company on the line as collateral. Then, he failed to repay the loan plus interest when it was due. I gave him an opportunity to settle his debt in another way, which I don't do with any of my clients, and he took it."

He should have just said that my father sold me.

"You're a loan shark?" I ask, staring into his eyes, trying to gauge his reaction.

"Among other things."

He takes a sip of wine, and I'm taken aback by his lack of denial, leaving me in disbelief. The rumors swirling around about him being connected to organized crime might actually hold some truth.

"And you just wanted me as payment?"

Shocked doesn't even describe how I feel right now. Sold by my own father, I now find myself seated beside the man who purchased me, who claims he's fixated on me and has admitted to stalking me.

"I'd much rather have you than any fucking company, that's for sure."

"Lucky me," I mumble.

Despite his lack of words, his smirking face reveals his amusement at my comment.

"Why do they call you Beast?"

"Because I've earned the name. I'm not ashamed about anything I've done or what I do to keep my people safe. I get what I want, including whatever it took to get you. But some parts of my life will never touch you. I promise."

"How did you earn the name?"

"How do you think?"

Did I really think he'd give me a straight answer?

I sigh. "So, the rumors are true?"

"Depends on what rumors you're referring to."

Annoyed, I roll my eyes, unable to hide my frustration. "You know exactly what I'm asking, Florian."

The intensity of his stare is so strong that it's almost uncomfortable. I want to break eye contact, but I don't. He may have a reputation for intimidating others, but if I'm going to be his wife, he needs to understand that he cannot wield that power over me. I refuse to look away and meet his intense gaze head-on.

After a few moments, when I say nothing or change the subject to give him an out, he sighs, leaning back in his chair. "Actually, I don't know what you're asking, Arabelle. There's a lot of shit that's been said about me in the tabloids, which I assume is where you got your information about me. And a lot of shit is said by people who claim to personally know me and by people who definitely don't know shit about me at all. So, most of what you think you know about me is bullshit."

As I lean back in the chair, I let out a deep sigh. "You know that's not an answer. I want to know why they call you Beast and how you earned that name."

"What you're asking isn't something I'm going to discuss with you in a restaurant. When we're able to have more privacy, sure. I'll divulge more to you about my life you haven't been able to find out in the papers. At least the parts that may affect you and that you're curious about."

When it comes to Florian Larsson, I'm definitely filled with curiosity. He's definitely a savvy businessman. I can tell that by the way he's carefully navigating this conversation. His honesty has thrown me off kilter, which I believe may have been his plan the entire time. It doesn't anger me, but it does pique my curiosity about him even more. I'm interested in finding out why he's called Beast.

He's a highly accomplished individual. He took over Larsson Industries, which came across more like a hostile takeover than him inheriting it from his father. So, what does that say about his relationship with his father? Is it shit like the one I have with mine?

"Who's the woman in the pictures?" I ask, shifting topics. Maybe I can get a straight answer this time.

He laughs. "Why? Are you jealous?"

"No. I have no reason to be jealous of someone I don't know, Florian. However, I'd like to know if my future husband plans to fuck this woman while we're together because you two look very cozy together."

"Did you read the stipulation in the contract?" he asks. "I'm sure if you didn't, your attorney did when he advised you on it."

"I did."

"And you still ask me that question?"

"Florian, I'm not clueless even though you may think I am. You are a gorgeous man, and she looks at you like you hang the moon. Every photo of you, she's on your arm, so she's definitely someone you are close with. I refuse to have blinders on, despite some stipulation in a contract. Even if you want me to."

"I'm not that kind of man, Arabelle. If I'm committed to a woman, it's her and only her I fuck. I've never made that commitment to any other woman except you. Adahlia, or Addie as I call her, is someone I've fucked, yes, but that's all it is. There was a time I thought of marrying her for business purposes, but that isn't a need anymore. So, I'm not."

"Is that what I am, too?" I ask. "A business deal?"

With a hint of a smile on his face, he leans back in his chair and takes another sip of wine. "No, Arabelle, definitely not. You're so much more to me than any business deal, and I can't wait to show you."

I've been around powerful men. There's a certain aura that radiates from them. My father used to be one of those men until his gambling addiction took over, and he became less like the man I grew up with and more like the pariah he is today. Florian has that same type of energy. I definitely need to find out all I can about Florian Larsson.

While he says this Adahlia is not an issue, the way she looks at him tells me that she definitely doesn't see their relationship the way he does. Just as I'm about to ask more questions about how he's going to handle that situation once we're married, his phone rings, interrupting us. Annoyance takes over his face as he retrieves it from his pocket and glances at the caller ID.

"I'm sorry, Arabelle. I have to take this."

"It's fine."

While I'm eating, I attempt to listen to his conversation. I know it's wrong to eavesdrop, but I want to know more about him. Unfortunately, I don't recognize the language, and by the time he's done with his call, I've finished my food.

"I'm sorry, Arabelle, but I must cut our dinner short. Business has come up."

"Oh!" I wipe my mouth with the table napkin and toss it on the plate. "It's no problem. I have a photo shoot tomorrow, anyway, so I need to get some sleep."

"I want to get some things straight about our engagement and any other concerns you may have. But we can talk about those another time," he says, standing. "I would like for us to get married as soon as possible."

He takes his wallet out of his back pocket, counts out several bills, and then casually tosses them onto the table.

"Wait. What's the rush?"

He pulls my chair out, and I stand.

"I would like us to get to know each other first. This is a big step for both of us."

"How about we discuss this more over dinner in the next few days? Do you think you can work me into your schedule?"

I release a breath. I'm glad he's open to talking about our arrangement more instead of jumping right into a marriage.

"I'll make the time."

"Great. Hugo will take you home."

"You don't have to do that. I can call a rideshare. It's no problem."

He shakes his head. "From now on, Hugo will take you wherever you need to go. Now that you're my fiancée, my men will always be around you."

"That's not necessary, Florian. No one other than my father even knows about this. I really think you are overreacting."

When we exit the private dining room and walk through the restaurant, I don't miss the curious glances from patrons. More than likely, they recognize Florian. We return to the hostess station. I retrieve my cashmere wrap, which Florian helps place around my shoulders, and my clutch.

We stop on the sidewalk in front of a blacked-out Range Rover. Standing by the rear door of the vehicle is a tall man wearing a black button-down shirt and dark gray slacks, with a scar running down the left side of his face.

"You can't argue with me on this, Beauty," he says. "I have enemies. This is for your safety and my peace of mind."

I look at the man with the scar, who I assume is Hugo, then back to Florian and sigh. "Okay."

I'm used to doing things on my own, but if he feels safer with someone driving me, then I'll let Hugo drive me around. At least, for now.

The man unlocks the door, and I slip into the back seat.

"Hugo will take you wherever you need to go."

"Thank you, Florian."

As he edges closer, I entertain the thought that he might actually kiss me. The eagerness to feel his lips on mine shocks me. I lean in, but instead of his lips touching mine, he kisses my forehead. Disappointment washes over me.

"Now isn't the time for that," he says, reading the disappointed look on my face. "But soon. I'll call you."

He takes a step back and firmly closes the door. Perhaps this marriage won't be as terrible as I thought. At least, in the charming and handsome department, Florian checks all the boxes, but something lurks just beneath the surface of that calm exterior. Something dangerous. I'm not so sure my heart will survive it.

15
FLORIAN

It only takes me half an hour to reach the warehouse in Hell's Kitchen. When I arrive, both Asva and Alrick are already waiting. When I received the call from Alrick while I was with Arabelle, I was beyond livid. I can't stand interruptions, and that was the first time we were alone together like a normal couple. I wanted to get to know her outside of what I've had my men dig up on her or what Hugo can tell me by following her every move. I'm interested in getting to know her. The real her.

But duty calls.

"What do we have?" I ask as soon as I step out of the car.

I can see the tension on their faces as I tighten the lapels of my peacoat around me. The temperature has dropped since I left the restaurant. Asva stands on my left and Alrick on my right as we make our way inside the warehouse.

"The guards came under siege," Asva reports, anger lacing his voice. "Most of the men were able to escape harm."

"Cops?"

"It's been handled," Alrick says. "The residents are keeping their mouths shut, and the O'Connors have already been in touch. They want to meet as soon as possible."

"Shit!" I run my hand through my hair. "How many dead?"

"Ten of our men."

"Their families?" I ask, trying to keep the anger and sadness out of my voice.

The families will need to be notified about their deaths. Every man who works for me is aware of the risk of not returning home, but it doesn't lessen the impact when it actually happens. But for their ultimate sacrifice, their families will never want for anything as long as they live.

"They're being notified as we speak," Alrick says.

I nod. I'll have to visit each one in the next coming days as they plan the funerals because that's what the leader of the family does.

"Once everything is set with dates for funerals, I'll go see the families, give them my condolences, and the first installment of their death benefits. How many of my father's men are dead?" I ask, rage building in me as I think of the sacrifice of good men because Olan doesn't want to understand that his time leading the Larsson Syndicate is over.

I have no doubt my father is behind this attack. I expected him to make his move sooner rather than later. I should have been more prepared than I was. He's trying to cripple me before taking me out, but this will be the last time I underestimate him. He will finally learn why they call me Beast.

"Olan lost fifteen," Asva says.

Red clouds my vision, and I stop in my tracks when we make it through the steel doors of the warehouse. The concrete floors are covered in blood, dead bodies riddled with bullet holes and spent shell casings. Some crates are flipped over and broken. Others are peppered with bullet holes, and brain matter is splattered on others.

"We captured two running out the back," Asva says as I survey the room, thinking of all the ways I'm going to torture anyone who had anything to do with this. "They're in the coolers."

I give a nod as I walk toward the freezers. "How much merchandise did we lose?"

"We can't tell yet, Beast," Alrick says. "I've called in extra help to go through the inventory. We should have an exact count by tomorrow morning."

By the look of the damage, he's cost me tens of thousands of dollars.

When we finally reach the coolers, an overwhelming rage consumes me. With a firm grip, Asva pulls the door open, the hinges creaking in protest. I step in, followed closely by Alrick and Asva, the sound of our footsteps echoing through the space. In the center of the room, two men are tied to chairs, their faces filled with fear and uncertainty.

There's no trace left of the supplies the Irish once stored in here. However, the drain in the center of the floor is quite useful. It makes the cleanup of bodily fluids a breeze.

"Who do we have here?"

I circle both men as they remain quiet. They've been stripped of all their clothing and are shivering uncontrollably in the bone-chilling temperatures. I hope they understand that their torment is far from over.

"Who sent you?" I ask.

There's no way any of my other enemies would dare attack me. Although they hate me, they're scared shitless of the reputation I've built for myself as the cruelest man in the underworld. Now, these two will see how cruel I can be.

Both men maintain their silence, but their eyes reveal so much hatred and fear. I crack my neck. I haven't had the chance to inflict pain on anyone in quite some time, and now, the monster inside me is itching to get out.

I retrieve a pocketknife from the inner pocket of my suit jacket prior to removing it. I throw the blazer to Asva, roll up my sleeves, and then remove the four-inch blade from its holder. "It's not wise of either of you not to answer my questions, gentlemen."

I run my thumb along the sharp edge of the blade, feeling a slight sting as a tiny drop of blood trickles out of the small slit in my skin. With my thumb pressed against my lips, I drink in the taste of my own blood before locking eyes with the two men.

"I've earned my name."

"You're nothing but the bastard son of a whore!" one of the men sneers with a thick Swedish accent. "No one is afraid of you!"

His voice drips with anger and hate. Most of my father's men hate me because my father made sure that everyone believed I was nothing. However, I made something of myself while they were still fighting and scrapping to crawl up the ranks. But if they'd simply gone along with the transition and did not remain loyal to Olan, their lives and their families' lives would have been so much better. Now, they have to die. And for what? For the ego of a man who cannot and will not ever admit defeat. Only his death will mark the end of the conflict between us.

Inside the closed space, my laughter reverberates and fills the air. I slice across the face of the man who spoke, feeling the warmth of his blood against my skin. "I may be a bastard, but I'm the rightful heir to the throne I sit on."

The sound of his screams fills my black soul with sadistic delight as his flesh slowly separates from his jawbone. The sight of his blood, crimson and vibrant, ignites a fire inside me. The sight of his bone makes me crave more.

As the stench of urine fills the room, I can't help but burst into more laughter.

"Did you just piss yourself, motherfucker?" I ask, laughing in their faces while they glare at me.

"Fuck you," one of the men screams, and I land a punch to his face.

"Now, I assume my father sent you?" I ask, ignoring his screams.

As the other nods, the one I sliced open responds with a grunt.

"Now we're getting somewhere, gentlemen." I stand back and cross my arms over my chest. "Now, what is he planning, and why hit my warehouse tonight?"

Both refuse to answer, which I should have expected. I guess slicing someone's face open isn't incentive enough for them to talk. I take the pocketknife and forcefully plunge it into the upper thigh of the other man, near his groin, then drag it down his leg, causing blood to gush from the wound.

"Oh, shit!" I cover my mouth with mock concern. "I think I've hit an artery."

Fear clouds the man's eyes, and I burst into laughter. However, he doesn't even have time to panic because, within minutes, he slumps over. Blood trickles down his thigh and pools onto the floor.

"*Odjur*, now we can't get any information out of him," Alrick says with humor in his voice.

"It doesn't matter." I shrug, eyeing the other man whose terrified gaze is locked onto me. "This one will talk, unless he wants to end up like his friend here."

I forcefully pull the other man's head back, his hair tangled and stained with his partner's blood.

"What is he planning?"

"He's...he's going after the girl," the man stammers, immediately answering my question.

Fuck!

I tighten my grip around the strands of his hair, mirroring the growing rage surging inside me.

"What girl?" I ask, even though I already know the answer. The rage coursing through me is too real to comprehend. "Adahlia?"

I hope it's Adahlia. Fuck, please let it be her. I don't give a fuck what happens to her, but my Beauty...if something happens to her, I won't survive it.

The man attempts to smirk, but the sagging flesh on his face makes it difficult. "This was the distraction," he forces out, his words distorted from the wound to his face. "She's the target." His attempt to laugh results in a strained, gravelly gargle. "Did you think you would win against him? Olan has eyes and ears everywhere, and soon, he'll have your girl, too."

My father is looking to destroy me. He must know Belle means something to me if I'm going to marry her, and I don't doubt Arabelle's father told him all about my deal. Coming here was a mistake because he's going after her.

I'm fucking terrified and seething as I pull my cell from my pocket and dial Hugo. He answers immediately.

"Beast?"

"Take Belle to the penthouse and secure her in the safe room until I get there. He's coming after her."

"You got it, Beast."

"Change in plans," I hear Hugo say before I end the call and focus on the man in front of me. I walk around the back of the chair and wrench his head back. "You chose the wrong damn side," I hiss in his ear, slice across his neck from ear to ear, then release his head.

Struggling against his restraints, he desperately attempts to reach the gaping wound on his neck as his body jerks—a natural reaction to having your throat slit.

"Hold his mouth open."

Asva walks up and forcefully opens his mouth, and his jaw pops. I pull his tongue out of his mouth and cut through the dense muscle, disregarding the blood that stains my hand.

"Nobody likes a snitch."

I toss the bloody muscle to Alrick, feeling the wetness and stickiness against my fingertips. He catches it effortlessly, tucking it away in his pocket as if it's the most normal thing to do.

"Send it to my father. Gift wrapped. And let him know it's from me."

"*Ja, Odjur,*" Alrick says.

Asva tosses me a wet towel and a bottle of water. I rub my hands, trying to remove the crimson stains clinging to my skin. I hate that I don't have time to get clean, but I have to get to Belle. She's mine, and I'll protect her even if it costs me my life.

Hugo informs me he's made it safely to my penthouse and secured Belle in the safe room. Although she's unhappy, he let her know it's for her safety and that I'm on the way and will explain everything once I arrive. Hopefully, she won't hold this incident against me. It's hard gaining someone's trust, and with her not knowing me, something like this could make it harder for me to get anywhere with her.

In less than thirty minutes, we pull up to my building, the familiar sight of its tall, imposing structure greeting us. The thirty-story, all-glass building was my first purchase after getting completely out from under my father. It cost a pretty penny, but it was well worth it because it houses most of my men. Despite the healthy cost, I looked at it as an investment in my organization and me.

Of course, all my men and their families love it. The majority of them don't come from money. Like me, they grew up hard and way too fast on the streets of Uppsala. And anything is better than living on the streets. But I made them a promise. They and their families would never want for anything again if they swore their loyalty to me. In exchange for their loyalty, they live a life most dream of.

Asva, Alrick, Daniel, and two additional members of my team form a protective perimeter around me as we navigate toward the exclusive entrance of the building. I stand in front of the retina scanner, its red laser beam scanning my eyes. The laser moves in a vertical and horizontal pattern, tracing my face.

"Good evening, Mr. Larsson," Megan, the artificial intelligence system, says in her smooth, melodic voice. *"Welcome home."*

The doors to the private elevator slide open, and we all step in. The private elevator and Megan are not accessible to everyone in this building. Only the men with Hugo and me have access to this elevator. Although this isn't the only way to access the twenty-ninth and thirtieth floors, it's the only one that directly opens into the penthouse. I only trust these men with me to give them direct access to my private residence.

"Twenty-ninth floor, *Megan.*"

Megan starts at my command, and I shift from foot to foot as the elevator slowly rises. Too slowly. I'm usually the calm one out of all of us but not now.

I can feel all their eyes on me because of the anxiousness sitting in my gut. I know Arabelle is safe because the state-of-the-art safe room in my bedroom is impenetrable. But I need to put my eyes on her myself. Hugo and all these men with me are highly trained, especially Hugo, and every one of them will die protecting her. However, I know in my heart and soul that no one can protect her better than me.

"Calm down, Florian," Alrick says. "This place is a fucking fortress. Nobody can get to her. And by any chance they do get past all the security features you have in place, Hugo's a damn one-man army."

I release a breath. "My mind knows this, but I can't relax until I see her and hear her voice for myself."

I catch Alrick's gaze, and there's a hint of confusion in his eyes, yet he says nothing. My closest men understand my obsession with Arabelle, including Alrick, but they don't understand how deep my feelings are for her. The feelings that go way beyond obsession.

The elevator stops, the doors slide open, and we're greeted by the barrels of two guns.

"Put the fucking guns down, Hugo," Asva hisses from in front of me.

Hugo chuckles, the sound echoing through the room as he holsters both weapons. I'm the last one to step off.

"How is she?" I ask, making my way to my bedroom, where the safe room is located.

"She's fine. Scared and pissed," Hugo replies, chuckling. "I've never heard so many curses come out of someone so beautiful."

So, my beauty isn't as innocent as she seems.

While they make themselves at home in the living area and kitchen, I walk into the master bedroom, where the reinforced and fireproof safe room is hidden behind a false wall. This isn't the only safe room in this penthouse, but it's the most technically advanced and closest to me. Every condo in the entire building has at least one safe room.

After inputting the code known only to me, which changes every hour, I push the steel door open. As soon as I step inside the room, her pacing comes to an abrupt halt, and her gaze pierces me. The brief look of fear in her eyes infuriates me to no end. It wouldn't be there if it wasn't for that bastard I share DNA with.

As I stalk toward her, a wave of relief washes over me when her shoulders sag and a frown creases her beautiful features. Angry or happy, it doesn't matter. At least she's okay.

"What the hell, Florian?" she asks when I wrap my arm around her.

"Don't worry, I've got it under control." I trace my finger down her jawline, then across the vein pulsing erratically in her neck. Her eyes flutter before she looks up at me with her beautiful dark brown doe eyes. "But I'm going to need you to stay here with me until the threat is neutralized."

As she steps out of my embrace, the warmth of her touch lingers on my skin.

"You think they're going to come after me? Hugo said there was a threat."

"We just need to take some precautions."

There's no reason to freak her out or piss her off more than she already is with the news that my father is targeting her because of me. Or that her father is the one who put that target squarely on her back. While I can't stand my father, I believe she still has some love for hers, so I don't want to shatter whatever image she has of him.

"If you want this to work between us, Florian, start telling me the truth. Am. I. In. Danger?"

I sigh deeply, carrying with it a mixture of frustration and resignation. She's right. If I want this to really work between us, I can't keep this from her.

"One of my warehouses was hit tonight. Two of the men involved said it was a distraction. You were the target."

"What?" she shouts, her voice echoing through the room. "But we don't even know each other. How do they know about me?"

I don't want to tell her, but she has every right to know the truth. Whether her father knew what would happen, he's the one who had to have leaked my plans of marrying his daughter to Olan.

Pinching the bridge of her nose, she looks up at me, her long lashes framing her eyes. She's beautiful. Her dancer's body, the way her hair cascades down her back in tight coils, and even the angry glare she's giving me add to the natural beauty she possesses.

I pull her back into my embrace, feeling the warmth of her body against mine. I brace myself for her resistance, but to my surprise, she eases into my arms. I don't believe she even knows she's doing it.

"Marrying you is a big step for me. So, my enemies know you're important to me."

"How am I important to you?" she asks with her brows furrowed. "We haven't known each other long enough for that to be true."

"You already know how important you are to me, and you in my arms like this is the only place you want to be, too. Eventually, you'll admit it to me and to yourself."

It's the only place I want her to be.

I tighten my embrace around her waist because I know she's not going to pull away from me. I'm enjoying her body being close to mine.

She stays silent for a moment, her breaths shallow and deliberate, like she's trying to make sense of the chaos unfolding around us. She's trying to make sense of why she can't pull away from me and how she can be having this kind of reaction to me even when we don't know each other.

"It's always going to be like this, isn't it?" she asks, barely above a whisper. "Am I always going to be in danger?"

I lift her chin so I can look into her beautiful eyes. There's no point in lying to her. She'll know because now, her life is going to change. "No one will ever get near you, Arabelle. I promise. I'll die before I let anyone harm you."

"Don't say things like that when you don't even know me,

Florian. I don't want or expect you to die for me. I just want to know what's going on."

"I've known you a long time, Arabelle. You just didn't know me."

Before she can utter another word, I press my lips against hers, silencing any further questions or concerns. I'm not sure if she's truly prepared to hear the entirety of my confession. Not yet anyway.

She doesn't need to know that I've watched her while she slept. She doesn't need to know I've watched her come. All she needs to know is that I'm hers, and she's mine.

16
ARABELLE

I'm floating.

As warmth floods my entire system, my body feels weightless, like it's freely moving through the air. This kiss is unlike any I've ever experienced, leaving me breathless and craving more. I've never been kissed so passionately to where it feels like nothing else in the world matters, including the danger he's put me in. This is the exact feeling I was looking for when Dale kissed me. The kind of kiss that has your toes curling in your shoes and butterflies erupting in your stomach.

Arousal surges through me as I rise onto my tiptoes, my fingers entwined in his smooth, silky hair, yearning to bring him closer.

The heat of desire consumes me, its flames licking at my skin with an insatiable intensity I've never experienced before. It's like the world has stopped around me, and I'm doused in nothing but an intense craving for this man. A man I know nothing about.

I moan into his mouth, desperately trying to deepen our kiss, but he maintains complete control.

Oh my god. What the hell am I doing?

He just confessed that I'm a target for his enemies, and all I can think about is how soft his lips feel against mine. How magnificent his hand feels squeezing my throat, his cock brushing against me.

I'm going crazy!

"Relax, Beauty." His breath tickles the space just above my lips. "You're thinking too much. Let go. It's only about what you feel."

Let go.

It's so easy for him to say. I've been thrust into some mob shit because my father sold me to a mobster, and he wants me to just let go.

How the hell am I supposed to do that? How am I just going to let go and feel when I'm in danger?

"Just get out of your head and stay in the moment," he says, like he hears the conversation I'm having with myself. "It's just you and me, Beauty."

His nose glides along my neck, leaving a trail of soft, tender kisses in its wake, causing more arousal to pool between my thighs. "Florian..."

"I've dreamed of this moment so many times." The pressure on my throat intensifies, and my mouth parts in response. "I've dreamed of tasting your beautiful skin and your sweet pussy. I've dreamed about how you'll feel with my cock deep inside you. Will you scream my name or God's?"

"Oh my..."

An insatiable need of wanting him deep inside me surges through my body. I dig my nails into his arms, relishing the sensation of his muscles tensing beneath my touch. He traces his tongue along the curve of my breast, then glides up my neck, sending delicious shivers down my spine.

"I want to fuck you, Beauty," he whispers in my ear. "But I don't think you're ready for that right now."

No. No. No. My mind screams, *I'm ready*, but my voice won't say the words. So, I pull away, shooting him a glare that only does the opposite of what I want him to do. He chuckles.

"I didn't say I wouldn't make you come, love, just not with my cock. Not until we're married. So, I'll let you choose. Do you want my tongue, or do you want my fingers?" he asks.

"I..."

His smile turns wicked. "Don't worry," he whispers. "Either way, you'll come with my name on your lips. I promise."

"You're very sure of yourself, aren't you?"

It's the only thing I can come up with to tamp down some of my desire for him. The man has me so full of lust right now, I can't even make a decision.

"Why don't you strip while you decide," he says, not responding to my question.

However, the wicked gleam in his eyes makes me think he doesn't have to respond because he's getting ready to show me. I'm not sure I'm completely ready for it.

"Or would you like help with that?"

I'm ready.

Without hesitation, I spin away from him, hastily gathering my hair off my neck, granting him access to unzip my dress. I brace myself against the wall when he pushes me against it. Despite the roughness of his touch against my skin, a delicious shiver runs through me as his calloused fingers delicately dance across my body. As the wetness increases between my legs, I release a breath, feeling a mix of anticipation and desire.

How long has it been since I've felt the touch of another person?

His hand moves slowly, pulling the zipper of my dress down my back, inch by inch, until it rests just above my ass. With both hands, he gently pushes the top of the dress off my shoulders, his fingers grazing my overly sensitive bare skin. I close my eyes, savoring the warmth and gentleness of his touch.

"You are so beautiful." His lips brush the curve of my neck, leaving a trail of soft kisses that gradually descend to my bare shoulder as my dress pools at my feet. "I've imagined this moment with you so many times."

From behind, he firmly grabs one of my breasts, caressing and teasing my erect nipple with his fingers.

"How wet are you, Beauty?"

As another rush of desire soaks through my already drenched lace panties, I moan.

"Why do you call me that?"

His tongue lightly traces up the column of my neck, sending

another shiver coursing through me. A mix of pleasure and pain consumes me as he teases and pinches my nipple and firmly holds onto my hip with his other hand.

"Don't answer my question with one of your own, my love."

My love.

I don't know how to explain it, but I love that he called me that. It just feels right. Everything feels right.

The sound of my panties ripping fills the safe room. From behind, with his arm wrapped around me, he tightly holds my neck, his warm breath tickling the shell of my ear as his other hand sensually moves toward my core.

"I call you Beauty because you are. I call you Beauty because you are the most beautiful woman I've ever laid eyes on. And I call you Beauty because I'm your Beast."

I am overwhelmed by the sheer magnitude of possessiveness unfurling inside me.

He's mine.

"Now, how wet are you?" he asks again, bringing me out of my thoughts.

"Very," I whisper.

With a groan, he forcefully turns me around and positions himself in front of me, using his knee to separate my legs. He runs his fingers through my wet folds while never taking his eyes off me. Heat dances in his eyes, causing my breathing to quicken.

He senses my growing excitement and need. He delicately brushes his fingers against my lips before sliding them into my mouth. The taste of my juices coats my tongue, and I can't help but groan. He continues to push his fingers in and out of my mouth like he's fucking it.

"I've only been able to dream about how good you taste."

"Now you don't have to imagine anymore," I say, feeling a jolt of electricity after his fingers press against my lips.

I've never been so direct with a man, not that there was a man around to say these things to. However, there's something about him that stirs something deep inside me. For once, he makes me not want to be the ice princess my sister describes me as. He makes me want to let go and go with the flow to enjoy the moment.

Heat fills his eyes, and without a word, he drops to his knees. Even though I didn't make the decision whether I wanted to come by his mouth or his fingers, I'm glad he took the decision out of my hands.

I tighten my grip on his long locks freely hanging loose around his shoulders. When he watches me like I'm some goddess, an outpouring of confidence washes over me. I feel beautiful and incredibly powerful. To have a man as powerful and beautiful as Florian on his knees in front of me gives me the most incredible surge of confidence I've ever felt as a woman. The kind of confidence that can be very addictive.

With a swift motion, he tosses one of my legs over his shoulder, and I let out a surprised yelp.

As he licks my slit, my grip on his hair tightens, sending shivers down my spine. Leaning my head back against the wall, I close my eyes and let out a groan as he works wonders with his mouth.

"Florian," I moan, my voice filled with longing.

He flicks, nips, and bites at my clit before sucking the bundle of nerves into his mouth. I can't help but rock my hips against his face as I ride a wave of ecstasy.

I keep my eyes closed as I continue to grind my pussy in his face. The sounds of my moans, the wetness of my pussy, and him devouring me like a madman fill the space.

He sucks my clit harder, then pushes his fingers inside me, and my world tilts. White spots dot behind my eyes as I scream his name.

"Fuck, you are so fucking gorgeous when you come," he whispers against my wet folds. "My Beauty. Mine."

He teases my sensitive clit with his tongue as his fingers move in and out of me until I descend from my euphoric state.

He slowly pulls his fingers away and then gives me one final, lingering lick that sends shivers coursing through my body. He pulls my leg from his shoulder, and I lean against the wall for support so I don't sink to the floor.

That was the most intense orgasm I've ever experienced, even though I don't have many to compare it to. All I know is that I want more.

Opening my eyes, I let out a sigh and watch him as he rises from the floor, his face beaming with a devious grin that's covered in my juices. His mouth slams into mine before I utter one word. The musky scent of my arousal lingers around his face, lips, and tongue, eliciting a groan from me when the taste hits my mouth.

Our tongues war with one another for dominance, but like everything else in this new relationship, I fear Florian will ultimately be in control. I can't deny that the thought of doing whatever he wants intrigues me because I rarely give up control of anything in my life to anyone. I'm completely fascinated by the way my body responds to him and my willingness to do something that's out of my comfort zone just because he asks me to.

Even after he pulls away, his eyes still hold a fiery intensity. "There's more of that to come, Beauty, but first kneel before your Beast so I can watch how beautiful you look with your mouth stuffed full of my cock."

My entire body tingles with anticipation, and I immediately drop to my knees like he instructed.

"Good girl." He pulls his cock from his pants, then palms it. "Now open up."

17

ARABELLE

I can't believe I'm about to do this. Even though I'm on my knees with his beautiful cock on full display, and my pussy is soaked and throbbing while lust blazes in his eyes, I'm terrified. I have no idea how to do this.

"I can see your mind racing a mile a minute, Beauty. Stop thinking so much and live in the moment."

I might as well break the news to him so he can decide if he still wants to go through with this. Maybe he won't laugh in my face when he finds out I have absolutely no idea what I'm doing because I've never given anyone oral sex in my life.

Of course, I've watched porn like most people while touching myself, but that will only help me so much in this situation. From what I've seen, you definitely need hands-on knowledge, and that's probably even more true with a man like Florian. He's probably never been with someone as inexperienced as me. He's about to get the shock of his life.

I sigh. "I'm trying to live in the moment, Florian, but I think you should know that I've never done this before."

He pauses for a second, and his face remains stoic, but I can see surprise dancing in his eyes as well as concern. "You're not a virgin, right?"

I might as well be.

"Would it make a difference if I were one?" I ask, annoyance coloring my voice. "I want this, and so do you, so why would that even matter?"

He's the one who got me all hot and bothered with that sinful mouth of his. Now he's pulling away because he thinks I'm a virgin. That should have been a question he asked before he licked my pussy.

"Yes, it would make a difference, Arabelle. And it matters a lot. Even though I want to fuck you, I'm not going to fuck you in a safe room if you're a virgin. I may not be a good man, but I'm not a bastard, either. I would never have your first time be in a place like this. You deserve better than that."

My heart flutters inside my chest. That's one of the sweetest things anyone has ever said to me. I can't believe the hardened criminal I've read about is worrying about making something special for me. That makes me see him a little differently than the world likes to portray him.

As some of the annoyance melts away, my eyes soften. "No, I'm not a virgin, Florian," I say, putting him out of his misery.

He lets out a relieved breath like it's the best news he's heard all day, and I laugh.

"Listen, my long work hours have prevented me from having a romantic relationship with any man."

I don't know why I feel the need to tell him about my love life, but I feel like I owe him some truth about my life since we will be husband and wife. Hopefully, he hasn't built me up in his mind to be someone I'm not.

"I've been on one date since I broke up with the only boyfriend I've ever had when I was younger. That's who took my virginity. And that one date after him didn't end well for me. So, I've continued to focus on my career instead of on finding a romantic partner."

Something flashes in his eyes before he quickly shuts it down.

"Since that date, my love life has been virtually non-existent by choice. So, you have to excuse me if I'm a little gun-shy when it comes to anything dealing with sex, especially something I've never done before."

I gesture toward his erect cock, the tip glistening with a droplet of cum. I dart my tongue across my lips, just thinking about how he would taste in my mouth. It's something I'm very interested in experiencing, which is why I'm on my knees waiting for him.

A wide grin stretches across his face. "So, I get to be the first man you ever give a blow job to?"

The pride and excitement in his voice causes me to roll my eyes, but I can't keep the smile off my face.

"Yes, you will be my first. Now, if you don't come here before I lose my nerve, it's a first that will have to wait a little while longer."

He reaches his hand out to me, and I dip my brows in confusion.

"I thought I was going to do,"—I motion to his cock again—"you know."

He chuckles. "I'd rather you sit on my face while you suck my dick. I want to taste more of that delicious cunt of yours."

There's no way I'm going to turn that down. The man is a master with his tongue. It definitely beats having to use my fingers to get pleasure all the time. I didn't realize what I had been missing out on.

I grab his hand and walk out of the safe room into his large bedroom. I didn't have time to pay attention to the layout when Hugo rushed me in here, but holy god, the place is massive and beautiful in a masculine way. It's muted grays and dark blues. Even the light incense aroma lingering in the air screams all man.

Compared to the bedrooms in both my apartments, this one is triple the size. The personal living area features a long gray couch positioned before a massive TV mounted on the dark-blue wall, all overlooking a roaring gas fireplace.

I turn my attention to the large, dark mahogany four-poster bed that sits not too far from large panes of windows that make up one wall. The tint is so dark you can't see out of it. I would have preferred if they were clear, but that's my little secret to keep.

"This is amazing."

He's lying on the bed with his legs wide and his bottom lip pulled between his teeth, palming his beautiful erect cock.

"Come here, beautiful."

Without hesitation, I walk toward him, then climb onto the bed and slowly crawl up his body. Bravely, I stop at his cock, settling between his thighs on my knees, and gaze up at him. I knock his hand away, and he arches his brow at me.

With my gaze on him, I lick from the base of his dick to the head, swirling my tongue around the tip before sucking the head into my mouth.

"Fuck, Beauty," he groans, propping up on his elbows to watch me.

Since he's not telling me to stop, I assume he's okay with what I'm doing.

As I move my mouth further down his length, then back up, my hand follows in sync, creating a rhythm that heightens my pleasure and hopefully his.

"Yes, baby," he groans. "Just like that."

He intertwines his hand in my curls. The delicious sting of my scalp causes me to moan around his length.

I'm clumsy at first as I try to get a good rhythm with my hand and mouth, which he doesn't seem to mind. All I hear are curses and moans echoing from his lips. But the further I go and the more vocal he becomes, the more confident I am in what I'm doing.

"Beauty, that feels so fucking good," he says, tightening his grip on my hair as he lifts his hips from below, matching my movements. "Fuck! Fuck! I'm close, baby!"

With his shout, I speed up my movements, moving my head and hand up and down his cock faster and harder until his body stiffens under me. "Shit! Shit! I'm coming, baby! I'm coming!" he shouts, and his warm cum coats the inside of my mouth, and I savor every bit of it.

He falls back on the bed and sighs. I sit up on my knees and gaze at him, proud of myself because he has the most serene look on his face.

He hisses, and his body visibly shivers when I grab his semi-hard dick and move my hand up and down it again.

When he opens his eyes, the hunger in them is indescribable. "That was fucking amazing."

Once again, pride moves through me, and I can't help but grin like an idiot. "I'm glad you enjoyed it."

"Oh, I more than enjoyed it. Now, it's time I returned the favor. Come here, Beauty, and sit that tasty cunt on my face."

I can't help but laugh, but I don't deny that my need for him is growing. My thighs are slick with my desire, and my pussy is throbbing, anticipating the amount of pleasure I'm about to experience. So, I don't waste any more time. I do as he asks and sit on his face.

"Hold on," he says before he dives in.

I can definitely get used to this.

18

FLORIAN

CHICAGO

"Thank you for coming, Mr. Larsson. Please have a seat," Detective Regan says. "Can we get you gentlemen anything? The coffee isn't that good, but we do have a vending machine."

"No, we're fine. And it's no problem, gentlemen. Anything I can do to help. You all know, my attorney, Mr. Kellan McGuire."

"So, let's get down to it, gentlemen," Mr. McGuire says. "My client's time as well as mine is too valuable to waste."

Both detectives look at each other before focusing on me and Kellan.

These detectives have no idea who they are going up against. Kellan McGuire is one of the top criminal defense attorneys in the country. He also happens to be a member of the McGuire clan, where his father, Dylan, is the head of the Scottish mob in America. Kellan straddles both sides of the law and does a hell of a job while doing it. He has an acquittal rate of ninety-eight percent. And he'll make sure that I won't be included in those two percent of convictions.

"Do you know Pierre Gaultier?" Detective Regan asks.

"As I've told you before, I don't recognize that name."

"A vehicle was seen pulling out of an alley behind The Black Star Bar and Grill the night that he went missing."

"I'm sure a lot of people were in that area, detective," Kellan says. "Get to the point."

"The point is that vehicle can be linked to your client." Detective Regan leans his forearms on the table. "Can you tell me about that, Mr. Larsson?"

I look at Kellan, and he nods his head. "I'm not sure, Detectives, but I can get that information to you. I've recently visited Chicago and had a few meetings. It is possible I had a meeting there or in the area. I'll have my assistant get my itinerary for those meetings to you as soon as possible."

Detective Logan nods as he records my answers on a notepad.

"Do you know Arabelle Williamson?" Detective Regan asks.

"I do. She's my fiancée. Why are you asking?"

"Your fiancée?" Detective Regan asks. "Since when?"

"How does that help with your investigation, gentlemen?" Kellan asks. "Mr. Larsson has stated that she's his fiancée. Please move on to the next question. We have things to do."

"We're just trying to establish a timeline of events, Mr. McGuire," Detective Regan says.

"And what does that timeline of events have to do with my client's engagement?" Kellan asks.

"Because your fiancée was on a date with Pierre Gaultier before he went missing, Mr. Larsson. Do you know anything about that?" Detective Logan asks.

"I don't keep up with men my fiancée has dated in the past just as she doesn't keep track of women I've dated in the past, gentlemen."

Kellan looks at his watch. "Mr. Larsson can answer one more question, gentlemen."

"Did you have anything to do with the disappearance or murder of Pierre Gaultier?"

"Gentlemen, as stated before, I have no idea who this man is. And I'm sure my fiancée knows nothing about his death or disappearance either."

"If you need any more information from Mr. Larsson or his

fiancée, please don't hesitate to reach out to me," Kellan says as he stands.

"I don't believe you're telling me the truth, Mr. Larsson," Detective Regan says.

"Your belief has no bearing on the truth, Detective," Kellan says. "If you have proof of his involvement, arrest him."

When neither man makes a move to put me in handcuffs, I stand, then button my suit blazer, and follow Kellan out of the office. When we step outside the precinct, Kellan looks at me with his brow arched. "Fiancée?"

"Yes, I'm getting married."

"And when did this happen?"

I smile. "It was a last-minute thing."

"And what does this woman have to do with this case?"

"He tried to rape her, so he was dealt with," I say, shrugging.

I don't hide anything from Kellan. I make sure he knows everything so he can do his job to the best of his ability. He has no illusions about the man that I am. As long as he gets paid, he doesn't worry about the morality part.

"Enough said. How are you going to handle this because I know we aren't taking this to trial."

"My money has a very long reach, Kellan. You know as well as anybody that this case will disappear before it ever sees the light of day."

"I can't believe someone's tamed the Beast," he says, chuckling. "It must be a cold day in hell."

"Not quite yet. But if anyone can, it's her."

He nods, clapping me on the back. "If anything comes up, I'll call you."

He walks off, and I head toward my car. When I slide into the back seat, I pull out my phone from inside my blazer jacket. The car pulls away from the curb onto the highway toward the airport.

I dial Alrick. I've got to get the ball moving on how to get both Arabelle and me out of the shit. There's no way we will go down for that prick's death. He deserved everything he got. I wish I could have prolonged his suffering.

"Yes, Beast?"

"Alrick, I need you to get with Nero and head to Chicago. I need some information on Pierre Gaultier to disappear. He's death needs to be ruled something other than murder."

"How soon?"

"Immediately. I don't give a fuck how much you have to spend, or how many bones need to be broken, I want it done, now."

"On it," he says, and I end the call.

I sigh and close my eyes. Never have I put myself in such a predicament. I'm usually on top of shit, but with Arabelle being in danger, I didn't think things through. However, I won't let this get in the way of what I want. This prick's death will not be the cause of me not getting the one woman I want.

19
FLORIAN

Wedding Day

The attack on my warehouse is the final push I need to convince Arabelle to marry me as soon as possible, hoping that marriage will provide us with added protection. Well, that's the excuse I gave her. I can increase the level of security around her, but my priority is to have her by my side sooner rather than later especially with cops sniffing around. My sanity can't take her being any other place than with me.

After I ate her out one more time, we finally relaxed, and I explained my position on why we needed to get married as soon as possible. Although I could see in her eyes she wanted to protest because she didn't think we knew enough about each other, she did at least give me the opportunity to explain my stance. However, it took me finally explaining to her the attack on my warehouse, its implications for us as a couple and for my organization, my father's role in it, and his threats to her before she finally agreed.

Although she's not too fond of going to the courthouse to get married, she also doesn't want to have a grand church wedding, which surprises me. What woman doesn't want the pomp and circumstance of a huge wedding, especially a woman like her? But I don't question her about that decision. Everyone wants different things. However, I do believe it has something to do with her family. I don't think she wants them anywhere near her big day. More than likely, she fears they would ruin it somehow, which I can understand because her father is a bastard, and her sisters are not ones who would let her have a moment in the spotlight. Her fame and fortune are the reasons they hate her. However, I promised her some kind of destination wedding with just the two of us at a later date so we can have pictures of our big day. She reluctantly agreed, so today is our wedding day, and I'm excited.

"Are you ready to do this?" Asva asks as we walk up the steep concrete stairs of the courthouse. "You can turn back now if you change your mind."

I laugh while holding on to a stunning bouquet of red roses that I picked up this morning myself. "No chance I'm changing my mind. She's the one."

"*The one*?" Asva asks with his brow arched.

I nod with a grin on my face. From the moment I saw her dance, I knew she was the one for me. Today, I'll make it official. I want everyone to know that Arabelle Williamson is mine.

"I know it's fucking weird coming from me, but yeah, Arabelle Williamson is the one made for me."

"You know, word has gotten back to Adahlia," he says, which causes me to stop in my tracks, the joy of the moment draining from me immediately.

I want this day to go by without any surprises, but of course, someone would try to interfere.

"And?"

"And she's throwing a fucking fit, Florian."

I respond with a slight shrug. "Not a surprise and also not my problem, Asva. I've always been upfront with Addie. She's always known what my stance is on our relationship. There's nothing I can do if she doesn't want to take the hint. We fucked, and I've told her that it's now over."

"I know that. We all know that. But apparently, she doesn't," Asva says. "She's throwing a fucking tantrum."

"Still not my problem. She can bitch, cry, whine, and complain all she wants. Arabelle will be my wife, and no one's going to stop me.

She can move on to the next willing cock because mine is done and belongs to only one woman."

"Just make sure you watch your back," he replies, "because it definitely can become your problem pretty quickly."

"That's what I have you for. My problem solver."

Although he's usually quiet, he's a highly efficient killer. If Adahlia becomes a problem, I'll either send Asva to handle her, or I'll deal with her personally.

"Any direct threats?" I ask as we wait for Hugo and Arabelle to arrive.

Everyone, I'm sure, knows by now that I'm getting married, but only the men here know it's happening today.

"None," Alrick answers instead of his brother. "If there are, they are keeping silent right now. But you really need to head Adahlia off before she gets out of hand, Florian. Don't underestimate her. A woman scorned and all that bullshit."

Alrick and Asva are both right. I shouldn't underestimate Addie, but I hope she's more talk than action. I'd hate to kill her if something happens to Arabelle. I don't particularly like to kill women, but I will if she fucks with me, and Arabelle is harmed.

"Have Nero keep an eye on her," I say as I watch Hugo pull the black Range Rover to a stop in front of the courthouse steps. "If she makes a move, just take care of it. I will deal with the fallout afterward."

"*Ja,* Beast," Asva responds.

Hugo jumps out and then goes to the other side and opens the back door. The moment Hugo helps her out of the SUV, my breath gets caught in my throat. It's like watching an angel.

Her tight, cream-colored, off-the-shoulder dress accentuates her petite frame, and her matching heels highlight her toned legs. Her hair is elegantly pulled into a bun with sprigs of baby breath intertwined, which emphasizes the string of white pearls draped around her slender neck and the teardrop pearl earrings swaying gently from her ears.

"Beautiful," I mumble.

"You're one lucky man," Asva says, clapping me on the shoulder as we all watch her walk up the stairs with the grace of a queen.

"Don't fuck it up," Alrick chimes in.

I have no intention of fucking it up. Arabelle will be my wife until I'm cold in the grave and beyond.

"Trust me, I will not fuck this up. This is my dream come true, and it will be 'until death do us part.'"

When she reaches me, I clasp her hand and press her knuckles against my lips, feeling the warmth of her skin against mine.

"You look amazing."

Despite the nervous energy emanating from her, a genuine, breathtaking smile spreads across her face.

"Thank you. You look handsome, too."

Her smile is contagious, and I find myself unable to resist smiling back.

"Are you ready?" I ask, handing her the bouquet of roses I made for her.

She takes hold of them and brings them to her nose, closing her eyes and inhaling deeply, savoring their fragrance. When she opens her eyes and focuses on me, she takes a moment to breathe in the crisp, clean air before exhaling slowly.

"I am."

I give her a wink, intertwine our fingers, and we enter the courthouse together. As I walk inside, I'm walking toward my future. *We're* walking toward our future.

"Where are we going?"

Despite the quick ceremony, I sense the exhaustion in her voice. Not only did I get my fill of her most of the night, but she also had an early start this morning to get ready for the wedding. The wedding ceremony didn't match my vision of marrying Arabelle, but it fulfilled its purpose. Once things calm down, I'll give her the wedding she deserves.

"It's a surprise," I tell her as we navigate to the back of the house.

I decided to give her a tour of our new home. I know she's used to doing things herself, but now, she doesn't have to.

"You can do anything to the house that you want."

She nods, her eyes still scanning the surroundings. With each step, she takes a moment to inhale the sweet, fragrant scent of the roses that fill every room. I make sure I replace them every other day with fresh ones.

"I love these roses." She pauses in front of another vase brimming with them. "They're so beautiful. Where do you get them? I spent a lot of time trying to track down the florist."

"I grow them."

I nudge her forward, encouraging her to discover her surprise.

"I wasn't expecting that."

I chuckle softly, but I remain silent, savoring the moment. I grow all these roses in honor of my mother. Her favorite flowers were fragrant roses, and she couldn't help but stop and inhale their sweet scent anytime she came across them. I have an entire indoor greenhouse full of them. It's something I don't share with anyone.

"I don't like surprises."

"You'll like this one."

She sighs heavily. "Well, can you at least tell me if we're almost there?"

"You're an impatient little thing, aren't you?"

When she stops, she huffs and crosses her arms over her chest in irritation. I give her a gentle push, encouraging her to move forward, and she resumes her strides.

"Well, if you tell me what I want to know, I'll stop being impatient, Florian."

This is the Arabelle who fills my senses with love and joy. The one I want to spend the rest of my life with. I don't want someone who'll tiptoe around me, afraid to be themselves because of who I am. I need a partner. Someone on my level.

Arabelle is definitely on my level.

Correction. She's leagues above me.

I grab her by the arm, stopping her in front of the door that leads to the in-house dance studio that I had custom-built for her so she can stay at home and practice dancing.

"This is it. Close your eyes."

She starts to protest.

"Please," I tack on to keep her from arguing with me.

My mother always used to say that a spoonful of honey is the best way to calm a bee.

Her eyes meet mine, and for a moment, I catch a glimpse of something before she conceals it. She's been doing that for most of the day. I've noticed her gaze lingering on me when she believes I'm not looking. However, I see everything she does.

Reluctantly, she sighs but complies with my request. "Is this it?"

"Yes." I twist the doorknob and give the door a firm push, feeling a rush of cool air brush against my skin. "You can open them now."

She slowly peels her eyes open and gasps. Her hands tremble as they rise to cover her mouth in disbelief. She takes tentative steps inside the room, her eyes darting around, taking in every detail.

I absolutely don't know shit about ballet, so I reached out to Madame Rostova, Arabelle's dance instructor in Los Angeles, to ensure the best design for this room. Anything Arabelle needs to excel, if I can't provide it, I'll find someone who can. Hopefully, this is up to her standards, but if it isn't, then I'll tear everything out and have it done the way she wants it.

According to the old ballerina, the high-density foam beneath the special Marley vinyl flooring helps lower stress on the bones and joints, reducing the risk of Arabelle getting injured. Also, along with *Megan,* I had a state-of-the-art music system installed. This way, Arabelle can simply ask *Megan* to play any musical number she needs, eliminating the need for her to struggle with CDs or music apps on her phone. The studio is flooded with natural light, thanks to the floor-to-ceiling windows that make up one wall of the room. Along another wall, there are mirrors and a floor-mounted barre for her to use. She has everything in this one room to make sure she performs to the best of her abilities.

"This is amazing." She kicks off her heels and walks barefoot across the floor toward the barre. With a gentle touch, she runs her fingers across it with the largest smile on her face. "This is...wow." She turns and walks back to me, her gaze never leaving mine. "You had this built for me?"

I push my hands into my pockets to stop myself from reaching out to touch her. "You deserve nothing but the best."

She reaches up, and her fingers delicately trace the contours of my face. I shut my eyes, savoring the sensation.

"I can never repay you for this, Florian. No one has ever done anything so sweet for me. I'm at a loss for words to explain how much this means to me."

I open my eyes. My skin is buzzing from the simple touch of her fingers. I pull her close to me and waste no more time. I want this woman. All of her.

20

ARABELLE

"How often do you get to come to a performance?" Florian asks as he takes his seat.

When I attempt to take my seat beside him, he surprises me by pulling me firmly into his lap.

It's our first date as a married couple, and I can sense his desire to create a memorable experience for me. I must say no one has ever treated me the way Florian has, and no one has ever been this considerate of what I might like.

We have a private box at the ballet, and outside, Asva, Hugo, and Alrick stand guard to ensure our night remains undisturbed. I've noticed the increase in security since our wedding, even though he doesn't think I have. No matter how much I press him for information about what's going on, he remains tight-lipped about the reason for all the extra guards, saying that he has everything handled, and it's nothing that I should be worried about. But I am worried, and I have a hunch it has something to do with his father. Anytime he's pissed off about anything, it's about his father.

"I haven't been to a performance where I haven't been a part of it since I was a kid. I don't have time for anything outside of work."

I squirm in his lap as his erection pushes against my ass. He grips my hips tighter to stop me from moving.

"Well, that changes now, Mrs. Larsson." He kisses my bare shoulder, then traces his fingers against my skin. "You can't work all the time."

I look over my shoulder and smile, feeling a rush of warmth

spread across my face at the look he's giving me. Whenever he addresses me as Mrs. Larsson, I can't help but feel a flutter of excitement, like a schoolgirl with a secret crush.

"With your empire, I'm sure you're just as much of a workaholic as I am."

"Touché," he says, his voice filled with a deep, smoky resonance, and a fiery intensity is burning in his eyes. "So, I guess it's something we both need to remedy, then. Less work, more play."

"I don't mind playing," I whisper, and his deep chuckle vibrates around me.

The lights of the theater dim, and a hushed anticipation fills the air, signaling the start of the performance. As his fingers touch my bare arm, a tingling sensation shoots down my spine, leaving me breathless. The atmosphere is so charged, and it's something I've never experienced before. I'm not sure if it's excitement for the performance or the intimacy Florian and I are sharing.

My choice for the evening is a chic, knee-length black dress that hugs my body to perfection and leaves my shoulders bare. Now, it's slowly inching up my thighs, giving him the perfect access to my core.

With a smile on my face, I turn my attention to the performance, trying to ignore the need to spread my legs wider so he can reach my pussy. But I don't know how long I'll be able to focus on the performance. Florian's gentle touch has moved from my arm to my inner thigh, sending a shiver down my spine.

Even though the darkness surrounds us, and there's no way anyone will be able to see us, the thrill of the possibility sends a surge of arousal through me, drenching the black lace panties I'm wearing. I think he knows I enjoy the thrill of being watched, and the ballet offers the illusion of all eyes on us while also providing the cover of darkness.

As his soft lips pepper kisses across my upper back, the fingers of one of his hands tease the hem of my dress, which is pushed above my hips now.

I look over my shoulder and take notice of the intense desire reflecting in his eyes. "Keep your eyes on the performance, Mrs. Larsson," he whispers, his fingers grazing the curves of my breasts. "You wouldn't want to miss anything, would you?"

My attention snaps back to the stage, but it's interrupted by his large hand caressing my breast through the thin fabric of my dress. A faint moan slips past my lips, causing my eyes to flutter slightly.

He pushes the top of my dress down, exposing my breasts to the cool breeze in the theater, which instantly makes my nipples harden.

"Florian," I moan. The sensation of grinding my hips against his straining erection through his dress slacks causes me to burn with a more intense desire for him.

"Be quiet, Beauty." He twists and pinches my nipple, and his other hand lightly brushes the fabric covering my heated core. "You don't want anyone to hear us, now, do you?"

I purse my lips, attempting to stifle the moans and whimpers, but his touch is driving me crazy. I want to feel him deep inside me, stretching me, where I'm so full it's like I might explode. So, I can't stop the moans and whimpers.

"Or maybe you do," he whispers, tracing delicate circles over my clit, the sensation seeping through the fabric of my panties.

"Oh my god."

"My Beauty isn't as sweet and innocent as I think she is, which is fine with me if she's not. Maybe she wants everyone to see my fingers playing with her pretty cunt. You're so wet. Is that it, baby? You want someone to see me playing with this tight pussy?"

"Florian...please," I plead, feeling his agile fingers teasing my sensitive spot, causing another surge of desire that saturates my underwear. "I need you."

"Be more specific, Beauty. Tell me exactly what you need, and I might just give it to you."

The intensity of his twists and pinches to my nipples increases, and while it's painful, I enjoy it so much. I love it.

"I want you to fuck me."

"In the theater?" He chuckles. "With everyone watching?"

He increases the gentle pressure on my clit.

"Yes," I groan. His hand on my throbbing core sends waves of pleasure through me. "Please."

"Take your panties off."

Quickly, I stand up from his lap, feeling a rush of excitement as I slide my panties down my legs. He unfastens his dress slacks, revealing himself to me. He firmly grasps my hips, guiding me to straddle his throbbing member. Slowly, I lower myself onto him, and we both hiss from the sensation.

"Fuck," he grunts, maneuvering me up and down his shaft, ensuring that every inch of him is deep within me. "That's it. Take all of me."

"Oh god," I groan, feeling the intense pleasure as he thrusts up into me while I bounce on his long, thick cock.

The orchestra's music provides a melodic backdrop to our passionate lovemaking, masking the intensity of our sounds.

"Not God," he grunts, his rough nails digging into my hips, intensifying the tingling sensation that spreads throughout my body. "But I am your Beast. Now come for me."

He pinches my clit, and waves of pleasure move through my entire body, then I lose myself in ecstasy.

"Florian!" I shout, my voice mingling with the music of the ballet while my body convulses as my orgasm barrels through me like an out-of-control freight train.

"Fuck, Beauty, I'm coming," he groans, and with each pulse of his release, he stiffens beneath me, filling me with his warm cum.

We both sit in silence, trying to catch our breath. As we both come down from the intense pleasure, I giggle as he sighs.

"I can't believe I just did that," I whisper, my voice filled with a mix of disbelief and awe. "Can we do it again? I really want to do it again."

He chuckles, but just before he responds, a gentle tap on the door interrupts our wonderful moment.

With a sigh, I rise to my feet and adjust my dress, pulling it back up to cover my chest before smoothing it down my hips. Ignoring his cum leaking from me, I reach for my underwear to pull them up, but he reaches out his hand. I hand them to him, and he gives them a long sniff before tucking them into his pocket.

"These are mine now." He tucks his now flaccid cock back into his dress pants. "Stay here," he says before walking to the door.

As he opens the door to the private box, a symphony of hushed whispers and muffled curses fills the air. After he closes the door, I notice a shift in his demeanor when he returns to sit beside me.

"What's wrong?"

He sighs. "My father's here, and he wants to meet you."

"Can't you let this go, Florian? Maybe if we just stay out of his way, he'll leave us alone."

"You don't understand what he's done to me and my family, Beauty."

"Maybe I don't understand, but I don't want to be dragged into the middle of whatever you two have going on. Could you just let it go just for me? I'm begging you."

Now the way he's looking at me is different. Gone is the man who's shattering the thick walls protecting my heart. His eyes and face are blank, devoid of any emotion or expression, which isn't normal when he looks at me. Most of the time, so many emotions are dancing in his eyes, but not now. The man I'm starting to have feelings for is definitely not the same person sitting beside me.

"I'm not doing that, Arabelle," he says, his voice distant and detached. "Not for you. Not for anyone else. He deserves everything that's going to happen to him and more."

I can't explain the amount of hurt his words cause, but that hurt only lasts for a short while. Then, nothing but anger fills me. I think about the life I had to give up, the dream of finally finding someone who will love me because of a debt my father owed. I ask him to give up one thing for me, and it's an instant no.

"After all that I gave up for this, and your answer is no? Either let it go for me or give me time to sort things out for myself, Florian. I don't want to be involved in whatever you have going on between you and your father. I refuse to."

"Then you can have your time."

With a nod, I divert my attention back to the performance. The silence between us is deafening. The distance between us seems insurmountable.

I feel his intense gaze, like a laser beam, piercing the side of my face, but I refuse to acknowledge him. I'm done having this conversation with him. I won't remain in a relationship where I'm not a priority and revenge is, especially if it puts my safety at risk. I've already had to hide in a safe room because of his father. If Florian would simply let go of this vendetta against his father, we could move on with our lives, build some type of future together. If he's not willing to do that for me, for us, then I can no longer stay in this relationship because it means he doesn't value me enough. It's as simple as that. He's made his choice, and now, I have to make mine.

21

FLORIAN

Despite her pleading to put her first, I couldn't bring myself to abandon this war against my father because he will never let it go. I have to finish it because it's the only way I'll have any peace. It's the only way we'll get any peace. He'll always come for me because I've taken everything that's important to him, which means she's in danger as long as he's breathing. So, when she asks for time away, I agree.

It's not because I'm letting her go. That will never be an option. But it'll give me time to kill him and give her time to cool down. She'll eventually understand that not only am I doing this for me, but I'm also doing this for her.

When he showed up to the theater, I couldn't put it off any longer. Not even for her. It didn't take Nero and Asva long to find my father and bring him to me. His ego refused to let him hide from me. So, they snatched him from one of the brothels he likes to visit after giving the madame a hefty sum of money to keep her mouth shut. He never believed I would make a move against him.

"Are you sure you want to sit in on this?" I ask Didrick for at least the fourth time while we're on our way to Hell's Kitchen.

I know Didrick feels the pressure to prove himself to me and our father, but deep down, he's not cut out for this lifestyle. He's not cut out to witness this type of brutality, and I have bigger aspirations for him than this life.

My other brothers are lost causes, and I'm sure, after I kill Olan, they'll come after me. However, I'm not worried about that. I'll be ready for whatever they want to do or whatever they have planned. What does worry me is the impact all this will have on Didrick. He's clean now. I don't want to send him spiraling back into addiction to numb his feelings about the gruesome death of his father and his role in it.

Maybe I need to put him in therapy once Olan is dead since, technically, I'll be his guardian until he turns eighteen.

Didrick wants to prove to me he's ready to enter this life, but deep down, I know he's not prepared. He doesn't have what it takes to live this life. He's too sensitive.

I also know he wants to prove to Olan that he isn't a complete waste of space, even though none of that matters to me as long as we're not under Olan's thumb.

Since getting out of rehab seven months ago, Didrick has made significant progress. He's like a new person. He's looking to do more in life than get high, like go back to school and get a job. I hope that dealing with Olan won't destroy all the progress he's made.

"How many times are you going to ask me that?" Didrick asks, irritation lacing his voice.

I really don't care if he's irritated with the constant questions. He needs to make sure this is something he wants to do. Once he decides it is, there's no turning back.

"As many times as it takes for you to be damn sure this is what you want to witness."

"And why wouldn't I, Florian?" he asks. "He's treated me like shit my entire life."

"I know he's treated you like shit, but he's also your father."

"He's yours too, and you have no problem doing whatever you are about to do to him."

"We are not the same, Didrick. Although he is my father, it's only by blood." I let out a weary sigh, feeling the tension in my body as I pinch the bridge of my nose. "He didn't raise me, Didrick. We didn't live under the same roof. He had nothing to do with me growing up, other than when he came to my home to fuck my mother and tell me I wasn't worth shit and that he wished she had aborted me."

The horror and pity on his face mean nothing to me. He needs to understand the differences in our childhoods. Yes, Olan is father to us both, and he's treated us both like shit, but being treated like shit as his bastard was totally different from what Didrick and my other brothers experienced.

"I'm not telling you this for your pity, Didrick. I'm over what happened to me as a child, even if I'm not over what he forced my mother to go through. But you need to know that, even though we both had it bad as his children, we have two very different histories when it comes to Olan. You're his son. I'm his bastard."

He fails to see this is the most important distinction between me and him. I have no emotional attachment to Olan, which is why I can separate our connection by blood. He made me this way, which is something he didn't do with his other children.

Didrick lets out a sigh of frustration, his hand sweeping across his forehead. He looks different from the way he did when Alrick found him behind my warehouse. He's got a buzz cut, which makes him look older, and the most shocking change has been his weight gain. He looks so much healthier. Happier.

"That may be true, Florian, but I still need to do this for me. I need to prove to myself that he doesn't define who I am. I need to show him that he doesn't hold that kind of power over me anymore. He needs to see that I'm my own person, and that I'm somebody without him."

I understand the need to do all that because I can admit it was something I needed to do when I was his age, too.

As I look at him, I observe no sign of doubt in his eyes. If this is something he truly believes he needs to do to move on with his life, I won't stand in his way. I just hope he prepares for the consequences of watching his father die a painful and brutal death.

"I won't try to convince you not to do this anymore, Didrick, because you have made up your mind. However, there's only one rule that you must follow."

"Whatever you need me to do, I'll do it, Florian."

"You do as I say."

"That's it?"

"That's it." I shrug. "This is my world. This is my business. I run a very tight ship, and what I say goes. I need you to understand that, in this situation, I'm not your brother, Didrick. I'm the one they call Beast. And I don't bend to anything or for anyone."

"Do you actually use that name?" he asks, smirking. "I've heard our brothers call you that."

"I do, and I fucking earned it."

The smirk on his face immediately disappears.

"Every man in that room is under my command. All loyal to me and me only. If you step foot in that room, that means your loyalty is to me, too, not to our father. Do you understand?"

"I do," he says without hesitation.

"Make sure you believe what you say, Didrick because if my men think you aren't with me, that's a death sentence. Blood or not, loyalty is everything to me and to these men. These men are my family, and our father is the enemy. Nothing you can do will save him, so make sure when you step out of this car, your loyalty is to me. If it's not, that means you and him will leave here in body bags."

His eyes widen. "Are you trying to scare me?"

"No, I'm not trying to scare you, but I'm telling you how it will be. This is the reality of this situation, and I'm treating you like an adult. The blood we share doesn't change the outcome of what happens today. *Far* will die. Hopefully, you won't join him. If you get out of the car, I have your complete loyalty. If you decide that you're not ready to make that commitment to me, I understand, and I won't hold that against you, but those are your two choices."

As the car comes to a stop, I take a moment to give Didrick one last look before opening the door and stepping out of the vehicle. He has a lot to think about and a short amount of time to make his decision. If he remains inside, I have my answer. He isn't ready to witness the death of our father. If he gets out, then he's with me. It's a tough choice for a kid his age, but a necessary one.

After a few minutes, the car door opens. He steps out and then looks at me. I give him a curt nod and walk inside the building with him following me. There's no more time to discuss his choice. He has made his decision. I just hope he can live with it for his sake.

As usual, the men who work in this warehouse don't pay attention when I arrive. Without fail, I make it a point to visit Hell's Kitchen at least twice every week so they can get used to my presence. If my men know that I'm always hands-on, then that leaves little to no room for anyone to make mistakes. However, today, I'm here for a totally different reason. Today, I'm here to kill my father.

"Are you sure Didrick being here is such a good idea?" Alrick asks.

"No, but he wants to be here, so I won't stop him."

"Can you trust him?"

His question gives me pause because I truly have to think about how to answer it. I want to trust Didrick, but the thought lingers in my head that maybe he's been totally corrupted by our father, and there's nothing I can do to change that fact.

There are only a handful of people I trust. Alrick and Asva, most definitely, are a part of the small number of people, as well as few of my other men I surround myself with, including Hugo and Nero. But those who are my blood relatives, I don't trust at all, including Didrick. Of course, I want to trust him but wanting to and actually doing it are two different things.

"You know there's only a few people I trust, Alrick, and he isn't one of them. At least, not yet. But my concerns, as well as my expectations, have been made very clear to him. So, he's a friend until he's not."

Alrick's gaze shifts to Didrick, who scans the warehouse with curiosity as we stroll by my men who are stacking crates of guns and ammunition before returning his attention to me. Alrick knows exactly what that means, and a sly smile creeps across his face. If Didrick does anything to interfere, Alrick or Asva will kill him.

We make it to the back of the warehouse, and Asva opens the cooler doors. As expected, the twins have already restrained Olan and stripped him of all his clothes. I have no sympathy for the bastard. He doesn't look like the strong man he likes to portray himself to be to the men who are loyal to him. He looks like a cowardly motherfucker who is finally going to meet his maker.

"You go in first, Didrick." He looks at me with eyes as big as saucers. "Let him think you are here without me."

"But why?" Didrick asks.

"Because I said so."

He looks at me, his gaze lingering for only a moment before finally nodding. I can sense his nervousness as he steps inside the room alone, his eyes darting around anxiously. His trembling hands and unsteady stance betray his overwhelming fear of Olan—a reaction to being in our father's presence that will take him years to get over.

"What do you think he'll do?" Alrick asks.

I shrug.

This is Didrick's test. I need to see how he will react when he sees Olan in this vulnerable position. Will he plead with me to let him go? Or will he sit by and let happen what's supposed to happen? Hopefully, he remembers my warning.

I watch from the threshold of the door with my arms crossed over my chest. Olan's shoulders sag in relief when he sees Didrick walk into the room. He thinks he will save him. Desperate times call for desperate measures if he believes the addict he kicked out of the house will save him.

"Thank God, Didrick!" With every ounce of strength he can muster, Olan tugs at the restraints holding him in place. "Get me out of here! Florian has lost his fucking mind!"

Didrick's head tilts to the side, a questioning expression on his face. "You think I'm here to save you?"

"Of course!" Again, Olan tugs at his restraints. "I need you to cut this damn tape, then call your brothers so I can tell them where we are. I need all my men to gather and hit this place again."

Didrick crosses his arms over his chest. "After everything you've done to me, why the hell do you think I would do that?"

Olan stops pulling at the tape and glares at my youngest brother like he could kill him for even asking the question. This is the type of man Olan is. He tries to intimidate you into doing whatever he wants.

He starts this brainwashing at a very young age, so when you're old enough to resist, you won't even think about it because you're scared to death of how he'll react. I'm proud that Didrick doesn't cower to Olan's attempt to intimidate him even though it's ingrained in him to do whatever Olan says.

"Because I'm your goddamn father!" he shouts. "Cut me the fuck loose, Didrick! Now!"

"Fuck you," Didrick says. "You can rot here for all I fucking care."

Although I would have liked for him to be more forceful with Olan, at least he's finally making a stand for himself. I'm proud of him for being able to do that at such a young age.

"You ungrateful little shit!" Olan sneers with such malice in his eyes and voice, you'd think Didrick was just a stranger, a random person on the street. If you were on the outside looking in, you wouldn't believe that this man was actually speaking to his son. "I've done everything for you! Every fucking thing, and you're treating me like this? Wait until your brothers find out."

Didrick laughs, but there's no humor in it. Immediately, the anger drains from his face and is replaced with heartache. "Kicking me out of the house after you got me addicted to heroin is doing everything for me? You're a piece of shit!"

Now that's news to me. From what Olan told me when he came to me and asked me to pay Didrick's drug debt, Didrick was in a bad accident and became addicted that way. I guess there are some more questions I need answers to.

As I enter the cooler, Olan glances at Didrick and then shifts his attention to me. "You! I'm going to fucking kill you!"

"Yes, it's me, Olan."

I approach my younger brother. "Now, tell me how our father got you hooked on drugs and why."

Now that I've heard that Olan is behind Didrick's addiction, I'm going to need to hear the entire story. I'm sure he used Didrick to get to me because he knew that I would help him if the price was right—the price being Larsson Industries. However, I'm not sure what part Didrick played in this little scheme, but I hope he wasn't a willing participant because I actually believe he has a chance at a long and prosperous life. As long as he didn't cross me or try to fuck me over.

22

ARABELLE

I don't know why I thought Florian would listen to me. Despite the beautiful ring on my finger, we're still strangers. I'm his wife in name only, despite the intimacy we've been experiencing lately. To me, it's more than sex, and we actually have a connection. I thought that maybe, just maybe, his feelings for me were getting stronger like mine are for him. Obviously, I misread what we shared. I linked our intimacy with feelings, and now, I realize they are not the same thing.

He and his father are on a collision course headed straight for disaster, and I don't know if Florian will survive it. Truthfully, I want nothing to do with it. I want us to build this relationship so we both can have a life that isn't full of misery. So, I thought he'd at least put me first since, according to him, he wants this to be a real marriage. According to him, he's wanted me for a long time. But, of course, he didn't put me ahead of his vendetta. Even when I gave him the choice of staying or leaving, he chose for me to go, which stung a little.

"Are you all right?" Dale asks.

My eyes fill with tears as I shake my head, standing next to the only person I can call a friend. "I don't know why I thought this would be easy, Dale. This is the hardest thing I've ever had to do."

With his arm around my shoulder, he pulls me into a warm embrace. When I left Florian's home, which is now our home, Dale was the first person who came to mind. Although I've distanced myself from Dale because of his feelings for me, I have no one else to turn to. I can't rely on my sisters because they would probably be happy to learn I'm going through this, or they'll tell me to suck it up and get over it because I'm lucky to even be married to the great Florian Larsson. My father would only be worried about how it affected him. So, I don't regret not reaching out to them.

"You always see the best in people, sweetheart. So, you thought you could be yourself, and everything else would fall into place. But Florian is a different kind of man. A man you didn't quite prepare yourself for."

"So, you're telling me I'm an idiot?"

I sure as hell feel like an idiot.

"No, you're not an idiot, Arabelle. You're just too kind sometimes, especially when it comes to your family. Do you feel like you're in danger?" Dale asks.

Unfortunately, I don't have an answer to that question. It's not as simple as black and white. Florian and his father walk in the gray, which makes everything difficult to answer.

"Not entirely," I say. "At times it feels like I'm living a fairytale. He's sweet. Attentive. He makes me feel like a queen. Then there are times I understand why they call him Beast."

"Has he hurt you?" Dale asks, his voice dripping with anger.

"Of course not!" I shout, offended that he would think Florian would harm me, or that I would stay with someone who physically harmed me. "He wouldn't hurt me, Dale. Not intentionally anyway."

Dale rests his elbows on his knees and exhales. "Arabelle, why did you come here? To me, it seems as though you have developed feelings for him, and he hasn't hurt you. So, why are you not with your husband?"

"I gave him an ultimatum, and I thought he'd choose me."

"And he didn't?"

I let out a sigh. "He didn't."

Dale leans back in the chair. "And what ultimatum did you give him?"

"Stop fighting with his father, or give me some time to sort out what I need to do."

"And he gave you time?"

"He did. But I thought he would pick me and stop this shit with his father."

"You don't know what's actually transpired between them?"

"I don't, but it still stings that the man I married let me walk out the door. He didn't even try to stop me, Dale."

"Men don't do well with ultimatums, love. Maybe what he's trying to handle with his father, he needs to do not only for you, but for him. I know very little about Florian and his father, but from what I hear, his father is a real piece of work."

"I don't know anything about his father, either. Florian refuses to talk about him, but I believe he's not a nice man because of how Florian reacts anytime Olan's name is mentioned."

"And there has to be a reason for that," Dale reasoned.

"I jumped the gun, didn't I?"

Dale laughs. "I would say so, but I think you expected what anyone would in your position. You expected your spouse to put you first, and that's okay, Belle. Don't beat yourself up over it. But you also have to remember your relationship is very different from most people's. It's not the typical relationship. Now, don't get me wrong. I'm not a fan of Florian's for reasons you already know, but I want you to be happy, and even though you had this little misstep, you seem to be very happy with him."

I understand that completely. This is a marriage with no love involved, even though I can admit things are rapidly changing between us, at least on my end. I have to give him some grace. I can't have things the way I want them immediately.

"You're right."

"I am most of the time," he says, and I nudge him.

"Thank you for meeting with me," I say, and he smiles. "I hope I didn't ruin any plans you have."

"Anytime, sweetheart. Anytime."

"So, what's been up with you?" I ask, changing the subject.

I have to stop thinking about Florian. Nothing is going to change when it comes to him and his father. So, there's no use in my dwelling over it. I'll make things right between us once I go back home.

The moment Dale's face lights up with a smile, I immediately know why.

"You met someone, didn't you?" I ask, and he nods. "Oh my god, Dale! That's wonderful."

It makes me happy that my friend found someone who will treat him like he deserves.

"She's wonderful, Belle."

"Tell me all about her, then."

"First, thank you for not letting me confuse my love for you with true love."

My smile is uncontrollable.

"You always told me there was someone out there for me," he continues. "And for a long time, I believed it was you, but when I met Aurora, it was instant. And I knew she was it for me."

"I'm so happy for you, Dale. When do I get to meet her?"

"As a matter of fact, she's coming to town during your next performance. She's a huge fan of yours."

"A fan of mine?"

It's always a surprise to hear someone is a fan. I'm just a girl who loves to dance. Nothing more, nothing less.

"Why does that always surprise you?" he asks. "Don't you know that you're Arabelle Williamson, one of the top ballerinas of our time?"

I roll my eyes. "Whatever. Anyway, make sure you let me know for sure when she's in town because I want to meet her. So, bring her backstage. I'll make sure I set it up."

"She'll love that, Belle. I appreciate it."

"Anytime, Dale."

"So, what are you going to do about Florian?" he asks, moving the conversation back to Florian.

"I guess I'm going home with my tail between my legs to apologize."

I have to swallow my pride. I can't expect him to put me first when he doesn't even love me. It's unrealistic of me to expect him to change his life just because I want him to, considering we haven't been married for long. I shouldn't have given him that ultimatum, although I believe whatever is going on with his father will affect me.

We need to have a serious conversation.

"Florian!" I take my coat off as I move through the foyer. "Florian! Are you here? We need to talk!"

"So, you're her?" a voice says that's not my husband's or any of the staff as soon as I step into the living room. "So, you're the one who took him from me?"

I stop in my tracks. "Excuse me? How did you get in here?"

She rises from the couch and approaches me, just as beautiful as her pictures. Her silky blonde hair extends past her breasts, nearly brushing her slender waist. I almost take a step back from the intense hatred in the arctic blue eyes staring back at me. I believe he said her name is Addie.

"You heard me," she sneers, ignoring my question. "You took him from me."

"I'm not sure who you are or what you're talking about, but you need to leave my home. Now!"

"Your home?" Her frown deepens as she looks around the living room. "You know, for as long as I've been with Florian, I knew nothing of this place. He always took me to his penthouse. Anyway, if it wasn't for your father, I wouldn't have known to find you here."

How in the hell did my father know about this place?

"My father?" I ask. "And how do you know my father?"

"How I know him isn't important. He just gave me a little insight into a clause in that contract you signed for Florian. But I wasn't expecting you."

The infidelity clause.

That's when I take a close look at her clothes and what she's wearing. The dress she's wearing barely reaches past her ass and clings to her body like a second skin. She's beautiful, but the way she's dressed, she was definitely here to seduce my husband.

"Anyway, this place isn't quite up to my taste. Where's the gold trimming, the expensive artwork? The fur rugs?" With pinched brows and a look of disgust, she continues to survey my home. "Florian can do a lot better than this monstrosity, and he can do a lot better than you."

It's not up to her taste, but it's definitely up to mine. I can't help but feel like he designed the entire estate with me in mind, and I take offense to her statement about our home and about me.

Situated on Mecox Bay, the luxurious home offers over forty-five thousand square feet of living space and is nestled on its own charming cul-de-sac. It has five bedrooms and six bathrooms, along with two very large fireplaces, stone countertops, and both marble and hardwood flooring throughout the entire mansion. While it's a little large and extravagant for just the two of us, it's absolutely perfect in my eyes.

"What does he see in you?" she asks, scanning my figure before locking onto my face. "You're just...normal."

I can see the hate she has for me in her eyes. I have to figure out a way to get out of here.

"Well, that's something you'll have to ask Florian. Right now, I've got some things to take care of. So, if you'd like, you can wait here for him."

As I turn on my heels, the sharp pain of her nails digging into my arm jolts me to a stop. I whip around, pulling my arm from her grip. My heart pounds in my chest when I come face-to-face with the cold, steel barrel of a gun.

Slowly, I raise my hands, taking a small step away, trying to put some distance between us.

Maybe I can run?

"Put the gun down."

"I can't do that," she says, her eyes wild with fury. "He won't answer any of my calls, and I've done everything to get his attention. So, if he wants to save you, he'll have to come to me."

My mind immediately went to Hugo, but he's not expecting her. However, she doesn't know that. Maybe the threat will get her to change her mind about whatever she has planned.

"You won't get out of here alive."

"Then you'll die along with me. Head to the door. And don't try anything. It will mess up my plans if I have to shoot you now."

She pushes me toward the door, and I don't resist. She's crazy, and I have no doubt in my mind that she will kill me if I don't comply.

"You don't have to do this."

She laughs, but her laughter is devoid of any joy or amusement, sending a chilling sensation through me. "Yes, I do have to do this, Arabelle. Like I said, he'll come for you. Then, I can kill you, and we'll live happily ever after."

As soon as I open the door, I expect Hugo to make an appearance. When he does, he doesn't have time to say anything or pull his gun because immediately, her gun goes off.

"Hugo!" Horrified, I scream as I watch blood collect around his limp body on the concrete.

"Get in the car!" she shouts, pushing me from behind. "Now!"

I can't tear my eyes away from Hugo as he fights to catch his breath. "Hugo! Please!"

"Get in the fucking car!" she screams, diverting my attention from the man I've grown fond of.

"Please let him be all right," I mumble.

"You need to be more worried about yourself. You have three seconds to get in the damn car, or you'll join your friend sooner than I'd like."

Without hesitating any further, I enter the car from the passenger side. "You drive," she commands, and I maneuver over the center console to the driver's seat. "Now go!"

I start the engine and drive down the driveway.

She keeps the gun pointed at me.

"You still have time to stop this because you won't get away with this," I say, making sure to keep my eyes on the road.

"Maybe I won't, but if I can't have him, then neither will you."

I inhale deeply and exhale, allowing her words to sink in. Florian will come for me. I know he will. But I hope he's prepared for me not to make it out of this alive. I realize I also have to accept this.

23
FLORIAN

Pure rage consumes me as I listen to Didrick reveal how my father intentionally got him addicted to drugs, knowing I would try to save him. He only found out when he overheard Olan talking to my other brothers about it. What kind of parent would do that to their child?

"I'm sorry, Florian," Didrick apologizes again. "I didn't know. After the accident, I just wanted the pain to end, and after his doctor gave me the first hit, I just couldn't stop."

I firmly grip his shoulder. "This isn't on you," I assure him.

His eyes reveal shame, and I understand why. However, the man who caused his suffering and mine acts like an innocent man and is sitting right in front of us.

"All's fair in war, boys," Olan says with a smirk. "You have too many weaknesses, especially that ballerina, Florian. If I can exploit them, so can others. You might want to remember that."

"Asva, take Didrick to the penthouse," I order, never taking my eyes off our father.

"But I thought..."

I raise my hand, stopping Didrick's protest. I'm not letting him see what comes next, especially not with what Olan has done to him. I won't be the reason he spirals back into addiction.

"Not this time."

He stares at me for a moment before nodding. I can see the disappointment on his face, but I hope he knows this is the best thing for him. Whether he's here or not, he'll no longer have to worry about our father.

He looks at my father, and the smirk that crosses my father's face will only last for a few moments. Didrick walks closer to Olan and spits in his face.

"Rot in hell, asshole," Didrick says.

Our father chuckles as Didrick's spit slowly slides down his cheek. "You're an addict. A loser. I should have had that doctor give you a fatal dose and been done with you."

Didrick pulls back and punches him in the face. When Olan screams, it's like music to my ears. I've dreamed of the day I would hear his screams.

"Fuck you!" Didrick yells. "Fuck you! You piece of shit!"

While I believe Didrick needs to get all this shit off his chest, I don't believe he'd be able to live with himself if he killed Olan or even watched him take his last breath. So, I signal to Alrick to grab Didrick before he gets carried away. It can be very cathartic to beat someone's ass.

Alrick snatches Didrick, pulling him out of the room with Asva following. Then Asva closes the door, leaving only Olan and me.

I take off my suit jacket and casually throw it onto the table near the wall. I can feel Olan's eyes on me, watching every move I make, anticipating what I'll do next. But he has no idea what's coming to him.

I carefully roll up the sleeves of my dress shirt to my elbows. Tattooed on my right forearm is the goddess Freja in a chariot pulled by cats, which represents my mother. Tattooed on my left forearm is a colossal beast, his teeth displayed and blood dripping from its long canines holding a sickle. Its arm is tightly wrapped around a ballerina, symbolizing my wife and me. The two most important people in my life. One I couldn't protect from him, and the other one, I'll die trying to.

I position the chair in front of me and take a seat facing him. "Oh my, my, my, how times have changed, dear old dad. Look at who is the prey and who is the predator now."

"Let me out of these restraints so we can see how much times have changed, boy. I'm always the predator, son."

I laugh. "How does it feel to know this is your final day on Earth?"

"My sons will come for me."

The confident tone of his voice only adds to my amusement. Even if they know where he is, they won't be able to save him because they'll die as soon as they step inside my building.

I have the feeling my brothers would rather our old man die. They want to be free of him as much as I do.

"Will they?" I ask with my brow arched.

"They will, and they will make you pay for this."

I couldn't stop the laugh from leaving my lips. "Well, if they do come, which I think is highly unlikely, but if they do, they'll die right along with you, Olan."

His eyes narrow. "You'd kill your own flesh and blood for power?" He scoffs. "You've become exactly the man I thought you would become. That's why I wanted that bitch of a mother of yours to abort you. You're nothing. I can't even believe you're a result of my seed. You're no son of mine."

I throw my head back and burst into laughter again. "I might be nothing to you, but I'm more of a man than you'll ever be. I've got both your empires, and you have nothing."

I rise and remove the knife from the holster attached to the waistband of my slacks. Holding the blade in front of me, I flip it back and forth so my father can see his fate.

"What are you planning to do to me?"

There's no trace of his previous bluster and confidence in his voice. Now, it trembles with fear.

I slide my finger along the sharp edge of the steel blade, never taking my eyes off him. "Anything that I want to do to you, Olan. You will get no mercy from me, just like you gave her no mercy."

"Son, you don't have to do this," he pleads, but those pleas fall on deaf ears. "We can rule together."

"Together?" I step closer to him, tightening my grip on the knife's handle. "Why do you think I'd want to rule anything with you?"

"You're my son!" he yells, never averting his gaze from my knife. "If it wasn't for me, where the hell would you be? You can't kill me! You need me!"

I press the knife against his cheek, then pull it down and watch his skin split into two. As Olan screams, the sound reverberates in my ears, causing a dark pleasure to rise within me.

"That is a very good question, *Far*."

With a chilling laugh, I trace the knife along the other side of Olan's face, relishing the sensation of the knife slicing through his skin.

"Where do you think I would be if it wasn't for you, Olan?" I ask, even though I don't give a fuck about the answer.

He's cost me so much, and he'll die for it. Today is the last day I'll have to worry about Olan Larsson.

Defiant as always, Olan glares at me. "Dead, just like your whore mother."

His laugh reveals his blood-stained teeth.

Tamping down my anger, I shrug at his insulting comment about my mother. He knows she's a sore spot for me, and he'll say and do anything he can to get under my skin, but not today. Today, I'll celebrate his downfall.

"Maybe I would be dead." I shrug. "But that was your mistake, Olan. You should have killed us both when you had the chance. Instead, you wanted to make us suffer because of your lonely existence as a man."

"Fuck you!"

"How does it feel knowing that the kid you tormented for so long will be the one to kill you?"

He lets out a laugh, but it comes out muffled and distorted due to the blood pooling in his mouth. He tries his hardest to spit it out, narrowly missing me. A glob of blood and mucus lands at my feet.

"You'll pay for this," he says. "As a matter of fact, there's nothing you can do to save her now."

Fear floods my senses, leaving me paralyzed in its grip. "What have you done?"

"I've ended you!" he shouts as best he can, his laughter echoing through the room. "I'm going to show you that you're still that same little boy who will always crave my attention. And now you have it, my son. How does it feel?"

I shake my head, trying to clear the fear closing in on me. "Where is she?"

His piercing gaze locks onto me, and a victorious grin spreads across his face. "Dead."

Torturing him is not important now. As long as he's dead, I'm good. She's more important than he'll ever be.

With a loud yell, I forcefully drive the knife under his chin, plunging it through his head. I ignore the sound of his final breath escaping his lips. Watching him die isn't as important anymore, and he no longer deserves my attention.

Arabelle's gone.

I rush out of the room, feeling the adrenaline coursing through my veins along with pure terror and rage. Asva and Alrick fall in beside me, their footsteps matching mine as I pull out my phone and dial Hugo's number.

"What's wrong?" Alrick asks.

I end the call when he doesn't answer and dial him again. After a few more tries, he finally answers, but heavy breathing comes over the line.

"Florian, what's going on?" Alrick asks. "Talk to me."

"Hugo!" I shout. "Hugo!"

Silence.

"I'm sending help, Hugo. Hang on. Asva, take Nero and get to the house. Something's happened. Alrick, you come with me."

With another burst of adrenaline, I hop inside the passenger side of the SUV, feeling the powerful acceleration as Alrick peels away from the warehouse. I end the call to Hugo and immediately dial Arabelle's number.

"Hello, Florian."

When Addie's voice comes over the line and not Arabelle's, anger rushes through me, causing my hand to clench around my phone.

I'm going to kill her.

"Where's Arabelle, Addie?"

"No 'how are you doing?'" she asks, laughing like a crazy lunatic. "No 'I've missed you too, baby?'"

"Addie, stop fucking playing with me. Where the fuck is Arabelle?"

She huffs. "Get a grip on yourself, Florian. Your precious Beauty is fine."

Arabelle's blood-curdling screams send shivers down my spine, and my heart drops to my feet.

"At least, she's fine for now."

"I'm going to fucking kill you when I see you!" I yell. "Let her go!"

"If I die, so does she, Florian. And I know how much you don't want me to die, my love."

I need to think rationally and calm down before it costs Arabelle her life because, clearly, Adahlia has lost her fucking mind.

"What do you want, Adahlia? I'll give you anything you want if you just let her go."

"What I've always wanted, Florian. You. I want to be your wife."

"Where are you?" I ask, raking my hand over my face in frustration and ignoring her statement. I have one fucking wife, and Adahlia will never be her. "We'll meet and talk."

"At our special place. I'll be waiting."

The only response I get on the other end is silence. Anger roars through me as I pound my fist against the dash.

"I'm going to fucking kill her," I say and punch the dashboard again. "Head to the penthouse. They're on the rooftop."

My men and their families may find it odd that Arabelle and Adahlia are together, but no one will stop them from entering the building. Everyone knows Arabelle is my wife, and they know Adahlia comes to my penthouse often.

It's not surprising she chose the rooftop. Our conversations up there revolved around our lives and the dreams for our future outside of what we needed to do for our families. It was too bad that it was also the place where she'd lose her life.

As the elevator doors slide open, a gust of wind sends a chill down my spine. Alrick is getting more men, but I've ordered them to hold back to avoid spooking Adahlia. Right now, my only concern is getting Arabelle away from her unharmed. Alrick already knows to take steps to make sure Arabelle's safe, and that Adahlia dies if anything happens to me.

With my hands buried deep in the pockets of my peacoat, I approach Adahlia, who is standing behind a trembling Arabelle, a gun pointed at her head.

"Hands up!" Adahlia orders. "Or I'll kill her, Florian! Don't fucking play with me!"

I continue to walk toward them, but I do raise my hands in the air as a sign that I don't mean her any harm.

"What's this all about, Addie?" I ask. My eyes shift toward Arabelle to make sure she's all right. She looks terrified, and there's a mark above one of her eyes. Other than that, she looks fine. I return my focus to Adahlia. "Why are we here?"

In a display of annoyance, Adahlia rolls her eyes. "You know why we're here, Florian. Don't play stupid. You married this bitch when it should have been me. Did you think I'd just let her get away with taking you from me? I'm my father's daughter, after all. You should know better than to screw me over!"

She tightly clutches Arabelle's hair, forcefully pulling her head back, eliciting a piercing scream.

"Addie! Addie! Take a deep breath and calm down. Leave her out of it. None of this is her fault. Your problem is with me, so talk to me. We're friends, aren't we?"

I'm only a few feet from them, but the closer I get, Adahlia steps closer to the edge of the building.

"Friends?" she screams. "We're more than friends! I love you!"

Her face is flushed, and her eyes dart around with a wild intensity I've only seen in people who are cornered and have lost their shit. If I don't act soon, Arabelle will be hurt or worse. And I will never let that happen. It's going to be her before I let anything happen to Arabelle.

When I'm close enough where I know Arabelle won't be hurt, at least not from the gun, I spring toward Adahlia, simultaneously shoving Arabelle aside. The sharp sound of the gun reverberates through the air, jolting me into action, and Adahlia loses her balance when I push her over the edge.

"Florian!" Adahlia screams. "Please, help me!"

I walk to the edge of the building and look over the edge. She's clinging onto a metal pipe that's fixed to the concrete of the building. It's groaning from her weight.

"Please, help me," she pleads, her tear-streaked face filled with desperation. "I love you, Florian. You can't let me die."

As I reach down, my fingers wrap around her delicate wrist, feeling the pulse of her heartbeat. She tightly grips my hand, her knuckles turning white when she lets go of the pipe.

However, I know how this ends. Pulling her up would put Arabelle at risk. She's already proven that she's a threat, and she will never leave us in peace if I let her live. There's only one thing that I can do.

My face breaks into a wicked smile, and she instantly recognizes her mistake of placing her trust in the Beast.

Wrong move.

Her relief immediately turns to fear, and tears fill her eyes.

"Florian..."

Arabelle's voice, filled with pain, echoes in my ears from behind me, prompting me to release Adahlia's hand without a second thought. Her screams of terror echo through the stillness of the night, blending with the distant hum of the city. While I'd love nothing more than to watch her fall to her death, I have more important things to attend to.

I rush toward Arabelle, my heart pounding in my chest. When I reach her, I kneel beside her. "Are you hurt?" I ask, looking over her body for any injuries.

She reaches for the bruise over her eye and winces before dropping her hand. "Bruised, and I have a massive headache, but I think I'm going to be okay."

I help her to her feet, feeling the warmth of her body against mine when I wrap my arm around her shoulders. I guide her toward the elevator, eager to get off this fucking rooftop and safely inside my penthouse. The place will be swarmed by cops in no time.

"Is she dead?" she asks when we step inside the elevator.

When I press the button, the door closes, sealing us inside, she presses her head against my chest. "She is."

She lets out a sigh of relief. "And Hugo?"

I tighten my embrace. "I don't know."

Hopefully, he isn't going to die. He's like a brother to me, but right now, I'm more concerned with her well-being. I failed to protect her, the one thing I promised her I would always do. Now, I need to make it right.

24

ARABELLE

As I sit in Florian's penthouse, a chill runs down my spine as I watch him carefully light the fireplace. The cold from being on top of the roof and the ice pack against my eye has penetrated deep into my bones.

I tug his coat around me, relishing in his intoxicating scent. It has a soothing effect. It's kind of unnerving how quiet he's been since everything that's happened. The absence of his voice only amplifies the tension in the room.

"What now?" I ask.

He momentarily stops what he's doing, like he's in deep thought, before picking up where he left off. "We give our statements to the cops. I don't like to deal with them, but with Adahlia's body at the base of the building, it's something we can't avoid."

"Did you let her fall?"

He faces me, his eyes locking with mine before he takes a few steps and positions himself directly in front of me. "Do you really want to know the answer to that question? Think really hard before you answer, Beauty."

Did I really want to know if he let Adahlia fall to her death? Although I know my husband is a dangerous man, would he go as far as killing for me? I'm scared to know the truth, but I think I need to know the truth if I want to know the real man.

I respond by nodding. I need to know how far he's willing to go to keep me safe since I'm starting to realize how dangerous my life is now. How far will he go to keep our children safe?

He sits next to me and looks into my eyes. The intense emotions swirling in his gaze are almost heart-stopping, but I'm not in the right frame of mind to decipher any of it.

"I told you from the beginning that I will do everything in my power to keep you safe. Adahlia dying was the only way to keep you safe. So, when she pleaded for my help, I reached out for her hand. Once she grabbed onto mine, I let her fall to her death."

I let out a gasp, and he takes hold of my hand.

"I'm a man of my word, Beauty. No one will ever harm you. No matter who it is."

"She wasn't working alone," I mutter.

Although I don't know what he'll do once he finds out my father was involved, I don't want him dead over it, even if he does deserve it.

"I know," he says, anger clouding his eyes. "My father knew Adahlia was coming after you. And one of the men whom I thought was loyal to me was loyal to him. That's how she got in."

"What?"

"Nothing for you to worry about anymore."

"You killed your father? You killed the man who let her in?" I ask even though I already know the answers.

His father is dead, and the man who let her in will be dead if he isn't already.

A younger version of Florian appears from the kitchen before he can respond. "What's going on?" he asks.

"Didrick, this is my wife, Arabelle. Arabelle, this is my brother, Didrick."

"You're married?" Didrick asks, looking from his brother to me. "When the hell did that happen?"

"I am. We'll talk about it later," Florian says. "Right now, the police are on the way.

"The police?" he asks, concern and fear covering his face. "Does it have to do with *Far*?"

"No, it doesn't, but I do need you to stay in your room until they leave."

"Okay." He nods. "No problem. Whatever you need me to do. Nice to meet you, Arabelle," he says before disappearing down the hallway.

When the door to his bedroom clicks, Florian sighs. "He's had some issues with drugs. He's just come back from rehab, so he'll be staying here under my care until he turns eighteen."

I've had a lot of experience dealing with addiction, and he's so young. I hope Didrick's recovery is better than my sister's. Hopefully, he'll take sobriety more seriously than Raven.

"My father told Adahlia about the infidelity clause in the contract."

Even though I don't want him to hurt my father, I can't keep him from knowing. I don't want any secrets between us, especially one this serious.

Florian exhales and pinches the bridge of his nose. I can feel the anger radiating off him. I understand why he's angry. My father deserves to pay for what he's done. However, I still don't want my father to die because he made a stupid decision.

"He was trying to save me from you."

His gaze meets mine, yet his expression remains devoid of any emotion, making it hard for me to read where his head is.

"Don't kill him, Florian. Please."

His fingers gently trace my jawline, causing my eyes to flutter. "Still trying to save the bastard, I see."

"He's my father, Florian. I don't want him dead for doing what he thought would help me. He doesn't know the real you, Florian. Not like I do. He was trying to do what he thought was the right thing for me."

He lifts my hand to his mouth and presses a kiss on my knuckles. "He doesn't deserve you, you know?"

I gaze into his eyes and quietly mutter, "I know, but he's still my dad, even if he is shitty at the job."

"Okay, my Beauty. He'll live this time. But you let him know it's because of your grace and mercy that he has another chance at life because this day could have ended much differently."

"Thank you."

"Anything for you, baby. Are you warm enough, or do you want me to turn up the heat?"

"I'm warm enough." I lean closer to him. "What do we tell the police?"

"The truth." He shrugs. "We did nothing wrong, Arabelle. There's no need to lie about what happened. Adahlia kidnapped you, brought you here so that I would come for you, and when I tried to rescue you, she fell over the side of the roof."

And you let her go.

His phone rings, and he quickly retrieves it from his jacket. Then there's a knock on the door. With the phone pressed to his ear, he stands, walks to the door, and opens it. Two men in suits talk with Florian for a few moments, and then Florian steps aside, allowing them in. Florian ends his phone call and escorts them into the living area.

"Gentlemen, this is my wife, Arabelle Larsson," Florian says when he sits beside me, slipping his phone into his blazer before he grabs my hand. "Have a seat."

With a motion, he directs the two men to sit in the chairs across from us.

"Beauty, they want to ask you some questions," Florian says.

I nod, pulling his coat closer around my shoulders. "Okay, that's fine."

"My name is Detective Roberts, and this is my partner, Detective Reyes. Can you tell me what happened?"

"I came home—"

"From where?" Detective Roberts interrupts.

"From my attorney's home. Dale Austin."

Florian tenses as soon as Dale's name is mentioned, so I squeeze his hand, hoping it will calm him down. I've come to know that he's very possessive when it comes to me, and his anger makes me nervous. He has absolutely nothing to worry about when it comes to Dale.

The investigator jots down notes in a tiny notebook. "And Dale Austin will verify this?" Detective Reyes asks.

"Of course."

"Can you please continue?"

"I came home..."

"Here?" Detective Reyes interrupts again.

"No," Florian answers for me instead. "Our home outside the city. This is just one of the many properties that I own."

Both detectives nod as they continue to scribble on their notepads.

"When I came in, she was sitting in the living room. At first, I didn't see her because I was looking for Florian, but he wasn't there."

"Mr. Larsson, where were you at this time?" Detective Reyes asks.

"I was checking on one of my properties. We had some things get stolen from my construction site."

"Okay," Detective Reyes responds, shifting his attention back to me. "Mrs. Larsson, how do you know Ms. Karlsson?"

"I don't know her," I respond, causing his brows to furrow in confusion.

"If you don't know her, what did she want, and how did you both end up here?" Detective Roberts asks, confusion blanketing his face.

"She was upset that my husband and I are married."

"And how do you know Ms. Karlsson, Mr. Larsson?" the detective asks.

"We fucked," Florian says so calmly I can't help but look at him.

"Nothing serious, I assume?"

"Not on my end," Florian says. "I ended it with her when I got engaged to Arabelle."

"I see." Detective Roberts nods. "Mrs. Larsson, what happened next?"

Florian holds my hand tightly, and I respond with a smile. Is it weird that I find comfort in his presence even after he admitted that he killed her to protect me?

"She forced me outside and shot my bodyguard."

"Why do you need a bodyguard?" Detective Reyes asks.

Despite his lack of familiarity with me, he is certainly aware of who Florian is. There's no way he doesn't know. I won't answer questions they already know the answers to.

"My wife is one of the world's most well-known ballerinas," Florian answers. "Of course, she'll always have protection around her."

They seem to accept that answer, but I'm sure they will investigate to make sure he's not lying about who I am.

"And then she brought you here?" Detective Reyes asks, seeming to accept Florian's response.

"Yes, then she forced me onto the rooftop. Florian came and rescued me."

"How did Ms. Karlsson end up falling off the building?"

"I lunged at her to get Arabelle away from her because she had a gun pointed at her head," Florian says.

"And is that how you got the scratches on your hand and wrists, Mr. Larsson?"

Florian's gaze moves to his hand, and so does mine. I didn't see them earlier, and I'm not sure if he did, either.

"Those came from me trying to save her," Florian says. "She was hanging on to the metal pipe fastened to the side of the building. When I tried to pull her up, she couldn't hold on."

"So, you're trying to tell us that you tried to save the woman who had just kidnapped your wife?" Detective Reyes says with his brow arched.

"That's exactly what I'm saying, Detective," Florian responds, and both detectives look at each other in disbelief before turning their attention back to Florian. "Listen, gentlemen, I've known Adahlia a very long time. Since we were kids, actually. We grew up together in Sweden and reconnected once we both came to the States."

"And you think your marriage drove her to do this despite your years of friendship? That seems a little excessive, don't you think?"

"It was excessive, but it doesn't change the fact that my marriage to Arabelle pushed Adahlia over the edge. We had a long sexual relationship. When I had events to attend, she was always my date, but I made it clear to her that it would never move beyond friendship. I think she went a little mad when she found out about my marriage. However, that doesn't mean I wanted the woman dead."

His words are so convincing, even I would have believed them if I didn't know the truth.

Florian stands. "My wife has been through enough today. Now, if you have any more questions for my wife or me, please contact my attorney, and he'll set up an appointment."

Despite closing their notepads and standing, I can tell from their eyes they still have more questions they want answers to. But there's nothing more I can tell them. I've shared everything I know with them.

Florian hands Detective Reyes a business card, then guides them to the door. As soon as I hear it shut, I exhale. I close my eyes, wishing it were any other day, but it's not. I was held captive at gunpoint, witnessed a person being shot, and narrowly escaped getting shot myself. Is this how my life will be from now on?

"Beauty."

My eyes open and meet a pair of steely gray eyes that seem to pierce straight into my soul.

"Let's get you to bed," he says. "Then we'll discuss things more in the morning. Is that fine with you?"

I nod and rise to my feet. It's been such a long day. All I want to do is curl up in bed and sleep.

His arm encircles my shoulders, bringing me closer to him. "How's Hugo?" I ask as we walk down the hallway to the bedroom at the very end.

"Touch and go. Alrick and Asva are at the hospital with him."

The sadness in his voice tightens around my heart. Even though I don't know any of these men, I know they're his family.

"Don't worry, he'll pull through. He's strong. There's no way he'll give up."

Instead of responding, he tightens his embrace as we step into the bedroom. This is my new life. It's dangerous and unpredictable, something I'm not used to. However, I believe the man whose arms I'm in right now will do everything in his power to make sure I'm safe. He proved that tonight.

"Let's get you cleaned up and into bed."

25
FLORIAN

While filling the bathtub with warm water and her favorite oil, I can't stop thinking about the terrified look on Arabelle's face when Adahlia held that gun to her head, and how close I actually came to losing her. Never have I ever feared anything so much in my life, but at that moment, I was absolutely taken over by fear, terrified that I would have to walk through this life without her.

Now that everything is over, and it's sinking in that she almost died because of me, I can't blame anyone but myself. I'd been warned about Adahlia, and I should have taken the threat from her more seriously. However, I never thought she would dare turn against me. We were friends before we were lovers. I told her over and over again where our relationship stood, but I guess none of that mattered to her. She was determined we were going to be together—only what she wanted or believed mattered.

I also should have taken the threat from my father more seriously, too. Alrick warned me time and time again to end things quickly. But my ego and pride got the better of me and wouldn't let me look at him as more than someone to play with before I finally crushed him.

I won't ever make that kind of mistake again.

Every threat to her will be dealt with immediately. Except her father. Of course, I'm not happy about that, especially after what he did. He's the reason Adahlia even knew about the infidelity clause. If it wasn't for him, it's possible none of this would have even happened.

However, I will respect her wishes unless he presents himself as a very serious threat.

If it wasn't for Arabelle, her father would be dead just like Adahlia and Olan for her almost taking away from me. Even though he didn't intend for the events that happened to happen, he put her life at risk all because he plotted against me. All because he wants her back in his life so she can keep saving his ass. He believes I'm the one causing her to stay away, which couldn't be further from the truth.

He thought Adahlia could seduce me into breaking my vows, thereby breaking the contract Arabelle signed. However, nobody can ever make me break my vows to the one woman who owns my heart and soul. My vow to Arabelle is until death do us part, and that's not happening any time soon for either of us. She will always remain with me in this life and the next.

First, I turn off the water. Then, I light the candles placed around the master en suite. I want to make sure she's as comfortable as she can possibly be after the day she's had. At least this will take her mind off what happened with Adahlia and, hopefully, Hugo as well.

In the short amount of time we've been together, she's become really close to him, which is what I had hoped for. You can't have trust in someone you don't like, and someone actually liking Hugo is always a toss-up. He's the type of person who burrows under your skin in a good or a bad way. You'll either hate him or love him, and he's made a very good impression on Arabelle despite his dark, off-the-wall sense of humor. She's just as worried about him as I am, but she's trying to be strong for me because she knows he's like a brother to me.

Sighing and pushing the thoughts of Hugo and everyone else to the back of my mind, I try to firmly plant my attention on her. There's nothing I can do for his situation, but there is absolutely something I can do for her.

Having dimmed the overhead lights and decreased the tint on the windows so it's clear, I make my way back to the bedroom and discover she's standing where I left her. By the wide-eyed look on her face, it's like she's finally coming to terms with how close she came to death. I wish it was possible to take away all her fear, but I know I can't. It will always be in the back of her mind what Adahlia did and my role in the situation. However, I will make sure she knows that I will never put her in that position ever again.

As soon as I extend my hand toward her, she grabs it, which sends a rush of relief moving through me that I can't explain. I gently squeeze her hand, pleased that she's not pulling away from me even after I confessed to killing Addie.

I walk her inside the bathroom and as soon as she enters, she lets out a gasp, facing the windows.

"Wow...Florian. This view is amazing."

"It is. It's one of the reasons I purchased the building."

While she stands in front of the wall of windows, I move behind her, giving her a bit of space just in case she needs it. Still, I remain close to her.

I admire the breathtaking New York skyline along with her. It's night now, and it's a spectacular spectacle of lights and silhouettes of New York's iconic architecture rising across the city. It's a view I've fallen in love with.

"The building?" she asks, looking over her shoulders at me with a crease between her eyes, like she's not sure she heard me correctly.

"Yes, the building. I own it."

She faces me. "The entire building?"

I burst into laughter. "Yes, Beauty. The entire building. I own it."

As I take off my shirt, she's no longer focused on me owning the building. Immediately, her lips part as she watches me with such intensity. So much desire.

"Are you enjoying the show?"

With a mischievous smile playing on my lips, I shed my dress slacks and black boxer briefs, presenting her with an unhindered view of my erect cock, palming my hard length in my hand. Her focus shifts to my bare feet as I make my way toward her on the heated white tile. When I reach her, I grab her hand and place it on my dick.

"This is what you do to me, Beauty." She looks into my eyes as her smooth palm holds my cock. "Whenever you're around, I have a constant hard-on."

I relish the gentle touch of her smooth hand as she starts caressing my hard, velvety steel with delicate, tentative strokes.

I don't want to miss any emotion on her face or the feeling of her hand moving up and down my shaft. Pulling my lip between my teeth, I gaze down at her, images playing in my head of what I would love to do to her body and her luscious lips wrapped around my cock.

"I won't come in your hand, Beauty."

As her grip tightens, I can't help but smirk at the challenge she presents to me. I can tell by her movements she's new to all this, but she's eager to please me, or at least prove to me that she can do it. But we'll have time for that at some other time. I'll give her all the lessons she wants.

I knock her hands away from my body, quickly pull her shirt over her head, and tease her sensitive nipples with the gentle touch of my thumbs, eliciting a pleasurable groan from her.

"No bra?" I whisper, pushing her closer to the wall of windows until her back is flush against the large panes of glass.

She shakes her head, never taking her eyes off me as I twist and pinch her nipples.

"Can anyone see us?"

Her question comes out in a breathy moan, and my smirk turns into a full-blown smile as I shrug. We're already both standing naked in front of the windows. "Even though we are high up, it's possible."

Her pupils dilate with the thought of someone seeing us, and her breaths pick up.

"Would you like someone to see us?" I ask even though I know the answer.

I push her leggings down to her ankles. She steps out of them when they pool at her feet, and then the sound of her panties ripping fills the space.

"Maybe."

Even though she sounds innocent, I know that she's not. I will always believe it's one of the reasons she likes her apartment in Los Angeles. Even the apartment she has in New York has a lot of windows, although not in the bedroom.

The windows in her bedroom at her apartment in Los Angeles allow anyone to see inside her room at night. They allow anyone to see what she's doing, even when she's masturbating, which I think she loves. It's one of the reasons I contemplated buying the building across from hers.

"I can't wait to experience the real Arabelle." I pinch her nipples harder, eliciting a deep moan from her that travels straight to my cock. "Are you the prim and proper ballerina everyone thinks you are, or are you the dirty little girl I believe you to be?"

"Let's find out," she whispers without hesitation with a mischievous glint in her eyes.

"Are you sure?" I ask. Although she's been through hell today, maybe she wants to have a little fun to take her mind off things. "Because, right now, the windows are clear, and someone might see us."

Her eyes light up with excitement. She gazes out the window for a moment longer like she's scanning the building across the street to see if anyone can see us, before she shifts her focus back to me and smiles.

"I'm sure. I need you, Florian. Fuck me, please."

The amount of desire that barrels through me almost puts me on my knees. However, I stiffen my spine. Fucking her wasn't in my plans, at least not until I got her in the bath where she could decompress. However, if what she needs is for me to fuck her right now, I'm sure as hell not going to deny her.

I adjust my position so that anyone watching can clearly see both our profiles. These windows have a tint, but I can adjust the level of darkness to my liking. Right now, they are clear. If she wants someone to see us, she will definitely get what she wants.

"On your knees, then balance your ass on your heels," I command. "And don't do anything until I tell you to, Beauty."

She moves in front of me and kneels at my feet without hesitation. As she settles into the pose I want her in, I take a step closer to her. Close enough to where I can comfortably slide into her mouth when the time is right.

"Hands palm down on your thighs, and don't move them."

She does as I ask, and I grip my cock, moving my hand up and down my shaft. Her beautiful eyes widen as she gazes at me with such intensity, and her mouth slightly parts on a breathy moan. I doubt she's ever watched a man masturbate unless it's been in a porn. Maybe I should ask her.

"Have you ever watched a man masturbate?"

She shakes her head. "No, but I like it so far."

I chuckle. "Are you wet, baby? Is watching me touch myself making you wet?"

She pulls her bottom lip between her teeth, nodding, her eyes fixed on my cock.

I reach for her mouth and pull her lip free with my thumb. "Open your mouth and get me wet."

She opens her mouth wider, and I slide in, groaning from the warmth and wetness of her mouth. "Fuck! That feels so good," I mumble, hating that I have to pull out because I'm not ready to fuck her mouth just yet.

After a few thrusts in and out of her mouth, I pulled completely out, causing her to whimper, clenching her fists. A smirk plays on my lips when I notice her growing frustration. She's itching to touch me so bad and keep me in her mouth, but I'm proud of her for obeying my command.

"I know you love the taste of my cock and watch to touch me so bad, Beauty, but it's not time yet," I say as I grip my length tighter and return to jacking myself off now that she's got me wet enough.

Lazily moving my hand up and down my shaft, I watch how fixated she is on the movement of my hand. How closely her eyes track my hand up and down my cock. I watch as she squirms while closely watching me. Her tongue darts out of her mouth, wetting her lips, and I imagine how it will feel moving along my shaft.

My body shivers. I let out a long groan when my hand grazes my sensitive head as I imagine the tip of her tongue caressing me and providing the sensation instead of my palm.

"Florian..." She moans and squirms, and her fists clench tighter where they rest on her thighs. "Please."

I pull my bottom lip between my teeth as I push myself closer to the edge. I can't ignore the passion in her voice.

"Please, what, Beauty?"

"Let me taste you."

I definitely can't deny her, especially not while she's so beautiful on her knees in front of me, waiting to obey me, serve me.

"First, I'm going to come down your throat." Gripping her head, I push my cock deep inside her mouth. "Then I'm going to come inside that tight little cunt of yours. Would you like that, baby? Would you like me to flood your mouth with my seed?"

She eagerly nods her head around my length. I pull out where the tip is only left in her mouth before guiding her farther down my dick until the tip hits the back of her throat. She gags as I hold her head still. Tears and panic fill her eyes.

"Breathe through your nose, baby. I'm not going to hurt you. Trust me."

She nods as best as she can, and fear is replaced by passion in her dark orbs, which pierce my heart and soul. Immediately, she relaxes and breathes through her nose.

"Don't move, Beauty. I'm gonna fuck your mouth."

The sensation of her hum vibrates through my entire body, and I relish in the intense feeling moving through me. With my hand intertwined in her tight curly hair that she's wearing loose tonight, I fuck her mouth like it's her cunt.

Fuck, she is taking me so well. I lose myself in the feeling as I take my pleasure from her. I thrust harder and faster, enjoying every sensation moving through my body. I'm not sure if anyone is watching, but I saw movement in one of the apartments across from this one. I hope they are enjoying the show because it's not often that I will share something so intimate with strangers. It's only because it's something she wants.

"I think we have an audience, Beauty," I say. "Show them how my dirty girl takes all this dick."

I open my eyes to her looking at me with desire and, dare I say, love in her tear-filled eyes.

At the thought of her truly loving me, a tingling sensation covers me from the soles of my feet to the crown of my head. Euphoria takes over my entire being. I hold her head still and release thick ropes of warm cum into her welcoming mouth.

While she hasn't voiced it yet, probably because of how this relationship started or she's waiting for me to express how deep my feelings are for her first, I know she has deep feelings for me. I can see it written all over her face.

My entire body tingles as my orgasm barrels toward me. I hold her head still and give in to everything I'm feeling at the moment. I throw my head back, moan, and release inside her mouth in one of the most powerful orgasms I've ever had.

When I look down at her, I pull myself free and run the pad of my thumb over her swollen red lips. "Breathtaking," I whisper as the most beautiful smile crosses her face.

I reach out my hand to help her stand and then pull her into my arms. "I love you, Beauty."

Her body stiffens in shock, but I don't expect her to respond, so I crash my mouth into hers, silencing any response. I don't want her to feel obligated to say it back to me. When she's ready to tell me, she will. I'll just have to wait to hear those three little words from her lips.

26
FLORIAN

Six Months Later...

The days and months since Olan's death have been quiet. Thankfully. Even with Adahlia's death, I expected her father to try to get even with me. Grumblings started circulating that Andreas was going to make his move to avenge his daughter's death. So, in a meeting that I requested, we spent hours talking about what led up to Adahlia's death. Our conversation went on late into the night. And, of course, he blamed Arabelle and me, but Adahlia was the cause of her own death. Not me and certainly not my wife. I broke things off with her. She should have gone on with her life. If she had, she'd be alive today.

Andreas knows I have the upper hand in negotiations because his daughter kidnapped my wife, which is something I could use to declare war on his organization, even though that's not what I want. I don't blame Andreas for what his daughter did. And Arabelle and I just want peace. We were ready to move forward in our lives and forget the past. So, because Adahlia acted without her father's knowledge, I was willing not to drag his entire organization into a conflict he knew he couldn't win. I like Andreas. We work well together, and it was in our best interests if he remained the leader of his family.

Once I made sure he understood what the consequences of her actions could be and how they could affect him and his organization if he moved forward with whatever he planned to do, he decided that wouldn't be the best course of action to take. Which was a relief for me.

Now, the only issue we have is Arthur. Of course, I let him live because she asked me to, but I know, eventually, he'll try to worm his way back into her life. At this point, I'm not sure how to handle it. Neither he nor those two ungrateful bitches she calls sisters deserve anything from her. It's up to me to protect her, and that means if I need to protect her from her family, I will.

Eager to see my wife's performance, I let all the thoughts of what needs to be done drift from my mind as I slide into the private box at the theater and settle into my seat. This will be her first performance as principal dancer, a moment she's been working toward for years.

Some rumblings have remained surrounding Pierre Gaultier's death, the man who drugged Arabelle and tried to rape her, which kept the theater from announcing it sooner.

Detectives questioned her and me for hours, again. However, this time Kellan was present during her questioning. After some persuasion in the form of a lot of cash from me, and the threat of death, the medical examiner ruled the man's death a suicide. Despite the family's disagreement with the findings, she had hospital records on her side, and as soon as I threatened to go to the media about her attack, they dropped their accusations. Nothing will derail my Beauty's chances to have her happily ever after.

I sigh as I hear voices drifting in from outside the private box. I want to enjoy just one night without having to deal with something.

Asva's heavy hand lands on my shoulder. "Williamson wants to talk," he whispers.

"Of course he does," I huff in annoyance.

"We told him that it was a no-go, but he's causing a scene."

I can't enjoy one day without someone wanting to interfere.

Arabelle's decision to sever ties with her family when she signed the contract was a courageous one, and I believe it was the right choice for her. She's had absolutely no contact with them and has stopped funding their extravagant lifestyle. With the flow of money stopped, the Williamson family is almost in the same position they were in when Arthur came to me looking for help. It's why he's here now because I know it's not to see his daughter's performance.

I let out a weary sigh, feeling the tension in my body as I pinch the bridge of my nose. I just want one fucking day to watch my wife do what she loves.

"Let him in," I mutter, even though I prefer to watch the show in peace.

I guess this meeting was bound to happen.

After a few moments, Arthur slides into the seat beside me, the leather cushion sinking under his weight.

"To what do I owe this pleasure, Arthur?" I ask, never taking my eyes off the stage. "I know you aren't looking for me to bail you out again, are you?"

The first act has begun, and Arabelle won't join until near the end, allowing me plenty of time to handle my father-in-law before she performs.

"I want to see my daughter," he says, ignoring my question about him needing more of my money. "But she's not answering my calls."

I guess he's learned his lesson about coming to me to bail him out.

"And what does that have to do with me, Arthur?"

"You can't keep her away from me, Florian," he says, fury lacing his voice. "She's all I have."

"You mean she's the only one of your children with enough money to keep you above water."

"You can't keep her away from me," he repeats. "She's my daughter."

"And she's my wife. However, I'm not keeping her away from you, Arthur. You did that all by yourself. I don't control her. She's the one who made the decision to cut you out of her life."

"I don't believe that," he huffs. "Of course, she is upset about this marriage, but she wouldn't do that to her family. She always sticks by us."

"I don't give a fuck what you believe, Arthur. Did she not say she was done with you when she signed my contract?"

His silence says it all. He can't put this on me. It was a decision Arabelle made on her own. She found out what kind of man her father truly is when he decided that his comfort meant more than his child. He just didn't believe she would stand by her decision and completely cut them out of her life.

Reluctantly, I tear my eyes away from the performance to glance at him. The last time I saw him, he looked so much younger compared to now. Don't get me wrong—he looked like shit then, but he's definitely looking worse now. I guess money problems can age you.

"But you should thank her because I know what you planned with Adahlia," I say so there's no confusion on his part, and so that he realizes the mercy I've given to him. Only because his daughter asked me to.

"Florian...I'm...I'm sorry," he stammers.

I raise my hand, silencing his lies before they can escape his lips.

"I don't need your apologies, Arthur. They won't do any good anyway, but I'm not mad at that, even though I should be. It was a clever ploy. But that plan almost got your daughter killed. Now, that's something I will never forgive. Or forget."

His eyes widen in alarm as he comprehends the gravity of the threat. And let's be honest—that's exactly what it is, and that's how he should take it. Even in the darkness of the theater, I see the fear dancing in his dark eyes. He should be very afraid of what I can do to him because he's forever on my shit list. All my Beauty has to do is say the word, and Arthur Williamson will no longer breathe.

"I didn't know she would try to hurt Arabelle," he says, trying to make excuses for putting Arabelle in danger. "She was only supposed to seduce you so Arabelle could break the contract. I would never hurt my daughter."

"And yet, you gave her to me so you can have your precious

company." I turn my attention back to the performance. "That says more about you than you can ever imagine, Arthur."

"Listen!" he shouts, jumping to his feet, then pointing his finger at me, which causes me to give him the attention he so desperately wants. "If you keep my daughter away from me, you'll regret it! I'll make sure of it!"

I'm glad the music is loud enough to drown out his outburst, creating a shield of sound that keeps unwanted eyes away. I don't take threats lightly, and his words have given me all the reason to view him as the threat he truly is.

"Is that right?"

With a wave of my hand, Asva seizes Arthur, tugging him closer to the door, immersing them both into the darkness of the box. I rise from my seat and stalk toward my father-in-law, my eyes fixed on him like a predator. As I pull the small knife from its sheath nestled in the waistband of my tuxedo pants, he desperately fights against Asva's grip. When I stand in front of him, fear is etched across his face. He should have thought about that before he tossed his threats about so carelessly.

"She'll never forgive you if you hurt me," he says, his voice trembling.

I firmly grasp his shoulder, digging my fingers into muscle. My smile widens as I lean close to him. With a swift motion, I drive the knife into his stomach and twist the hilt, eliciting a guttural grunt from him.

"Then I'll make sure she never finds out it was me," I whisper in his ear. "See you in hell."

After removing the knife from his body, I retrieve my handkerchief from the inside pocket of my tuxedo and use it to clean the blood from my hands and the blade. Finally, I place it inside Asva's jacket pocket so he can get rid of it.

The utter horror that's mixed with pain on Arthur's face is hilarious. He quickly forgot who he was dealing with.

"Make sure no one sees you on the way out. And dump him

where it'll take at least a week to find him. Maybe one of the old gambling houses."

Asva nods.

I turned my attention back to Arthur, whose dark shirt will do a very good job hiding the blood gushing from his stab wound.

"Just because I know my Beauty will be devastated when she learns of your death, I'll give her the opportunity to say goodbye to you."

"You won't get away with this," he groans.

"Maybe I won't, but you won't be around to find out. And she'll finally be rid of you once and for all."

Ignoring the groans and curses coming from Arthur, I sink back into the comfort of my seat as Asva helps him out of the room.

He's on the verge of death, and I feel absolutely nothing. He's nothing but a burden to his daughter, which means he's better off dead.

As Arabelle makes her way onto the stage, her father's presence fades away and is replaced by a rush of adrenaline and excitement. It's like seeing her all over again for the first time. It's like I'm experiencing the joy of falling in love with her all over again, and my face betrays my pride with a constant smile. With every step, turn, and leap, she's the epitome of grace and beauty. And I can proudly say that she's all mine.

27
ARABELLE

The past few weeks have been a hazy blur, with days and nights blending into one another. Being named principal dancer has been a relief and exciting, but like everything in my life, nothing ever goes as planned.

My father's body was discovered in a dimly lit alley outside the gambling house he often visited, after being missing for nearly two weeks. He had been brutally stabbed and bled out from the knife wound to his stomach. The police believe he owed people money, which didn't shock me when they delivered the news of his death. They also believe his debt may have been the cause of his death. While they haven't found the man or men responsible, that's the theory the police are currently pursuing in their investigation.

Despite cutting him out of my life, I can't deny that his death has impacted me. I've been devastated ever since I got the news, and I've been mourning the father from my childhood, not the addicted leech he'd become.

"Are you ready, sweetheart?" Florian asks, his warm fingers intertwining with mine.

My husband is becoming someone I trust and depend on. Every time he surprises me with how gentle, caring, or understanding he can be, he sinks his claws deeper into my heart. He's not just my biggest supporter, but he's also the one who always stands up for me and protects me. He has become the person I love more than anyone else.

I look over at him and feel a warmth spread through me as I smile at him. Today is the day we bury my father. Even though it's a somber day, with him gone, I'm looking forward to finally closing this chapter of my life.

I release a breath. "As ready as I'll ever be."

He gives a curt nod, and Hugo steps out of the car. The constant security presence is still something I'm adjusting to. But after the incident with Adahlia, I've never been more grateful for the watchful eyes of men like Hugo, Nero, Asva, Alrick, and the rest of the men who have become my second family. Overbearing family, but still family. They are all like the big brothers I've never had.

The door opens, and Florian steps out first. That's something else I've had to get used to. I can't leave any vehicle until I am given the *all-clear* signal. A reality of my new life.

After he engages in a brief conversation with Hugo, he reaches his hand out to me. I grasp it and step out, and the scent of freshly cut grass and flowers from the cemetery immediately fills my nostrils. The last time I visited the cemetery, I went to have a heart-to-heart with my mother about marrying Florian. It might seem crazy to seek guidance from the dead, but other than Dale, she's all I have.

My sisters skipped having the grand church funeral and opted for a more intimate graveside service, which suits me just fine. With the Devil by my side, I'm not sure if lightning wouldn't strike me dead as soon as we entered the church.

If he's the Devil, then what am I?

It's a question I've asked myself a lot since our marriage, and the only answer I've been able to come up with is that I'm the Beast's wife. It's a role I embrace now.

As we approach the large crowd gathered near the gravesite, my grip tightens on my husband's hand. Florian lifts my hand to his lips, his touch sending a warm tingle through my fingertips before he gives me a reassuring smile. Despite his silence, the intensity in his eyes speaks volumes at this moment.

I'm not alone.

Despite the estrangement between my father and me when he

passed away, he left me everything he didn't lose. At first, I wondered why he would leave me anything, especially when I knew my sisters needed it more than me. However, it finally dawned on me that he knew Florian would take care of everything because of me.

Once again, my husband covered all my father's debts to prevent them from being transferred to me and my sisters. And while they still hate me and are still ungrateful, I don't want them to be in the same position as my father. I have Florian for protection. They have no one. They'll have a clean slate to make something of their lives, but I won't hold my breath waiting for a thank you that'll never come.

As soon as the crowd notices us, the air fills with murmurs and chatter. I'm not sure if it's because of Florian's reputation or mine. Or if it's just people who are aware of the estrangement between me and my father.

Either way, I lean closer to my husband, trying to gather some strength from him. He gently presses his lips against my forehead, leaving a lingering warmth, which calms some of my nerves.

I hate the scrutinizing stares aimed at us, but I don't know what I was expecting.

When we reach where my father's coffin is placed, as I expected, at least one of my sisters attempts to stop me—Angela. Raven is trashed, sitting not too far from the coffin. She probably can't stand steady on her feet to confront me even though I already know where she stands. Her thoughts aren't going to be different from Angela's.

"What the hell are you doing here?" Angela sneers as she tries to grab my arm, but Hugo stops her from touching me. "We don't want you here! It's your fault he's dead, and you have the nerve to show up here! Get the fuck out of here!"

Of course, they blame me for his death because I cut him off, and if I hadn't, he wouldn't have been killed for the money he owed. They'll always find something to blame me for, even though it's his fault he ended up dead.

With Hugo's massive figure looming over us and creating a barrier between my sister and me, Florian lets go of my hand and takes a step toward my sister. I've never seen him look so lethal other than when Adahlia fell from the rooftop. His eyes are filled with a chilling intensity that would make a grown man crumble under his icy glare.

"If it wasn't for your sister, you wouldn't have anything," Florian says with a chilling calmness that sends shivers down my spine. "And if you keep this up, I'll make damn sure that happens. You'll be left with absolutely nothing. Be glad she allowed you to remain in the house because if it was up to me, you and Raven would rot in hell right beside your sorry-ass father."

Angela's eyes narrow on me. "You're just going to stand there and let your husband threaten me and talk about our father that way? He killed him!"

Florian stiffens beside me.

He wouldn't do that to me. I know he wouldn't.

"He did not kill him, Angela, and no one's threatening you," I say, even though I know Florian's words are a threat. A threat I know he'll follow through with if Angela keeps acting like a bitch. "I'm here to say goodbye in peace. That's it."

I'm so tired of constantly dealing with them. I've had absolutely no contact with them at all, which they should be happy about. I just want to say my goodbyes, and they'll never have to see me again. Thankfully.

"You deserve nothing from him!" she screams, drawing even more unwanted attention to us. "He gave you everything! You took everything from us!"

"As always, with you, it comes down to money, Angela. Like Florian said, I'm letting you remain in the house, which is something I don't have to do. You should be grateful I don't throw your ass out on the street, especially since you believe I'm the cause of everything that's wrong in your life. It's time to grow up and pull your own weight because you'll get absolutely nothing else from me. Now, please leave me the hell alone so I can say goodbye to our father."

"Fuck you, bitch!" Angela screams. "You'll pay for this!"

I ignore her threats and curses because I know whatever she says or does won't touch me. My husband won't let anything happen to me.

"I don't want to do this anymore, Florian. I'm ready to say goodbye so we can leave."

I'm so tired of having to deal with them because I've done all I can for them. I'm ready to wipe the slate clean and move forward in my life without them in it.

He nods and motions to Hugo, who then creates a path for me through the growing crowd. Still, my sister's voice echoes behind me, so I push it to the back of my mind. It's more important to me to say goodbye to my father than to engage with my sister. Nothing good will ever come of it.

I approach the beautiful dark wood casket that my father picked out years ago. At least, after my mother passed away, he was responsible enough to take care of this part of his life.

When my hand touches the coffin's smooth surface, instead of the grief and anger I expected, I feel a wave of peace.

"I forgive you for all the hurtful things you said and did to me."

I'm not forgiving him to give him some type of absolution, even though he's no longer here. I'm forgiving him for me. I don't need that kind of hate in my heart when I leave here today. I want to be free.

I once loved this man. He made my dreams come true. He also, along with my sisters, became my nightmare. I can't say I'll miss the man he became, but I will definitely miss the man he once was.

"Rest in power, Daddy," I say, then turn on my heels with my husband by my side and leave the cemetery.

It's hard to give him my love now, but I can definitely wish that he's finally at peace. And now, this chapter of my life is finally closed. Now, on to bigger and better things.

28

FLORIAN

She's been quiet since we returned home, and I can see all the questions in her eyes. We ate dinner in absolute silence, only the sound of our clinking silverware filling the room. After she moved to her studio for a few hours, I remained in my garden. She needed space to come to terms with what her sister told her.

Now I'm just waiting. Waiting for her to ask did I kill her father, although she doesn't know how to. The distance she's put between us is immense because she already knows the truth. It kills me not to be close to her, touching her smooth skin. However, I did what needed to be done to keep her safe. He's a threat that no longer exists. And I'm not sorry he's gone.

If I could snap her sister's neck and get away with it, I would. If it wasn't for her, this issue wouldn't even exist. While I had good reason to get rid of Arthur, I never believed the subject would ever come up.

She's sitting at her vanity, brushing her hair, and staring off in the distance. She's imagining all sorts of things. She wants to believe she has married the man of her dreams who wouldn't dare kill her father, when she knows in her heart who I am.

I've been sitting at the foot of our bed, and she hasn't acknowledged that I'm even in the room with her. It's fucking pissing me off. I'm ready to get this over with so we can move on with our lives.

"Ask what you want to know, Beauty."

She stops brushing her hair, and I can see the tears gathering in her eyes through her reflection in the mirror. My heart twists inside my chest, but I don't move. I don't move to comfort her. She needs to do this. She needs to know the truth.

"Did you do it?"

"I've done a lot of things, Beauty. Be specific."

I know I'm sounding like an asshole, but I want her to ask me the fucking question and not sidestep shit with me. If she wants to know if I killed Arthur, all she has to do is ask the question. I'm not going to hold shit back from her.

She jumps up from her seat and faces me. The tears gathered in her eyes finally spill over.

"Did I kill your father? It's okay to ask it."

"Florian..."

"Say it!" I yell, and she flinches. "Say it. Ask me the fucking question, Beauty."

She releases a breath and glares at me. I wait until she gathers the courage to say what she needs to say. She's a strong fucking woman and should not be scared to ask her fucking husband anything she wants to know. Even if it might make her hate me, I will not lie to her.

"Did you kill my father?"

"I did."

"You did?" she asks with disbelief in her voice. "You killed him?"

I rise from the bed and walk toward her, then stop directly in front of her.

"I did. He was a threat to you and..."

Her slap stings my face, leaving a burning sensation and a ringing in my ears. A smile crosses my face, and she stares at me like I've lost my mind. But I'm smiling not because I killed Arthur. I smile because I'm proud that she's found her voice.

"I hate you!" she screams. "I want a divorce!"

"No, you don't, Beauty." I stuff my hands deep into my pockets to keep from comforting her. "And that's what pisses you off. Not that I killed your father, but that you love the man who did."

"Get out, Florian!" she screams, her beautiful skin tinted red. "Get out! I want you gone!"

The truth hurts, but it needs to be said.

"You may want me gone, right now, Arabelle. But you will always belong to me. There's nothing and no one that will keep me away from you. I'm your Beast, just like you're my, Beauty."

I don't say anything else to her and leave our bedroom. I'll give her all the space she needs to come to terms that this is the man that she married. I don't let anyone threaten my family. And she is my family.

"How long are you going to be here?" Didrick asks. "It's been two weeks, Florian."

I sip my whiskey, trying to hold back my smile. I've been staying at the penthouse while Arabelle ignores me. She's pissed about what I've done, but she knows anything I do, I do it for her. It's been difficult.

"I know how long it's been, Didrick. I will leave when she wants me to come home."

"But are you doing anything to get back in her good graces, or are you just waiting for her to come around?"

I've sent her roses, notes, and even extravagant gifts. Alrick says she trashes the roses and has him return the gifts. But I'll break her down eventually. She loves me. I just have to remind her.

"Are you tired of me being here?"

"Yes," he says, flopping in the chair beside me. "I love you, but I like my space. I like having my girlfriend over where we can fuck and not have her worry about you hearing her scream my name."

I laugh. "Well, when Arabelle comes around, I'll get out of your hair."

"And you think she's going to come around?" He shakes his head. "You killed her father."

"With good reason."

"No matter the reason, Florian, I can't believe I'm having to give my older brother advice on women. She's not going to come around, Florian. Not until you can show her a different side of you."

"I am who I am. She's under no illusion of the man she married, Didrick."

"You are who you are, but you're also someone who loves a woman who is hurting right now. And you're letting her go through it by herself. Show her that you are there for her."

He throws his hand up before I can respond.

"And don't say you've been giving her roses and all that bullshit. She doesn't want that. She wants the man she fell in love with."

He gets up and heads toward his room. I down the rest of my drink as I think about what Didrick says. I know she loves me. I just have to remind her of the man she fell in love with. I don't know how easy that's going to be when she won't even answer my damn calls.

29
ARABELLE

The sweat stings my eyes as I pace my dance studio, the silence only broken by my own breathing. I just got finished doing a rigorous routine, trying to forget what's happening around me. And I still have no idea how to get over this. I don't know why I expected him to say something other than the truth.

How can I forgive or forget what's happened?

Florian is a dangerous man. He doesn't hide that side from me. And when it comes to protecting me, he's already told me he will always do what needs to be done. It's what I love most about him. He puts me first. But how do I stay with him after he killed my father?

"Arabelle, just giving you a heads up, Florian is on the way."

I pinch the bridge of my nose. "I'm not ready to see him, Hugo."

He sighs and props himself against the doorframe, crossing his arms over his chest. "It doesn't matter if you're not ready to see him. He's coming anyway."

"I know."

"Do you want to talk about it?"

I gaze at him.

A rare smile crosses his face. "You can trust me, Arabelle. He's my friend, but so are you."

Since he was shot, Hugo and I have become closer. He's like the older brother I never had, always looking out for me, offering advice, and being there when I need him.

I sigh. "I don't know how I can continue this relationship knowing that he killed my father."

"Florian is a man of his word, Belle. He's never hidden who he is from you, and you fell in love with him anyway."

"I know but this is different, Hugo. He killed my father."

"You need to ask yourself are you upset that he killed your father, or are you upset at yourself for still wanting the man who did it after finding out."

I face the window with my back to Hugo. He's hit the same nerve Florian did the last time I saw him. I do love him, but I hate I have no loyalty to my father.

"You don't owe your father anything, Belle. He stopped being a loving father a long time ago. He used you. He's caused you pain. And when Florian gave him a pass, he continued to try to hurt you. Florian couldn't let that drop. And I, as well as every man who works for him, would have lost all respect for him if he did."

"So, you believe he did the right thing?"

"I do. Just listen to him and hear him out."

The moment Hugo leaves, a crushing weight settles onto my shoulders, making it hard to breathe. I have a decision to make.

Memories of the past few months filter through my mind. All the tears, all the laughs. Despite the deaths and how our relationship started, it's not been all that terrible.

Whenever I'm with Florian he makes me feel like I'm the only person in the world. I'm loved and protected. I can conquer the world with him by my side. There's no doubt I love him just as much as he loves me.

"Beauty?"

Just the sound of his voice moves against my skin like a gentle caress. I've missed him so much it hurts.

As his footsteps echo across the hardwood floors my body trembles. The atmosphere sizzles with so much tension.

He stands directly behind. I sigh and face him. Immediately he wraps his arms around me, and I fall into his embrace. We don't say anything to one another. We just soak in the moment.

"I don't forgive you," I say against his chest.

"I know."

"But I want to. I want to move beyond this so I can forgive you."

He steps away from me and immediately I want to be back in his arms. It's been absolutely hell not having him around, but I needed time to sort out my feelings even if I still don't know where we go from here, or how to move on.

He pulls papers from inside his blazer jacket then rips them up. "What was that?" I ask.

He smiles. "That was the contract between us. I don't want anything hanging over our heads when we move forward from this. No contracts and no secrets. So, Mrs. Larsson, you are free to stay or go. I won't hold you in this marriage if you don't want to be here."

"You'll let me leave?"

His jaw twitches, and I know he's having a difficult time with this conversation. However, I want to see if he's really telling the truth. Will he let me go if that's the decision I make?

"I will. If that's what you want."

"Give me some time, and I'll give you my decision when I'm ready."

He nods, then turns on his heels and strides out the door.

30
FLORIAN

Six Weeks Later...

As I walk into our home, the absence of the usual laughter and hustle and bustle of the staff is immediately apparent. The haunting melody of Michel Fokine's "The Dying Swan" fills the air, which explains the silence. When Arabelle dances, everyone stops what they're doing to watch like they are watching an angel from heaven. When she dances, she tells a story, and her captivating presence draws you in, making it impossible to look away.

At first, it was hard for both Arabelle and I to come back home after Adahlia kidnapped her and almost killed Hugo. We stayed at the penthouse for a while before she got the nerve to come back home, which I completely understand. However, she missed the studio, and after our brief separation, it's the only thing that has made living here again normal.

Like I've done time and time again, I follow the melodic tunes down the hallway toward the addition I had built onto the back of our home.

The moment I step into the studio's entrance, I stop in my tracks. Hugo, Nero, Asva, Alrick, and a few other staff members are sitting on the floor around the room, their gazes locked on the captivating scene in front of them.

Leaning against the doorframe, I'm mesmerized by her elegant and beautiful movements. As she moves, it seems like she's gliding effortlessly, like she's floating on air. Her movements are graceful and fluid as she moves around the studio in a light pink leotard, pink spandex shorts, and pointe shoes the color of her ebony skin.

The wall of mirrors reflects every graceful turn and bend of her body, capturing her from every angle, while the recessed lighting and the natural light streaming through the windows illuminate her flawlessly.

So far, she hasn't noticed anyone watching her, not even me. She never does. And she's always shocked when they all praise her when she finishes. With her performance just a week away, she has dedicated at least two months to perfecting this piece. For a perfectionist like her, there's always something that can be tweaked in her mind, but when she dances, everything she does is filled with grace and precision.

Nothing can be more perfect.

When she closes her eyes, I see her swaying to the rhythm, completely lost in the music. Each note becomes a part of her blood, a part of her soul. It's one of the most beautiful and most magnificent things to witness. It's something I'll never get tired of experiencing. I come here often just to witness something that comes so naturally to her, and it's hard to reconcile how much effort she puts into it. The months and long hours she pours into one performance are astounding.

On the final note, she times her ending to perfection. It's one section she says she needs to work on. In the silent room, the sudden eruption of loud bravos and cheers startles her. She looks around the room, then smiles when she notices everyone. She stands, straightening her back, then curtseys while they continue to cheer her on.

I step into the room, and a wave of pride washes over me. This is my wife. The thought still boggles my mind often when I see her.

Once everyone notices me, they file out of the room, leaving us alone. As I walk toward my wife, I feel the warmth of her presence drawing me closer to her.

"I'm sweaty," she mumbles against my chest after I pull her into my arms.

"I don't care," I say, then feel the warmth of her skin as I run my tongue along the side of her neck, savoring the subtle saltiness.

Her laughter fills the air, resonating deep within me. "You're terrible."

"You have absolutely no idea how terrible I can be when it comes to you." I kiss the top of her head. "That was absolutely amazing, Beauty. I think Asva even had tears in his eyes."

Unable to contain herself, she laughs even harder. Asva would be the last person to cry over anything. He's the most serious person I've ever met, but just like the rest of us, anytime we watch her dance, she pulls emotions from us we don't even know we have.

"My ending is still off." She sighs, pinching the bridge of her nose when she pulls away from me. "So, I have a lot more work to do until I get it right."

I can hear the disappointment in her voice, but I can also see the determination in her eyes. Even though it looks perfect to me, whatever she feels is off, there is no doubt in my mind that she'll correct it before her performance.

"It's absolutely perfect, Arabelle. Ask anyone."

"You're supposed to say that because you're my husband, and they are my friends. All of you are biased."

She stands on her tiptoes and plants a gentle kiss on my lips. But I have other plans, and I deepen the kiss, then capture her moan with my mouth. Nothing compares to this woman. I'll burn the world down if it means I get to spend the rest of my days with her.

I pull back, ending our kiss and causing her to grumble. "I say it because it's the truth, my love." I brush my fingers down her cheek, causing her eyes to flutter. "Do you know how much I love you?"

I'm sure she thinks she does, but she has no idea. What I feel for her goes beyond the limitations of the word love. And to think that there was a time when I believed I could live without this. That I didn't need the love of anyone, only the revenge that I had for my father. However, Arabelle transformed my life in ways I never thought possible. She's no longer my unattainable beauty.

She captured the attention of the Beast, and she's captured my heart.

"I do know how much you love me, but I'm sure you'll tell me I have no idea," she says, smiling.

"Beauty, you are my world. I would be nothing without you. Never forget that."

"I love you, too, Beast."

She steps away from me, and I watch her walk toward the floor-to-ceiling windows of the studio, the sound of her pointe shoes tapping against the hardwood floor. Every step she takes is delicate, like she's floating on a cloud.

She looks over her shoulder with lust and mischievousness dancing in her eyes.

"You never answered my question."

My brows furrow in confusion. "What question?"

"When you first showed me this place, I asked could anyone see in here."

"I don't remember you asking me that."

To ensure no one sneaks onto the property, I have men patrolling the perimeter of our home. With her increasing fame, we've had multiple incidents of paparazzi attempting to trespass onto our estate, along with enthusiastic fans.

After the first few incidents, I beefed up security even more. While the paparazzi still camp outside the gates and have been caught hiding in trees trying to catch even the smallest glimpse of her, nobody has penetrated the walls.

With a smile on my face, I make my way toward her, my dress shoes echoing off the floor of her studio. She leans against the large panes of glass with a smile on her face. "Why do you want to know?" I ask.

My little ballerina is a total exhibitionist, and I love it. It's made for some fun nights at the penthouse. It also has me contemplating whether I need to have our bedroom and bathroom remodeled to include a wall of windows just for her.

She shrugs, a naughty smirk playing on her lips. "I just want to know."

"Hmm," I murmur, my hands finding her hips as I pull her close to me. "You just want to know, huh?"

She nods her head, her large doe eyes peering into mine.

Her leotard clings to her body like a second skin, accentuating her slender figure as I drag it down to her waist, leaving her breasts exposed.

Under my gaze, her dark brown nipples, slightly darker than her skin, harden like pebbles. With a delicate touch, I run the pads of my thumbs across them before squeezing them between my fingers. With a hiss, she arches her body in response to my touch.

"You would love it if someone saw me pleasuring you."

Although I'm a possessive bastard, there are ways to give her the illusion of someone watching us fuck, even though no one would ever have the pleasure of seeing her come undone from my touch. That's for my eyes only.

Swiftly, I turn her body and push her flat against one of the large-pane windows, causing her to yelp from the quick movement. I lean forward, my hard dick pressing against her soft ass.

"Is this what you want, Beauty?" I grind my cock against her harder, causing her to moan. "You want someone to see me fucking this tight body of yours?"

She whimpers, and the sound ignites something primal inside me. I snatch her leotard along with her spandex shorts down her body, undo my slacks, then pull my cock out. I don't waste any time before surging inside her tight warmth.

"Florian!" she screams at the top of her lungs.

"So fucking tight," I groan. "So wet. You are made for me, Beauty. This cunt is made for me."

"Oh god."

The side of her face is flat against the window, along with her palms and her body, when I see the shadow of one of my men.

"Open your eyes, Beauty," I say as I plow into her harder and faster. "Nero's walking by. Let him see me fuck my wife."

I let her step back to where she's not plastered against the window so she can watch one of our guards as he walks by the windows. He looks in our direction, causing her to gasp. You would think she's appalled at the possibility of Nero seeing us, but I know that's not the case. Her pussy is getting wetter, which tells me all I need to know.

"Dirty, dirty girl," I whisper in her ear. My cock slides in and out of her wet cunt effortlessly. "That greedy little cunt of yours is weeping. You love how Nero can see how well your cunt takes my cock, don't you?"

"Florian...please..."

"Please, what, my love?" I nip at her earlobe as my warm breath brushes against her skin, causing goose pimples to rise. "Fuck you harder? Fuck you faster? Make you scream my name?"

My hand grasps one of her breasts from behind, squeezing it hard. That's another thing about my woman. She loves a little of pain while I fuck her.

"Fuck me! Make me scream!"

I chuckle as I plow into her harder, faster, feeling her body respond to my touch. She's more verbal during our lovemaking, which I love. She's a reserved woman, not very vocal about many things that she wants, but during sex, she steps out of her shell, and I fucking love it.

I reach around her waist and play with her clit, causing her to whimper. Fuck, I love the little noises and sounds she makes. They go straight to my cock and work wonders for my ego because I know those sounds are only for me and caused only by me.

Nero's still standing in front of the window. Even though his gaze is not on us, it doesn't even matter because I'm pretty sure he can hear us. The room isn't soundproof.

"He's listening to you, Beauty." I moan when her pussy flutters around my dick. "How about you scream my name so he can hear who you belong to? Come for me."

I pinch her clit, and her body seizes as her pussy clamps around my cock. "Florian!"

I continue to plunge deep into her tight warmth as she pulls me over the edge right along with her. I pump inside her until I'm spent, and she sags against the window.

"That was..."

I turn her around in my arms. "You like that Nero can see and hear us?"

She says nothing, resting her forehead against my chest, and I tighten my embrace.

"No need to be embarrassed about what you like, Beauty. If I had an issue with it, Nero would be dead."

Her head pops up, and her eyes widen in disbelief as she stares at me like I've lost my damn mind. I respond with a nonchalant shrug because it's the truth. I don't care if he or anyone hears me fuck my wife. But no one will ever witness the way her body revels in pleasure unless I want them to. And if they ever did without my permission, I'd gouge their eyes out, then slit their throats.

As she remains pressed against the window, I trail my fingers along her smooth skin, eliciting a breathy moan. I drop to my knees, toss one of her legs over my shoulder, and dive in. Her hands grip my hair, pulling at the strands, and the sting on my scalp causes me to groan.

With every lick, I delve deeper into her wet folds, teasing her entrance before focusing on her swollen clit with gentle circles. As the mixture of my cum and hers coats my mouth, an electrifying surge courses through me, sending my mind and body into a frenzy.

I love the mixture of our cum, and I will never get enough of her. She's the reason I breathe. She's the lightness to my darkness. The other half of my soul. She's my fucking everything, and I will make sure she knows this until the day I take my final breath.

"Oh my god," she moans as I flick and suck her swollen clit. "That feels so good, baby."

I hum against her folds, pulling her closer to my mouth so I don't miss one drop. I suck her clit harder, forcing another deep guttural moan deep from the love of my life.

There isn't a day that will go by when I will not worship this woman for the goddess she is. Whatever she wants or whatever she needs, I will always go to the ends of the earth to give it to her. No matter what it costs me.

"That's it, my love," I murmur against her wet cunt. "Come for me."

My command is all she needs, and her grasp tightens on my hair, causing a sting to cover my scalp. Her legs tremble as a combination of my cum and her arousal floods my mouth, and I drink up every drop.

I continue to tease her until she comes down from another orgasm. I remove her leg from my shoulder, then rise to my feet. She leans against the window with her eyes closed and a serene look on her face as she waits for her breaths to even out.

When she finally looks at me, I recognize the same look she gave me the first time I met her at the ballet in her dressing room. It causes the same fire to churn in my stomach. I realize that our relationship didn't start out in the most conventional way, but this is the person I'm supposed to be with. My life would not be complete without her.

As I pull her into my arms, she nestles closer, her arms wrapping around my neck. One of the most beautiful smiles I've ever seen graces her face.

"I love you," she says.

"Say it again."

She cups my face with one hand, rises onto her tiptoes and kisses me, and it's like the first time we kissed all over again. However, before I can deepen the kiss, she pulls away.

"I love you, my husband, my heart, my Beast."

"I love you too, Beauty. Until my last breath."

31
ARABELLE

SIX MONTHS LATER...

I grip the balcony railing and watch as the white-capped waves of the crystal-clear waters batter the sandy shore below. This is one of the most serene and beautiful places I have ever seen.

The brisk winds of the Mediterranean Sea blow through my shoulder-length hair, which is now in tight curls because of the salty air. I deeply inhale the warm breeze. It's like heaven on earth.

His arms, warm and firm, wrap around my waist from behind, and his large hands resting on my stomach ground me in the moment. I lean against his broad chest, sinking deeper into his embrace, the scent of his smoky cologne filling my senses.

"How are you feeling today?" he asks, his soft, warm lips brushing the crook of my neck.

I look back over my shoulder with a smile, hoping to ease the concern I see in his loving gaze. "Not too bad today. I've only been to the bathroom twice since I woke up this morning. So, I say that's a plus."

I face him, then finger a piece of his shoulder-length hair, which is loose today because he knows how much I love it.

So far, this pregnancy has been kicking my ass. I'm on leave from the theater until I have our baby. Since I found out that I was pregnant, I've had nonstop morning sickness to the point where I've been dehydrated and hospitalized once. This morning was the first time

I've had a day where I haven't been bent over a toilet for the majority of the day.

He releases a relieved breath and slowly, the tension eases from his body as his hardened exterior relaxes. "Good." He lays his hand on my growing stomach and the grin crossing his face when he touches me always causes my heart to stop. "And the baby?" he asks.

"Doing backflips like she's training for the Olympics."

He chuckles, and it's like music to my ears. "Or maybe she's training to be a dancer like her mama."

"That's possible too. Olympian or dancer, I could live with either one."

His rare laugh fills the air once again, a warm and genuine sound that lights up his entire face. It leaves me completely captivated and fascinated by how much it changes his features.

It isn't often my husband finds humor in anything, but when he does, I fall in love with him all over again. It's like he drops his carefully erected walls. Then, and only then, does he let me see the true Florian Larsson. It's very rare because the man carries the weight of the world on his shoulders, and that weight has gotten heavier since I've been pregnant. He's constantly got his head on a swivel, making sure everything stays safe for his family. I've told him constantly that it's no way to live, but he always says that it's necessary to keep us safe.

Despite the constant pressures of this life, this trip has done wonders for him to relax a little before the reality of our world comes crashing back down on us when we return to the States. Here, he can be Florian. There, he becomes Beast, head of the Larsson Syndicate.

His face softens, and his eyes light up with a warmth that melts away all his troubles whenever he speaks about our daughter or when he excitedly surprises me with another gift he thinks I'll like, want, or need. When he speaks about his mother, that light shines brightly in his eyes. Other than that, he's all business.

I've gotten used to Beast, as most people know him. It's an intricate part of Florian. He's the protector. He's the savior. He's the provider. But he's also the one who, above all else, will do anything for me and our daughter that I'm carrying. Beast and Florian are one and the same. While it took me some time to come to terms with the important roles both versions my husband plays in my life, I've come to love them both very deeply.

"That dress looks so beautiful on you, Beauty."

My lips curve into a smile I can't control, a feeling of pure bliss washing over my entire body. This morning, when I woke up, I found a lovely cream-colored dress with a note from Florian asking that I wear it today. Although it's fancier than the dresses I've been wearing, I did as he asked.

The draped silhouette of the chiffon floor-length dress beautifully complements my growing pregnant belly, while the cinched waist adds a touch of elegance. Its design gives a Grecian goddess vibe and not maternity dress, which I love. It moves so fluidly with each step I take. It's absolutely gorgeous.

"Thank you. It's stunning. And you don't look so bad yourself. What's the occasion?"

He's wearing a tailored black dress shirt, the top buttons undone to reveal a glimpse of his chest, paired with matching slim dress slacks and black dress shoes. He's always in a suit or dressed up, but this doesn't look like his normal attire.

"I've got a little something planned for us that I think you will absolutely love."

"You always have something planned for us. What is it?" I ask with excitement in my voice. "Are we going on another tour?"

Even though Florian is constantly surprising me, I still hate surprises. I believe he's trying to change my mind about them, but I'd rather know what's going on instead of waiting until the end. I'm impatient, which is something he's gotten used to.

We've been out exploring the island and have gone to a couple of outdoor markets only a few times since we've been here. Because my morning sickness has been terrible, Florian has tried to make me as comfortable as possible. Now that my nausea is calm today, there's a lot more I want to see of the place.

"It's a surprise, Beauty."

I huff and frown, which only causes his smile to annoyingly widen. "Why are you smiling, Florian?" I ask with my hands on my hips. "You know I hate surprises."

"I do know you hate them, but you're going to love this one."

That's what he always says. I roll my eyes at him, frustrated that he likes to do this to me.

"Come with me," he says, intertwining our fingers before I can respond.

I don't hesitate to go with him as he pulls me toward the entrance of our home in Cyprus.

"Where are we going, Florian?"

"You'll see."

Florian wasted no time in making one of my dreams come true. Cyprus is one place I've always wanted to visit, but with my dance schedule, I've always had to put vacationing on the back burner. Now that I'm on maternity leave, we finally have time to do some of the things I've put off for years before our daughter is born.

I slide into the back seat of our car and sigh in annoyance. I'm pissed that he's not telling me where we're going, and it's very annoying that he knows it irks me and doesn't care.

After he slides in beside me, he grabs my feet, places them in his lap, and removes my sandals.

"God, Florian, that feels so good," I moan as he massages the soles of my feet.

I know he's trying to distract me, so I'm not irritated. It's definitely working.

He pauses for a moment, and I can feel the intensity of his desire in the way he gazes at me. "If you moan like that again, I'm going to have to stuff your mouth full of my dick."

Heat radiates across my face, making my skin feel like it's on fire. I can only imagine the look on Hugo's face upon hearing Florian's words. The man says what he wants to say no matter who's around. He has absolutely no filter.

"Florian! Hugo can hear you," I whisper yell, with wide eyes, as heat sears my skin and pools between my thighs. I want to ask him to follow through with his threat once we get to wherever we are going.

"Do you think I give a damn that he can hear me?" he says, pressing a button on the handle of his door. "But, for you, I'll fix it."

A dark screen rises, separating us from the front of the car to give us some privacy. Before I can reply, he returns to rubbing my feet, and I forget what I wanted to say.

I close my eyes and relax. His calloused hands feel so good. I also have a lot of swelling in my feet and ankles with this pregnancy. Florian has been amazing at giving me massages to help make me more comfortable during this pregnancy.

One of his hands trails from my feet up my calf, and I moan. I open my legs a little more and scoot a little closer to him. His deep chuckle vibrates through the car, causing my eyes to pop open. "What's so funny?"

"You're horny."

I roll my eyes again, letting out a sigh because he knows exactly what he's doing. With this pregnancy, I've been cranky, and the only way he's been able to calm me down has been by giving me amazing orgasms after his amazing massages. I'm definitely not complaining. He's a master with his tongue, cock, and fingers.

"Well, what are you going to do about it, Mr. Larsson?"

He lets out a chuckle, grazing his fingertips along the wet folds of my pussy. "No panties?" he asks with his brow arched.

"I didn't like that I could see them through my dress." I open my legs wider. "And it makes it easier for you to make me feel good."

He only smiles as he runs his fingers through my folds again, then makes small circles on my clit. "Florian..."

He pushes his fingers inside me and the sound of my wetness fills the car. "My dirty girl is so wet," he moans, licking his lips. "Is all this for me?"

He puts a little more pressure on my clit and continues to draw small circles on the sensitive bundles of nerves, which drives me absolutely crazy. My hips move on their own, wishing he could fill me with his cock.

"Oh god, yes, baby. All for you. Just like that."

"I wish I could lick this tight pussy." He pushes his fingers in and out of me while he continues to masterfully play with my clit, bringing me closer to the edge. "But we don't have much time, so if you want to come, baby, you only have a few minutes."

I groan, moving my hips faster to match his movements as delicious tingles cover my entire body. When it seems like I can't take any more of his ministrations, he pinches my clit, finally giving me what my body craves, and sends me crashing over the edge in pure bliss.

"Florian!" I shout, slamming my eyes shut as my orgasm barrels through me like a freight train.

"Fuck, you're so beautiful when you come," he says.

I continue to ride out my high, my hips grinding against his fingers as he moves them in and out of me at a lazy pace.

"Beast, I hate to interrupt, but we're here," Hugo says through the car's intercom, interrupting us.

The car comes to a stop, and it brings an abrupt end to my bliss.

I open my eyes as Florian removes his fingers from inside me. Then he licks them, removing all of my essence while intensely gazing at me, his eyes full of desire that no doubt mirrors mine.

I can never get enough of this man.

"Do you feel any better?" he asks, adjusting himself.

I'm still in a daze, so all I can do is smile, giving him a small nod as I do my best to fix my dress. He pecks me on the lips, then lowers the privacy screen.

"Okay, Hugo." He grabs my shoes from the floor of the car and places them back on my feet. "We'll resume this later."

"I'll make sure I hold you to that. Where are we at?" I ask as I look out of the window.

From where we are parked on the street, I can't see anything other than buildings and people walking down the sidewalks.

"I wanted to do something special for you," he says.

My eyes soften at the sincerity in his voice and in his eyes. "Sweetheart, you're always doing something special for me."

Florian showers me with the most wonderful gifts all the time. It's almost like he can't stand to see me go without, even if I never ask for what he's given me.

"You know you don't have to keep getting me stuff, right?"

"I do it because I love you, Beauty. You're a blessing to me, and it makes me happy to see you happy."

My door opens before I can respond, and Hugo sticks his hand out to me. I grasp it, knowing there's no use in arguing with Florian. He's going to do what he wants.

Hugo carefully helps me out of the car, making sure I have my feet planted firmly. I'm not so nimble anymore, so it takes me a little longer to exit vehicles now.

"Thank you, Hugo."

He winks and closes the door behind me. When Florian meets me on the sidewalk, he grabs my hand. I look at him in confusion because we're standing in front of a stone structure with a huge tower and a simple cross on top that looks like a centuries-old church. The exterior has a warm, golden hue under the Mediterranean sun that looks inviting, but I'm so confused as to why we're here.

"Where are we?" I ask.

He doesn't respond, just smiles and pulls me toward the entrance.

"Is this a church?"

He pushes the heavy wooden doors open.

"This looks like a church, Florian. Why are we at a chur—wow, this is amazing!"

Absolutely awe-struck, I scan the magnificent structure that looks like it had to have been constructed before medieval times. The walls and ceilings are adorned with beautiful biblical scenes that add a sense of reverence to the space. The chapel is filled with an eerie glow from the many lit candles lining the walls on huge candelabras. The candles look like they are straight out of a Gothic film, and the heavy scent of incense envelops the small room. Also adorning the sanctuary are statues of saints and biblical figures, each one exuding a sense of history and spirituality. I can't believe my eyes as I take in the luxury of the place, feeling a sense of wonder washing over me.

"I'm giving you a wedding," he says, his eyes sparkling with sincerity.

"But we're already married, Florian."

"We are, but I wanted to give you a wedding to remember, not the one you were forced into. We love each other now, Arabelle, and this time, when we say I do, it will be because of that love, not because of some fucking contract. This between us is real, Beauty. So, I want you to have a real wedding."

My eyes soften and fill with tears. Despite being known as a ruthless man, my husband's heart is as generous as anyone I've ever met. I gently hold his face in my hands before leaning in to kiss him. As he deepens the kiss, I feel his strong arms pulling me closer to him. However, before we get carried away, Hugo clearing his throat brings us back to reality. We're getting a little too comfortable in the house of the Lord.

"The priest is here," Hugo says from behind us, motioning with a jerk of his head.

I step away from Florian and focus on the altar of the church. In front of the sanctuary stands a man wearing a long black robe with a gold-embroidered cape draped over it and a stole around his neck.

Florian places his hand on the small of my back as we walk

toward the priest. When we reach him, he greets us with a warm smile.

"Mr. and Mrs. Larsson, it's so nice to meet you. I'm Father Adamos."

"Nice to meet you, Father," I say.

Florian nods.

"If you're ready," Father Adamos says, "we can get started."

"We're ready," I say, looking at Florian, who graces me with a wink and smile.

The priest nods. "Then let us begin. Please face each other," he says, holding a Bible in his hands. "Mr. Larsson, please take Mrs. Larsson's hands in yours."

We do as he asks.

I'm not really a religious person, and neither is Florian, but I appreciate the fact that he went through all this trouble to give me the wedding he believes I deserve. This is one of the sweetest things he has ever done for me. It will be something I will remember for the rest of my life.

The priest carefully flips open his worn Bible, its pages yellowed by age.

"'Submit to one another out of reverence for Christ. Blessed are they who fear the Lord and walk in His ways. You shall eat the fruit of the labor of your hands. You shall be blessed, and it shall be well with you,'" he says, closing his Bible. "Would you like to say your vows now?"

The smile that crosses Florian's face is heart-stopping. The way he smiles at me reflects his deep love and admiration for what we share with one another. We have been through so much together, and seeing these expressed on his face makes me fall more in love with him.

More tears fill my eyes.

"My Beauty, it's so hard to put into words what you mean to me. We didn't have the most typical relationship in the beginning."

Hugo's snort is so loud I burst into giggles as the priest to look at us in confusion. We definitely didn't start out like most people.

Florian glares at him, and Hugo throws up his hands. Then my husband faces me again, and it's hard to stop my giggles that have shifted to full-blown laughter.

"I'm sorry. Go ahead, baby," I say once I get myself under control.

"Where was I before I was so rudely interrupted?" I giggle again, and he smiles. "Yes, we had an unconventional start, but it led us down this path. It led us here today, and it has brought us together with an unbreakable bond. I will cherish you and our daughter until my last breath. I love you, Beauty."

"Mrs. Larsson, could you please say your vows."

Florian's gentle touch wipes away the tears that are cascading down my cheeks. "Wow, I wasn't expecting this." I release a deep breath, trying to calm all my emotions. "But I've come to expect the unexpected when it comes to you, Florian Larsson. When we first met, I never believed we'd get here, but I wouldn't want to be anywhere else. My prince, my Beast, I love you."

"Beautiful," the priest says with a huge smile on his face. "May this union be blessed with love, faith, and joy by the Father, the Son, and the Holy Spirit. What God has joined, let no man separate. You may kiss your lovely bride."

Florian steps closer to me, invading my space, and just like the first time we met, I'm trapped in his steely gaze. He pulls me as close as he can with my pregnant stomach and gazes down into my eyes with so much love, it almost knocks me off my feet.

"I love you, Mr. Larsson," I say with a smile on my face, giddiness moving through my body. "I guess since we did this the right way this time, now you're stuck with me."

He lets out one of his rare deep laughs that makes my knees tremble. "I love you too, Mrs. Larsson. And there's no other person I'd rather be stuck with."

When our lips meet, it's like an explosion, a kaleidoscope of feelings all at once. Happiness. Joy. Desire. Love. It engulfs me, consuming every thought and feeling, leaving no room for anything else. With this kiss, a torrent of love, hope, and dreams surge between us, flowing through our lips and into the very depths of our souls.

For as long as I can remember, dance has been my entire life—my one true love for so long. A lot of long days and lonely nights were spent perfecting my art. Perfecting the one thing that I loved and what I truly believed loved me in return. However, I would give up all the fame and all the fortune, just to have my happily ever after with my Beast. My true love.

EPILOGUE

FLORIAN

FIFTEEN YEARS LATER...

As tears fill her eyes, her grip on my hand tightens. From the private balcony of the theater that's reserved for us, we have a bird's-eye view of the bustling crowd below in the theater where she achieved the prestigious title of principal dancer almost seventeen years ago.

I can't help but smile when I see the look of wonderment and amazement on her face. She's even more beautiful than she was when I first met her in the dressing room of this very theater.

My eyes are drawn back to the stage, where our daughter gracefully moves across it, her first performance as a professional ballet dancer.

"She's beautiful," my wife whispers, and I couldn't agree more.

Carina's graceful movements on the dance floor evoke the same sense of awe that I felt when watching her mother dance on that very stage. It's like she's whispering words directly into your ear as she interprets the music she is dancing to.

"She looks just like you. The embodiment of grace, poise, and beauty."

My wife's smile has a radiant quality that can chase away any darkness, especially when she's proud of our daughter's accomplishments.

"She's so much better than me, Florian. Just look at how elegantly she moves across the stage. It's almost like she's floating," Arabelle says with awe in her voice.

It always amazes me when Arabelle talks about dancing because, after all this time, she still does not realize how good she actually is even as she's aged.

When Carina, our oldest child, decided to follow in her mother's footsteps, I supported her despite Arabelle's initial objections. Arabelle didn't want her to experience the same challenges she faced during her early years of dancing. The isolation. The mean girls of the dance world, which I was clueless about until I witnessed Arabelle having a run-in with someone after a performance. No, I didn't want my daughter to experience any of that part of dance, but Carina's natural talent can't be denied. Just like they did with Arabelle, the papers are labeling her as a prodigy. And she is. As soon as she saw her mother dance, her eyes lit up with excitement, and there was no stopping her. It's a talent that has to be fostered because it's too amazing to let the world not see how great she is.

When the final note sounds, the crowd erupts, and we join in, jumping to our feet and clapping along with them.

"Bravo! Bravo!" We all shout and cheer as the dancers, including Carina, take their well-deserved bows.

As we hold each other, tears of joy and relief fill our eyes. Hugo's hand lands on my shoulder. Glancing back, I'm met with the sight of prideful expressions etched on everyone's faces.

Not only is Hugo here, but Asva, Alrick, Nero, and Didrick have joined us as well. Carina thinks of them as her uncles, and there's no way they would miss her first performance. They all bitched about having to wear tuxedos but did it for her.

"She was amazing," I say as the dancers leave the stage.

"She was," Arabelle agrees. "I can't believe the performance she just had, Florian. This is going to open so many doors for her. It was absolutely perfect. She hit every mark she was supposed to. Do you realize how hard that is for someone her age?"

The sound of panic mixed with admiration is clear in my wife's voice. Having been here before, she's familiar with what lies ahead for Carina. I've only experienced this life through her and for only as long as she's been in mine. I have no idea what dancers face other than what Arabelle has experienced, but I trust my wife.

"She's going to be fine, Beauty." I try to give her some type of comfort. "I won't let anything happen to her."

"You'll have to increase her security."

"It's done."

"The paparazzi are probably going to be camped out at the house and her school now."

Since Arabelle's retirement, we haven't been bothered by the paps as much as when we first got married, but I have no problem doing whatever I need to do to keep Carina safe. She nods, relief on her face.

"Don't worry. I'll do whatever needs to be done, Beauty."

A gentle tug on my tuxedo jacket interrupts my thoughts. "Daddy?"

I look down at Anders, our youngest child, who's only four years old, and notice his wide-eyed curiosity. He bears a striking resemblance to my mother, except for his head full of dark curls, dark eyes, and brown skin.

I reach for him and pick him up. He wraps his arms around my neck, and a huge smile crosses his face. "I want to do that."

He points to the stage, and I ruffle his hair. He wants to do everything his sister does. He's even started watching both his mother and sister as they dance in the studio at home. It's not exactly the path I thought a son of mine would take. However, if he wants to dance, I won't stand in his way. I'll give my children everything my father didn't allow me to have. He has a choice of which road he decides to take when he gets older.

"You can do anything you want, Anders. Just say the word."

His smile is so captivating that it takes my breath away. All I can ever ask for is to see the joy lighting up his face. I didn't have the best childhood. My father refused to let me live the life I wanted to live.

But I refuse to be that with any of my children. They are allowed to become anything they want to be in this life. If I can provide it for them, then they will have it.

As our fingers interlace, Arabelle's smile lights up her entire face. "I love you."

I give her a playful wink. "I love you, too."

This is only the beginning of our journey together. My mother would be happy to know that I found happily-ever-afters do exist.

IF YOU LIKED THIS, YOU MAY LIKE

PIECES OF ASH BY KATY REGENCY

From *New York Times* bestselling author Katy Regnery comes a dark and twisted retelling of Cinderella—where survival is the only happily-ever-after.

My name is Ashley Ellis.

I was thirteen when my mother—iconic supermodel Tig—married Mosier Răumann, a man twice her age and the mysterious head of the powerful Răumann crime family. He promised us security. He delivered control.

When I turned eighteen, my mother died under suspicious circumstances—and I discovered the chilling plans Mosier had for me. Plans I never agreed to. Roles I refused to play.

With help from my godfather, I disappeared. But Mosier doesn't take no for an answer. His twin sons and loyal enforcers have been sent to bring me back, no matter what it takes.

They think I'm a girl running scared.

They're about to find out I'm not that easy to catch.

AVAILABLE NOW

ACKNOWLEDGMENTS

Thank you to all who support me. Without you none of this would be possible. I'd like to give a shout-out to my husband who encourages me to keep sharing my stories with anyone who's willing to take a chance. A special thanks to all the readers. Without you guys, I wouldn't be where I am today. If this is your first time reading my stories, thanks for giving me a chance. I hope you continue to enjoy the crazy world that goes on inside my head. To those who are not new, I'm glad you decided to stay on this journey with me. Hope you all continue to enjoy the ride!

USA TODAY Bestselling Author Courtney Dean was born in North Carolina. The wife and mother of two boys spends most of her days homeschooling them. When she's not just hanging out with her family, she's reading or writing stories about alpha jerks and the women who love them. She loves reading romance stories with a bit of suspense, thrill, danger, and paranormal novels.

www.courtneydean.com

www.ingramcontent.com/pod-product-compliance
Lightning Source LLC
LaVergne TN
LVHW030919080826
845145LV00013B/2965

* 9 7 8 1 9 6 9 8 7 6 2 2 6 *